PETTING GIRLS

'You better not fuck with me, bitch!' she spat as she reached her corner.

I shook my head and collapsed down into my seat, reaching for the water bottle held out by Kay. She'd scratched me quite badly, and I was in a fine state: filthy with oil and running sweat, my boobs already out and my corset up at the back so that my bottom showed. As I fought I'd be showing everything, and Angel was still fully covered, for all that her shorts were ruined. She wanted me down in the next round, and I had to make my decision.

'You can do it, Amber,' Kay urged from beside me. 'You're stronger than her, and she can't stand up in those boots anyway. I've put twenty on as well, at fifty to one. Everyone reckons it's a fix.'

'It is,' I breathed.

'You're not going to lose are you? Amber! Not to her!'

Why not visit Penny's website at:
www.pennybirch.com

By the same author:

THE INDIGNITIES OF ISABELLE
THE INDISCRETIONS OF ISABELLE
(writing as Cruella)

PENNY IN HARNESS
A TASTE OF AMBER
BAD PENNY
BRAT
IN FOR A PENNY
PLAYTHING
TIGHT WHITE COTTON
TIE AND TEASE
PENNY PIECES
TEMPER TANTRUMS
REGIME
DIRTY LAUNDRY
UNIFORM DOLL
NURSE'S ORDERS
JODHPURS AND JEANS
PEACH
FIT TO BE TIED
WHEN SHE WAS BAD
KNICKERS AND BOOTS
TICKLE TORTURE

PETTING GIRLS

Penny Birch

This book is a work of fiction.
In real life, make sure you practise safe, sane and consensual sex.

First published in 2005 by
Nexus
Thames Wharf Studios
Rainville Road
London W6 9HA

www.eburypublishing.co.uk

Typeset by TW Typesetting, Plymouth, Devon

Printed and bound in Great Britain by Clays Ltd, St Ives PLC

ISBN 978-0-3523-4607-0

The Random House Group Limited supports The Forest Stewardship
Council (FSC®), the leading international forest certification organisation.
Our books carrying the FSC label are printed on FSC® certified paper.
FSC is the only forest certification scheme endorsed by the leading
environmental organisations, including Greenpeace. Our
paper procurement policy can be found at
www.randomhouse.co.uk/environment

You'll notice that we have introduced a set of symbols onto our book jackets, so that you can tell at a glance what fetishes each of our brand new novels contains. Here's the key – enjoy!

cp (traditional)

cp (modern)

spanking

restraint/bondage

rope bondage/hojojutsu

latex/rubber/leather/enclosure

fem dom

willing captivity

medical

period setting

uniforms

sex rituals

One

Kay's tail wobbled slightly as I tapped the pig switch to her bottom. Her perfect, fleshy little buttocks were already marked by a faint criss-cross of red lines, and her beautiful creamy skin had begun to bead with sweat. Her mop of tawny blonde hair half covered the delicate oval of her face, but I could see that she had closed her eyes, and her mouth had come a little open, while her piggy snout was rising and falling gently to her breathing. Her upturned nipples were tight with excitement, her rounded, applelike breasts heaving gently. She was ready, and so was I, my nipples hard beneath my sweater, my fanny eager for the touch of her tongue.

'Down you go,' I ordered.

She went, down on all fours, to kneel in the lush grass, her face over the long zinc trough, her curly pink tail quivering eagerly above her bottom as she began to feed on the fruit peelings I'd put out for her. Her bottom was now revealed in full glory, the deliciously chubby cheeks rising above her slender thighs to form a plump, split ball that flared from her waist, open to show off the tiny, deep-brown dimple of her anus. I gave her a gentle cut of my switch.

'Knees apart, Kay, well apart.'

She obeyed, after just an instant of hesitation, still ever so slightly self-conscious about being bare for all that she was my girlfriend, done up as a pig and about

1

to be whipped to orgasm. I let her feed for a while, knowing how the humiliation of her condition would be rising in her head and with my own pleasure growing in response. Only when she had swallowed her second mouthful of peel did I start to whip her again, applying the switch gently across her buttocks to add to the tracery of lines. She wiggled them in encouragement and I began to beat her a little harder.

Her fanny was on full show, her shaved lips pouted out between her thighs, swollen and moist between, and just open enough to show the wet mouth of her vagina. I put the tip of the switch between, into the crease of her fanny, wiggling it gently to make her muscles tighten. She gave a low moan, her bumhole started to wink, and I knew that it would only take a few more touches. I began to whip her again, harder, much harder than she normally took. She began to gasp and her face came up from the trough, smeared with pulp and bits of skin. A piece of apple peel had stuck to her snout. I took a grip in her hair and pushed her head back down, rubbing her face in the slops as I began to whip her harder still.

'Eat it!' I barked, and she begun to gobble urgently at the bits of apple peel, orange peel and banana skins.

I got behind her, slid the tip of my pig switch between her fanny lips and began to wiggle it, right on her clit. Her bumhole began to wink again, the tight brown ring pulsing to show off a pink heart, while her whipped bottom was clenching hard and her fanny so open that I could have slid a finger in and barely touched the sides. After just an instant, the sound of her munching broke off and she was panting out her orgasm into the slops, her muscles in frantic contraction, her tail quivering over her upturned bottom, her titties bouncing and jiggling beneath her. Only when she finally began to go limp did I speak.

'Good piggy. Now my turn.'

She pulled herself up on to her haunches and turned to me. Her face was a mess, framed in bedraggled hair, smeared with pulp and bits of skin, her mouth slack in the aftermath of orgasm, her huge blue eyes wide and unfocused. I beckoned her as I put my back to the tree I'd made her hold while she was whipped. She shook her head to dislodge a piece of orange from her snout and came forwards, crawling. I put my hand between my legs, to find the crotch of my jodhpurs soaking and my fanny swollen and sensitive beneath. Kay poked her tongue out and waggled the tip.

My jodhpurs came down, pushed low, knickers and all, my dignity as her mistress forgotten in my need. With my fanny bare, I pushed out my hips and took her by the hair as she came forwards, pulling her face into my crotch. I felt the cool wetness of the slops I'd made her eat against my skin, and her tongue, moist and warm, burrowing between my fanny lips to lap eagerly at my clit.

I shut my eyes, revelling in the feel of her: naked, soiled and beaten at my feet, my own little piggy-girl, in tail and snout, her beautiful bottom whipped, her face smeared in my kitchen slops. Her hands came around me, to hold my bottom, kneading at my cheeks, and I was starting to come. Briefly, the noise of a car in the road distracted me, and then I was there, crying out in ecstasy with my fist clenched tight in Kay's hair and her tongue flicking hard on my clit, bringing me to a long, glorious peak that died only when I became aware of somebody calling out my name from the road.

'Amber!'

They couldn't see us. My house and the hedges shielded my play area completely, but it was still a shock, and all the more so because I recognised the voice – Melody Rathwell. I cursed under my breath as I struggled to pull my jodhpurs up, succeeding only in getting them tangled with my knickers. There was no point in pretending I wasn't there, as she was quite capable of waiting outside and I'd just end up looking silly. She called out again as I finally managed to cover myself up.

'Amber!'

'Hang on, Mel, I'll be with you in a minute,' I yelled back.

Kay scampered for the house, giggling and with her tail bobbing behind her as I made for the gates. I took my time, giving her a chance to get decent, not because of Melody, but because Morris was likely to be with her and Kay's not very good about men seeing her nude, no more than I am. Sure enough, as I swung the gates wide, their huge, gaudy Rolls-Royce was facing me, blocking most of the road, with Morris at the wheel and Mel standing to one side. She gave a casual one-fingered salute to a van driver who'd been waiting to get past and stepped close to kiss me as Morris drove in.

I caught her scent: cocoa butter and a rich musk, intensely feminine. She hugged me and slapped my bottom, immediately triggering the same ambivalent feelings she always provoked, the desire to drag her over my knee and spank her until she howled against the feeling that it would be utterly inappropriate and I should be the one getting my bottom warmed. She was fully dressed, but no less provocative for that, with a green skinny top tight over her big breasts and her tummy bare. Everything about her spoke of sexual aggression and, after closing the gate, I found my eyes on her rear view as she walked to where Morris was parking the car. Her heavy muscular bottom was encased in low-slung jeans that left the top of a scarlet thong on show, and good few inches of smooth, chocolate-coloured skin bare above.

Kay had come back out, now in a loose summer dress, no longer a pig, but still barefoot, her hair and face still wet, and presumably knickerless. I bit down a familiar pang of jealousy as she kissed Melody, but unlike me she didn't get her bottom slapped. I stepped close as Morris climbed out of the car, letting him kiss me so that he wouldn't get to Kay. He did anyway, patting her bottom as he spoke.

'Amber! You look great, just great, and Kay . . . wow, that's all I can say.'

His eyes moved between us in a brief inspection that nevertheless managed to be thorough, extremely lewd, and curiously professional, as if weighing us up for sale. I knew full well that the wet patch at the crotch of my jodhpurs showed the shape of my fanny lips, and found myself blushing as I ushered them inside. If Melody made me feel ill at ease, Morris was worse, and the fact that they were far and away the best customers for the kinky side of my business didn't help. Kay went to make coffee as the rest of us sat down around the kitchen table, and I let Morris speak, hoping he had some large and extravagant order for his SM club.

'It's the big one this month,' he said. 'Three thousand tickets already sold.'

'Excellent,' I answered, genuinely impressed.

His club had been growing steadily, yet for all its success it still represented just a tiny part of his income. He had kept it kinky, resisting the urge to tone it down for the sake of being able to use bigger venues, a refusal to compromise I had to admire. Three thousand was still a lot of people. Most would be men, most would be there just for the thrill of voyeurism. I felt a shiver run down my spine at the thought as he went on.

'You know we're doing a puppy-dog show?'

'I'd heard, yes, but it would be far too public for Kay, and –'

'No problem. I don't need you to compete. I need you to judge.'

'Judge?'

'Sure. Who better? You've got the name. You've got the experience.'

'And with me on the panel people will know you haven't fixed the result?'

He tried to look hurt but didn't really succeed. A refusal had already risen to my lips, but I bit it down. After all, what harm could there be in judging?

As usual, Morris' club was in a warehouse, in this case at Barking Creek, which seemed appropriate, a single vast room with the insides completely stripped out. He'd brought in lights, portable loos, a stage, cordons and various pieces of bondage equipment, but they still looked lost beneath the huge ironwork lattice that supported the roof. We'd arrived early, as requested, and only as it began to fill up did the air of industrial decay gradually give way to something more kinky.

Morris' guests ran the whole gamut of sexual display and sexual interest, from leather-clad professional dominas to out and out dirty old men, one or two of whom were actually wearing macs. Most of the other men were either in full leathers or posing pouches, a few in smart suits, but the women were far more varied. Before I'd finished the glass of champagne Morris had pressed into my hand on arrival, I'd seen a dozen striking costumes: rubber, leather and PVC in various designs, several schoolgirl outfits ranging from realistic demure to ones only appropriate for a strip show, Japanese girls in diminutive sailor suits with tight white panties showing beneath their tiny skirts, cabaret outfits, lingerie and, in one or two cases, nothing but make-up and a smile. These last included Sophie Cherwell and Annabelle Yates, who were on the door, stark naked but for electric-blue platform boots.

As I was to be a judge, I'd dressed in style: jodhpurs of black corduroy, a crisp white blouse, my hunting pinks, a necktie and riding boots polished until Kay had been able to see her reflection in them as she worked. She had been hesitant about coming, and I'd had to put her on a lead and in big rubber pants before she'd felt secure. They were very tight, and concealed nothing of the shape of her bottom. I'd made the hems uneven and glued on a sprightly little tail, sticking up over her bum to make her into a pointer puppy. She'd insisted on a top too, which I'd done in the same style, and I had named her Patch for the evening, not very original perhaps, but appropriate.

Once inside we were left to our own devices, sipping champagne and watching the place fill up. A long table had been placed on the stage, with three chairs behind it, obviously for the judges. That meant I had two colleagues, and I was interested to find out who they were. Morris had disappeared, Sophie and Annabelle were busy, and there was no sign of Mel, but I managed to collar her twin sister Harmony, who was handing out flyers.

'Who are the other judges?' I asked, almost shouting above the inevitable loud music.

'That guy Protheroe,' she answered, 'and Jean de Vrain.'

'Mr Protheroe! What does he know about ... about anything? Who's Jean de Vrain?'

'Protheroe paid Morris to be on the panel. Jean's a dom, very old school.'

'I've never heard of her.'

'No reason you should have. She used to publish a thing called *Slap Happy*, a domestic discipline magazine. That was years ago, but she tried to clear her old stock through the net and some busybody reported her. The local police are trying to prosecute.'

'What for?'

'They claim it's obscene. She's in Hampshire, and you know how the rural police love a vice case.'

'Poor woman.'

'I know. We're having a charity auction later to raise money for a fighting fund.'

'Good for you. Point her out to me.'

'She's not here yet, but you won't miss her, about seventy, steel-rimmed glasses, usually in tweed.'

I nodded and she turned away as a couple in black and red leather came towards her. Jean de Vrain was going to be easy to spot, and I was keen to meet her, and to sympathise. Being a member of a small village community myself, and supplementing the income from my saddlers with fetish gear, local disapproval was a constant worry. I was very careful, and kept my kinky activities strictly for those in the know, but having some prude find out what I was into was something I dreaded. It was hard to see how anything I did could warrant actual prosecution, but it is extraordinary how prudish some people can be.

Mr Protheroe was another matter, and something I wasn't at all happy about. He was among the worst of the dirty old men who attended Morris' paid spanking parties; he was flabby, balding, with a pear-shaped body, a red face, no neck and a permanent leer. If he looked revolting, his manner was worse. He had a thing about formal, old-fashioned spankings. Discipline for girls, he called it, but that didn't stop him groping his victims. For some reason he was obsessed with me, perhaps because he knew how much I hated it.

Just thinking about him made me acutely aware of my bottom, and I found myself tugging the tail of my pinks down to cover myself. Jean de Vrain could wait. Knowing Protheroe would be on the lookout for me, and not wishing to run into him, I took Kay out the back, to where a large service yard was screened from view by a high fence beyond which rose a small hill of scrap iron and the remains of cars. It was not the most romantic setting in the world, but it was peaceful, and we sat and chatted until Harmony came out to collect me.

The club was full: people were milling about across the whole great floor area and packed densely around the long bar and a cleared area in front of the stage. Protheroe was already in his seat, his great flabby buttocks sticking out at the sides. He was in suit trousers and a white shirt that could barely contain his body, while his face and the bald patch on top of his head were shiny with sweat. Beside him was a slim, elderly woman, in a tweed twinset with a pearl brooch on the lapel, evidently Jean de Vrain. She was small, barely taller than Kay, but there was a stern look to her, and what I was sure was disapproval as I mounted the stage.

'Sorry I'm late, I was outside,' I stated as I took my seat between them.

'Nothing a good spanking wouldn't put right!' Protheroe joked, chuckling as his eyes fixed firmly on my chest. 'Hello, Amber, you're looking well.'

I gave him a dirty look as Kay curled herself at my feet, then nodded to Jean de Vrain, who responded in kind. Morris was already on the stage, microphone in hand, and he began to speak as I made myself comfortable. We were certainly well provided for, Morris style, generous yet vulgar, with a champagne bucket in front of me and the necks of two bottles of pink Dom Perignon protruding from among the ice. Protheroe already had one open, and filled my glass as Morris began his introduction. I said thank you, eager to avoid any criticism of my manners and the inevitable suggestion for what should be done to improve them. As I took my first sip Morris stepped a little to the side and swept an arm back towards us, still speaking.

'. . . and to judge our show we have three experienced practitioners of the fine arts of kinkiness. To my left, Mrs Jean de Vrain, proprietor of *Slap Happy* magazine, for whom we'll be holding a charity auction later this evening, so be ready to dig deep for a worthy cause. At the far end, the infamous Mr Protheroe, who's spanked more naughty girls than he's had hot dinners. And last, but by no means least, Miss Amber Oakley, creator of the piggy-girl.'

He stepped aside with another sweeping gesture towards us and I found myself smiling nervously at the great ring of faces beyond the ropes. Morris continued to talk, explaining the rules, and I took a quick inventory of what was in front of me on the table: a sheet marked with the names of the owners and dogs, both puppy-girls and puppy-boys by the look of it, also a double column of boxes inviting me to mark each for look and performance, with marks out of ten. It seemed simple enough, and I was looking forward to it as the first contestants came out.

They were listed as Miss Barbara and 'Peebody'. I was not particularly impressed. Miss Barbara was genuine enough, if a little self-conscious, but very much a domina rather than a puppy mistress, all severity and pose in a rubber catsuit and holding a riding whip. Peebody was presumably supposed to be an Old English sheepdog, with a heavy corpulent body clad in white and grey fur. Unfortunately, the size of his haunches and the fact that he was walking bent double rather than crawling made him look more like a gigantic flea than a dog. He was at least enthusiastic, rolling over and fetching a ball in his mouth to Miss Barbara's commands, delivered in a soft Irish accent which rather detracted from her image as a harsh and sadistic mistress. After some reflection I decided on six for look and also for performance.

I was glad I'd marked him up because the next two had barely made an effort. Both were male and both were naked, their cocks and balls swinging bare between their legs as they crawled. The first was at least doglike, and was put through a range of tricks by his leather-clad master. The second didn't really perform at all, but just got punished, with a dozen strokes of a long wooden paddle applied by a mistress who looked as if she'd been paid to do the job. I couldn't bring myself to give them more than three in either category.

The fourth was spectacular: 'Rubba Dobie' with Mistress Angel. She was tall, black and elegant, with all the enthusiasm for her role I had found so lacking in the last mistress, better even than Miss Barbara. She was also properly dressed, in a smart grey suit, stockings and high heels. If she was fine, 'Rubba Dobie' was magnificent. He was entirely clad in shiny rubber, including a dog's head mask, all black except his genitals, which were bright pink and astonishingly detailed. The cock was a good foot long, a bulbous rubber truncheon ending in a wrinkly point, and grotesquely lifelike. A pendulous, heavily wrinkled scrotum hung behind beneath a pink anal star. He even had a knot: the bulge of flesh at the base of a dog's penis which swells to hold him in his bitch during mating. It was obscene, no other word did it justice, but I found myself unable to tear my eyes away as he was put through his paces by Mistress Angel: fetching and rolling over, begging, playing dead and finally attempting to hump her leg, which earned him applause from the audience and several hard slaps from her. I wanted to give him two tens, but settled for nines just in case.

There were only nine contenders, and the first four had all been male. I was beginning to feel a little cheated, and so was Mr Protheroe, who was shaking his head and grumbling to himself as he marked Angel and Rubba Dobie. The next one perked him up: Sophie had entered as Fido and came in crawling on all fours with Fat Jeff Bellbird in hot pursuit. She wasn't made up like a dog at all, but she was great fun to watch, running riot as she evaded Jeff time and again, nipping at the ankles of the audience and, when Jeff finally caught her, cocking her leg up and peeing on his trousers, with her fanny on full view to several hundred people. I gave her a four for look because however cute she was she'd made no more effort than the second or third, but a ten for a performance I was sure wouldn't be bettered.

Number six was also a girl, not somebody I knew, and she and her partner had entered as 'Command' and 'Obedience'. The names suited them: he a strict but ever so slightly nervous male dominant; she a plump young woman clearly new to submission but wanting nothing in enthusiasm. He put her through a precise regime, making her bark out the answers to sums, beg, catch a ball and roll over on her back. She did turn me on, especially lying tummy up with her thighs wide and her hands in the begging position, completely vulnerable, but like Sophie she was nude, the only difference a spiked dog collar. I gave her five and seven, then changed the seven to an eight.

Next came another gay male couple, and they were good, with 'Butch' naked but for an Alsatian mask and his master in full leathers. They went through a mock police dog training scenario which was both clever and well rehearsed, so I marked them seven and eight, which made them my second place team. The next was a mess, because the 'dog' was a cross-dresser and hadn't been able to abandon his main fetish for the sake of being a decent puppy-boy. A combination of huge floppy ears, a short floral dress and frilly pink knickers that almost completely failed to hide a large set of cock and balls failed to impress me, while his mistress once again looked as if she'd been hired for the evening.

Ninth and last was Miss Patricia Whitworth and 'Bitch'. I had fully expected Bitch to be a man, but as she trotted smartly out on her owner's lead I could see I'd guessed wrong. She was quite clearly a girl, or rather, a spaniel, with her body encased in woolly black fur save for where two sweetly rounded breasts hung down below her chest, and behind, where the rear of the puppy suit was split to show off her fanny and bumhole. The effect was deliciously rude, and gave me a pleasant-ly shocked feeling, which grew rapidly deeper as they went into their routine.

It was simple, and brief, but highly effective. Miss Patricia Whitworth, a smart young woman in a tight silk dress and a picture hat, extracted a tin from her handbag, a tin of dog food. A bowl and an opener followed, she decanted the vile pinkish brown mess into the bowl, stood back, and watched with her arms folded coolly across her chest as her girlfriend, who I could suddenly no longer think of as a puppy-girl, ate it. I just stared, revolted yet fascinated, both by the thought of making a woman eat a bowl of dog food and the strength of dominance and submission such an act represented. It was a messy business too, because although Bitch's muzzle was quite short, she was having trouble and, despite doing her best to snuffle the muck up and swallow it down, she ended up with her mask and what was visible of her face beneath well plastered.

The audience had watched in silence broken only by the occasional gasp of horror, but broke into whistles and applause the moment Bitch had swallowed her last mouthful. Miss Patricia Whitworth walked smartly off stage and we were done. I hesitated over my marking sheet, trying not to let the tingling in my fanny influence me unduly. Bitch was cute, and her costume good, but not as good as Rubba Dobie. I went for eight. The performance had been superb, as good as Sophie's, maybe less imaginative, but intensely humiliating. It had to be a ten.

That left me tied with Rubba Dobie and Bitch on equal marks and the second gay couple in third place. Jean de Vrain and Mr Protheroe leant in and Morris began to speak into the microphone once more.

'An easy winner, the last couple,' Protheroe stated. 'I gave them a double ten.'

'I have eighteen for them,' I said, 'and also for Angel and Rubba Dobie. How about you?'

'That revolting creature?' Jean de Vrain queried. 'I awarded zero for look, and –'

'Zero? But that suit was amazing. It must have taken months to make.'

'Merely because a great deal of effort has gone into something does not make it worthwhile,' she responded.

'I agree,' Mr Protheroe put in. 'It was just plain gross.'

'You wouldn't think so if you were gay,' I objected.

'Which I'm not, thank God,' he answered. 'I gave them five for look and eight for performance, which I think generous.'

'Very generous,' Jean de Vrain added. 'Zero and six.'

I stifled a sigh.

'That gives them . . . thirty-seven,' I said, 'and the last couple thirty-six and –'

'Seven and seven,' Jean de Vrain put in.

'– giving a total of fifty. How about Sophie? Fido that is?'

'The girl who urinated on the fat man's leg?' Jean de Vrain asked. 'Two and zero. She was absolutely revolting.'

'She was superb,' I protested. 'OK, she'd hadn't made any effort with a costume, but for performance. I gave her four and ten.'

'You shouldn't mark high for mere obscenity,' Jean de Vrain answered me.

I shrugged and turned to Mr Protheroe, a most unlikely ally.

'Eight and ten,' he said, 'which makes . . . fourteen . . . , and two . . . and eighteen . . . thirty-four.'

I shook my head. Sophie is ever so cute, but to give her eight just for going nude and five for Rubba Dobie was ridiculous. Jean de Vrain's attitude was no better.

'You're both being far too subjective,' I insisted. 'For the look you should judge on the quality of the appearance of the puppy-girl . . . or puppy-boy. For performance, on how well they behave, and I don't just mean obedience. It shouldn't matter if either their

14

appearance or their behaviour isn't in tune with your personal likes and dislikes.'

'I think I am quite qualified to make my own judgements,' Jean de Vrain answered icily.

'Absolutely,' Protheroe agreed, chuckling. 'So just you learn to respect your elders and betters, Miss Amber Oakley, or I may have to put you over my knee and spank your naughty bottom.'

He was laughing as he said it, and leering. I immediately found myself blushing crimson, but I wasn't giving up that easily.

'Never mind that,' I said quickly. 'But surely the time and effort that went into Rubba Dobie's suit must count for something?'

'It does,' he answered me. 'Five out of ten. I agree with Jean, the genitals were merely obscene.'

'Well, yes,' I admitted, 'but I still say we should be more objective in our judgement, and while I appreciate that you both have a great deal more experience than me when it comes to corporal punishment, so far as puppy play is –'

'You are well overdue,' Protheroe interrupted.

'Overdue? Overdue what?' I demanded.

'Discipline, I suspect Mr Protheroe means,' Jean de Vrain said quietly, 'and I am inclined to agree, a good spanking by preference.'

I opened my mouth, furious at the suggestion, but closed it again. Anything I said was just going to sound petulant. I quickly turned back to my marks and changed the subject.

'We'll have to agree to differ. Who else is in contention then? Not two or three?'

Both shook their heads, to my relief.

'I gave the second gay couple fifteen, seven and eight.'

'Four and five, nine,' Protheroe added.

'A four and a seven,' Jean de Vrain put in, 'an eleven, and therefore thirty-five.'

We went through the others, but it was clear none of them came close and Morris was hovering. I'd put the totals on my sheet and handed it up to him, then poured myself another glass of champagne as I sat back, feeling faintly irritated. Both Protheroe and Jean de Vrain had made completely subjective decisions, and it was only because they'd disagreed with each other so radically that we had a halfway sensible result. Yet the order had at least turned out fair.

'In third place,' Morris was saying, 'and taking home a cheque for one hundred pounds and a box of dog biscuits ... Mr Trainer and Butch!'

There was polite applause, and a few rude remarks. The couple did a quick lap of honour before coming to collect the prize, then stood below the front of the stage, with Butch squatting obediently at his master's side. I took another swallow of champagne as Morris continued, relieved that he wasn't reading out the actual marks.

'In second place, with a cheque for two hundred pounds and an economy-sized tin of Chunk, we have Mistress Angel and Rubba Dobie!'

The applause was a lot louder, and more sustained. They came out to take their prize and get into line beside the others even as Morris continued.

'And so, tonight's winner, with a cheque for five hundred pounds and a case of Puppy Chunk, which something tells me they may actually need ... Miss Patricia Whitworth and Bitch!'

They came out to wild applause, and I found myself smiling again. It was a just result, for all my colleagues' bizarre marking, and I at least had tried to be fair. The three winning couples gave a brief show of their dogs and the competition was over, leaving Kay and me free to amuse ourselves. The puppy show had left me quite turned on, and I wondered if I might be able to find somewhere quiet to play with Kay, but my first thought was to elude Protheroe.

16

I needed the loo as well, and made for the line of portables, each of which had a substantial queue. It wasn't particularly comfortable, as I needed to pee quite badly and there were various voyeurs hanging around in the hope that one of the girls would wet herself, so I was very glad when Patricia Whitworth joined the line behind me. Bitch was with her, still on a lead, just like I had Kay, and they immediately began to snuffle gently at each other. Ignoring the puppies, Patricia and I exchanged pecks and I congratulated her.

'Well done, you were great.'

'Thanks. I was really surprised, actually, I thought Mistress Angel and Rubba Dobie would win.'

'It was close,' I admitted, twisting the truth a little, 'but you had the edge. She's a spaniel, isn't she? My Patch is a pointer.'

I reached down to pet Bitch, rubbing her curly head. She snuffled my hand briefly and went back to Kay. Patricia ducked down to tickle Kay's chin. To my surprise, Kay let her, and I found myself glancing around the warehouse and wishing that Morris had set aside some private space. An area at the end was curtained off and divided into cubicles, but I knew Morris. Every hanging would have several sets of peep-holes for the voyeurs.

'Maybe we should get together sometime, Patricia?' I suggested as she stood up.

'Great!' she answered immediately. 'Patty will do fine, to you. I love the stuff you make, by the way.'

'Oh? What have you seen?'

'All sorts. There was this beautiful pony-girl at the last club, very tall, dark hair –'

'Vicky.'

'– and so elegant. She said you'd made her harness, and her tail. She showed me how it plugged in up her bum.'

'Always a favourite.'

'But the way the shaft went up between her cheeks, so that the hair seemed to sprout from her spine, pure genius! And the triple-ring device to hold her hair in ponytails. You're so clever.'

I was blushing despite myself, and smiling. She looked so enthusiastic, and I found myself focussing on her as a person rather than as Bitch's owner. She was nearly as tall as me, maybe five seven, slim and very poised. With her silk dress, big hat and carefully applied make-up, there was something old-fashioned about her, 1950s or even earlier. Her hair added to the effect, very dark and elaborately curled, as did the smart high heels, and what I was sure were stockings.

'I've been dying to meet you ever since,' she went on, 'but I didn't think I should introduce myself beforehand, and –'

'I wouldn't worry about things like that. Morris usually fixes his results.'

'He does? Don't tell me that, I was already feeling a bit of cheat with Grandma judging –'

'Grandma? Jean de Vrain is your grandmother?'

'Sure. I was the one who persuaded Morris to run the auction when she got into trouble. Are you going to do something for it?'

'I haven't been asked, but –'

The cubicle door opened and I nipped in quickly, not wanting anyone else to pinch my place. For a moment nothing mattered but getting my jodhpurs and knickers down and my bum on the seat, but the moment I'd let go and enjoyed the first wash of relief my mind had turned to Patty. She was lovely, and I was already hoping she switched because, while sharing Kay and her girlfriend would be good, having her across my knee and then between my thighs would be great, and under my bottom better still. It would even be worth taking a spanking in return, maybe being her puppy, if it was just the two of us.

18

I was feeling thoroughly pleased with myself as I tidied up, but also a little shocked at finding that Patty was Jean de Vrain's granddaughter. The idea of my parents finding out what I was into was a nightmare. It wasn't an age thing because my godfather not only knew but had introduced me to it, and to Morris in turn, but family is different.

She was just as eager to get into the loo as I'd been, but held out a card to me as we swapped places. I glanced at it briefly, noting an address in Lincoln. I'd given her Kay's lead, and she passed that to me too, but Bitch had disappeared. I was going to wait, and suggest we go out the back to find a little privacy for some puppy training, but spotted Protheroe coming towards the loos with an all too familiar leer painted across his sweaty, globular face.

Even to have to turn him down would be humiliating, as he should have known full well that I did not want to be spanked by him, so I tugged Kay into the narrow alley behind the line of loos. It was almost pitch black and the floor was criss-crossed with cables, but when we emerged I could see Protheroe where I'd been standing, looking around with a puzzled frown. Feeling rather pleased with myself, I made for the doorway that led out to the back, intent on some fresh air and perhaps to see if there were any quiet nooks to which I could invite Patty and Bitch.

I had to pass through a service bay, well lit and a lot quieter than the main area. Morris was there, talking to a huge man in an immaculate suit apparently made of white leather and stitched with thongs. I picked up their conversation as I drew close, the big man speaking.

'. . . great, Morris, just great. We have to get together on this. We've got clubs in New York, San Diego, LA, Jacksonville. Just think, what a show!'

Morris was nodding enthusiastically. I was going to pass with a polite nod, but he reached out and took my arm, introducing me immediately.

'This is one of my judges, Amber Oakley. Amber, meet Hudson Staebler. Hudson's from the US.'

'Fort Lauderdale, Florida,' the man filled in, extending one bearlike paw. 'Pleased to meet you, Amber. Great judgement call there, although for me I'd have placed the little blonde.'

'Sophie,' I told him. 'She only missed out by one point.'

He nodded thoughtfully.

'Great girl, Sophie,' Morris assured him. 'Anything you want, she'll oblige.'

He gave a meaningful wink, which left the American looking slightly surprised for an instant before he went on.

'I was just telling Morris here how we should organise an international competition. With the internet, there are puppy clubs growing up right across the States. What d' you think?'

'It's a great idea,' I told him, 'but I imagine we'd need to find some neutral ground.'

'Details,' he answered. 'It's got to be done, no matter where. Canada maybe.'

'Ireland?' I suggested.

He made an approving face. Morris spoke again.

'So what have you got for the auction, Amber? Going to let us have a pop at your Kay?'

'No ... I, er ... I haven't really thought about it. Perhaps –'

'You'll think of something,' he broke in, turning aside to greet Melody as she approached, along with Mistress Angel. I moved deftly aside to prevent Mel from greeting me with her usual slap, only to bump against Hudson Staebler, bum first, which left me feeling slightly awkward. Mel kissed me, grinning as she stood back beside Morris, who put his arm around her shoulder and greeted Mistress Angel, a little cautiously I thought. I'd realised she was tall, but in her heels she stood perhaps six foot, and with all the poise of a natural domina.

'Lost your dog?' I asked. She grinned, every bit as predatory as Mel.

'He's gone to change. So you reckon we were second best?'

'I had you equal first, and top for look,' I answered, before I could steel myself to respond to her scolding tone, but if she could play dominance games, so could I.

'I think you overdid it on the genitals,' I told her.

She shrugged.

'Not me, darling, him. I just walk the dog. So, Mel tells me you put up quite a fight in the wrestling ring?'

'I've won my share,' I answered carefully.

'And lost a few,' Mel added.

'Everyone loses sometimes,' I replied.

'Not this lady,' Angel put in. 'Are you entered next month?'

'No,' I admitted.

'Shame. You're cute, and I would just love to give you a good, public spanking, maybe piss on you after.'

'The feeling is mutual,' I answered, and had the satisfaction of seeing her eyebrows rise in affront.

'You two in the ring: that I would love to see,' Hudson Staebler laughed. 'But I wouldn't know where to put my money.'

I gave him a smile, warming to him. She looked so dominant, and most men simply wouldn't have had the guts to comment. It had hit home too.

'You'd better have your money on me,' Angel told him, and tried to give him a crushing look.

It didn't really work because for all her height she was still looking up at him, and he wasn't even wearing heels. I found myself smiling and turned to Morris.

'It's the wrestling next month then? Is Vicky entered?'

Morris had his glass to his lips and merely nodded.

'Vicky?' Angel queried. 'The pony-girl?'

'That's Vicky, but –' I assured her, then shut up because Mel was trying to wink at me without her friend noticing.

Whatever was going on, it was more complicated that I knew, and I quickly changed the topic of conversation.

'What are you doing for the auction, Mel?'

'Me personally?' she answered. 'Offering a topping scene, Angel and I together.'

'That should go well,' I admitted as Morris took over.

'A few things are fixed, and then people can make offers for whatever they want. We reckon we'll do better that way because then people get what they want, not just what's on offer, so they'll pay more.'

He was right, and I nodded in appreciation. Kay, bless her, had begun to pull on her lead, providing me with an excellent excuse to move on before Mel or Angel could make any embarrassing suggestions for what I might do, such as having my knickers auctioned off.

I did feel I ought to do something. Jean de Vrain was a mad old bitch, but she should have been able to publish her little spanking magazine without police interference. I felt for her, and knew that if I was ever in the same position Morris could be counted on to back me up. It was only fair that I did something, but I could hardly auction Kay. She simply didn't have the experience or self-confidence to cope. There was also the matter of not disappointing Patty, who I badly wanted in my bed.

My immediate thought was Sophie, who was sure to be game but was probably in the auction already. The same went for Harmony and Annabelle. It was always possible to offer a scene, like Mel and Angel, but I'd just end up thrashing some male sub, and it's not really my thing.

Kay had led me outside. She was well into her puppy role, not speaking, but she clearly had the same thing as I did on her mind. It was fully dark, but the yard was quite well lit by security lights in a neighbouring unit, and too open anyway. One or two couples had managed to find niches in which they were at least partially concealed, but that was just for sex. We needed more space.

I even walked Kay up to the far end to see if there was a way into another area, but the fence was ten foot high and topped with razor wire. The only other possibility was the curtained-off area in which the contenders for the puppy show had got ready. It was far from perfect, but perhaps good enough, at least to let the puppies play. I could worry about Patty later.

We went in again, and I fielded a glass of champagne from Annabelle, who was now acting as maid, still stark naked but for her boots, with her ankles hobbled and her tray chained to her wrists. As Mel's pet, I couldn't really play with her unless I was prepared to give Kay in return, so resisted the temptation of her slender, naked body and went to look for Sophie instead. I was feeling quite drunk, and quite horny, enough to wonder about putting Kay between my thighs then and there if the changing area was empty.

It wasn't, and I found Sophie, still stark naked, on her knees and down on Hudson Staebler's erection. I made to leave, but she beckoned to me, not even bothering to take her mouth off the thick, pale penis she was sucking. Her bum was red, and she'd clearly been spanked before being put to his cock. My face must have been more or less the same colour, but I held my ground, watching her suck with my tummy fluttering. He was quite big; his cock looked impressive even in comparison with his huge body. There was a casual, natural dominance about him as well, in the way he sat, obviously at ease, and not in the least embarrassed to have Kay and me watching.

I was half expecting to be invited to join her, and not sure if I could have resisted. Cock sucking is not

23

normally my thing at all, but there's a compulsion to seeing a man erect and in control of a girl, especially a really big man and a girl as cute and as submissive as Sophie. Fortunately, he came in her mouth before the blend of champagne and arousal could make me do anything silly. She swallowed like a good girl, came off his cock, thanked him, and turned to me, smiling.

'Hi, Amber, have you met Hudson?'

'Morris introduced us, thanks,' I answered.

'Me too,' she said laughing, 'and told me to suck him off, the dirty pig. I need to talk to you, later, as it goes –'

'Likewise. I was hoping to do something for the auction, and that you'd help me out?'

'If I can, but I'm already being auctioned for a spanking. I was supposed to stay pristine, in fact.'

She gave Hudson a look of mock disapproval. He laughed and slapped her bottom, then began to put his cock away, stuffing it into his underpants with some difficulty. I hesitated, feeling a little awkward. I knew Kay wouldn't want to play in front of a man, but the idea did appeal, and Sophie joining in even more so. All I needed to do was say the word and I could have what I so badly wanted, but the situation just wasn't right. Kay trusted me not to make her perform in front of men, and Hudson was so dominant that doing anything in front of him would be a gesture of submission for me. It had to wait.

'I could take an enema or something?' Sophie offered casually.

I nodded, knowing she meant it and amused not only by how filthy she could be, but how casual she was about it. Just the thought of anything so rude, even a fraction as rude, in front of three thousand or more gaping spectators was enough to set my stomach tight and sick, yet she had suggested it as if asking if I'd like a cup of coffee.

'Five minutes,' Hudson remarked. 'I'd better go to get a good place.'

'Shit,' Sophie swore, 'better get ready.'

She went to a bag and began to scramble into a schoolgirl outfit: tight white knickers, knee-high socks, tiny red tartan skirt, white blouse with nothing underneath, green tie and smart black shoes. I watched in appreciation, sure that there would be men in the audience who'd pay well for the privilege of taking her knickers back down to bare her for spanking, more than they'd have done had she stayed naked. She paused only to drain a miniature vodka down her throat, put her hair up into bunches secured by huge flowers made of pale blue silk and she was ready, or nearly so.

'How's my make-up?' she demanded, giving a worried glance into the mirror of her compact.

'Your lipstick's smudged.'

'Bloody Morris. I mean, I don't mind giving his friends blow jobs, but you'd have thought it could wait until after the auction.'

I nodded sympathetically and waited while she made some frantic repairs. Beyond the drapes the music had stopped and I could hear the excited hum of voices. The moment Sophie was ready we hurried out, to find Morris already on the stage, facing a throng of people pressed in around the ropes. Hudson Staebler hadn't managed to get his place, but I could clearly see him towering above everyone else a few feet back. We had a fine view from the side, so stayed put, with Kay kneeling beside me. Morris tapped the microphone and began to speak.

'Ladies and gentlemen, masters, mistresses, slaves and sluts, next tonight we have a special event, an event which ought to be a lot of fun, but which has a serious side. At the beginning of last month, the home of Mrs Jean de Vrain was raided by police and stocks of her vintage spanking magazine, *Slap Happy*, taken away, with a view to prosecuting her under the Obscene Publications Act. Jean is one of those rare few who has always stood for what she believes in, the right for every man and every woman to conduct their private life as they please, subject to consent. No doubt her persecutors think she is an easy target and, in bringing this prosecution, hope to establish a precedent for further action. So it makes no difference if you are into CP or not, if you're straight or gay, even if you only like to watch. This is a direct threat to your lifestyle, and so I ask you to dig deep for the fighting fund, but not for nothing.'

I found myself nodding in agreement. He paused as Mel and Angel stepped forwards, now both in full leather, spike-heeled boots, tight trousers and jackets with the zips drawn down to show the dark curves of their breasts, studded collars, peaked caps, all black and shiny. Both had their arms folded across their chests, and both carried plaited-leather dog whips.

'Not for nothing,' Morris repeated, with an admiring glance for his wife and her friend. 'First then, there will be a selection of treats, each going to the highest bidder. After that, I'll bring up my staff and others to the stage and any member of the audience may bid for whatsoever they please. So, to kick off, what am I bid for the rest of the evening as slave to the truly magnificent mistresses, Melody and Angel?'

Hands immediately began to shoot up from the audience, dozens of them, with the men calling out bids, some ridiculously low, but quickly rising. It was hard to see who was offering what, but Morris either had a better position or was simply making it up, pointing to people in the audience and calling out the bids in return, two hundred, three, four, then stopping at four hundred and fifty, which two men had called out at the same time.

'Well, gentlemen?' Morris demanded, only to have Mel take the microphone from him.

'They're no gentlemen,' she grated, 'more like grovelling little dirt bags. Come on out, the pair of you.'

They came, a middle-aged man in nothing but a leather posing pouch and an enormously fat cross-dresser in pink chiffon. Angel gave a sniff of distaste and bellowed an order.

'Kneel! Don't you know anything?'

Both knelt immediately. Angel stepped down from the stage and strode across the open space to where they were. Using her whip, she lifted one chin and then the other, looking down on them with an expression of amused contempt. The man in leather could barely bring himself to meet her eyes, I could see the shaking of his body from where I was. As he lowered his head, Angel spat, catching him on the little bald patch at the centre of his hair, extended one elegant leg to kick the cross-dresser over on to his side, then turned to nod at Mel.

'We'll take them both,' Mel announced, and passed the microphone back to Morris.

Neither man complained, but paid up promptly before they were quickly put on collars and leads and dragged away, the crowd parting before the two women. Sophie was next up, and she really played the part, jumping up on the stage, flashing her knickers in a mocking curtsey with her bum stuck out at the audience, then turning to blow them a raspberry and stand with her hands on her hips, so full of insolence and so challenging that I'd have been bidding myself if I'd been out there. All that was on offer was a chance to spank her, which she was usually up for anyway, but the bidding rose up over three hundred.

Jean de Vrain was seated on the far side of the stage, and smiling happily to herself as the successful bidder stepped out from the crowd. I vaguely recognised him as one of the men who attended Morris' paid parties, but I couldn't put a name to him. He was in a smart business suit, charcoal grey, with a red carnation in his lapel, very formal, also tall and quite well built, a man,

I was sure, who could deliver a serious spanking. Sophie didn't care, strolling out across the open floor to stand in front of him, one knee cocked out, her hands on her hips, daring him to do his worst. He lifted one eyebrow in disapproval, then spoke.

'A brat, I see. I wonder if you'll be so impudent once I've toasted your bare bottom. Fetch a chair.'

'Fetch it yourself, Fatso.'

He wasn't fat, but he did have the beginnings of a paunch, and for an instant there was genuine anger on his face before he recovered himself.

'Fetch it,' he snapped, 'or by God I'll make sure you can't sit for a week.'

Sophie stuck her tongue out at him. He'd begun to go red, but really he had no choice, and he knew it. There was a spare chair near where Kay and I were watching from, and he marched over to collect it. Placing it squarely in the centre of the clear space, facing the audience, he walked to where Sophie had been watching him coolly.

'Come on you, time you learnt your lesson,' he ordered, reaching out for her wrist.

Sophie skipped back out of reach and wagged a finger at him.

'Uh, uh, money first.'

He was going redder still as he quickly counted out notes to her. She stuck them down her front, then struck a pose as he put his wallet away.

'Well, I'm waiting. I thought you were going to spank me?'

His answer was to grab her by the ear and frogmarch her back to the chair. She squeaked a bit at having her ear pulled, and again as she was thrown down across his lap. He must have been genuinely angry because he didn't mess around, or draw out her exposure, but simply hoisted her school skirt high, whipped her knickers smartly down to bare her bum, and laid in.

28

He spanked hard, perhaps harder than Sophie had bargained for, especially without a warm-up. She tried to resist, but she was kicking in no time, and squealing, begging him to slow down. He took no notice whatsoever, laying in slap after furious slap to her bouncing bottom, with her arms flailing wildly and her head tossing in her pain. Her legs were going like pumps, and had quickly begun to come apart, showing off her fanny to at least half the audience, myself included.

It was a fine sight, as a well-spanked girl always is, but I took a moment to see how other people were reacting. Morris was wearing a quiet smile, more amused than anything, but then he'd seen her punished a hundred times and knew that if he wanted to relieve himself in her mouth afterwards she would be game. Jean de Vrain was also smiling, just, with a look of cool approval for what was being done. Most of the audience were rapt in attention, the girls aroused and gloating, the men leering, although a few of the more submissive ones looked shocked at what was being done to her.

Her bottom was cherry red by the time he stopped, and she slumped down over his knee, her head hung in defeat, her legs still apart, her moist, ready fanny on full show. If he'd fucked her then and there I doubt she'd have resisted, and as it was she let herself be taken by the hand and led away without so much as a murmur of protest. He'd earned whatever he was going to take, and I could hardly protest, but only hope she'd be back in time for me to auction her for the second time.

Harmony had already stepped forwards, her beautiful black skin glistening with oil, in nothing but her electric blue boots. Like Annabelle she was hobbled and had a tray chained to her wrists, on which was a single glass and a bottle of the pink Dom Perignon. Morris gestured to her as he stepped to the front of the stage and began to speak.

'Now we know what happens to sassy girls, don't we? Next a model of obedience, the beautiful Harmony, to serve as maid for the remainder of the evening, and when I say maid, I mean it. She'll do as she's told, so no doubt the lucky winner will need some refreshment, which is provided. The champagne's worth a hundred on its own, so do I hear two hundred?'

Several hands went up and the bidding began to rise steeply. The man who'd spanked Sophie very likely had his cock in her mouth at that instant, maybe up her fanny, but it had been no part of the deal. Harmony was available for anything their dirty little minds could dream up: sucking, fucking, whipping, even sodomy, and every little kink they could add on. It had to be a fix.

It was, although I couldn't imagine Harmony reaching the end of the night without being sore in several places. Hudson Staebler bid with an easy confidence, outdoing his competitors despite some determined opposition. By the time the bidding had passed six hundred, a hushed reverence had fallen over the hall, and she went for seven hundred and fifty. He came forwards to pay Morris, and didn't even hurry, opening the champagne and pouring himself a glass before clipping a lead to her wrist chain and taking her to one corner of the stage, where he sat her down on his lap, idly fondling her bottom as Annabelle stepped forwards.

She was still in nothing but kinky boots, only no longer hobbled and chained at the wrists. As always, she was shaved and, as she gave the audience a twirl, I could clearly see the tattoo on her pubic mound that marked her as Mel's property. I'd first known her as a domina, and a pretty fierce one too, but her fall had been absolute, and she now worshipped Melody and did exactly as she was told.

'Our house slave, Annabelle,' Morris announced, 'who has been instructed to go into the little booth you will note at the far end of the hall for a bukkake session. That means you get to come in her face for those few of you who don't spend half your life surfing the web for porn. Highest bidder first, twenty places in all, so what do I hear?'

They began to bid, fast and furious. It was a clever trick, ensuring that they collected far more than if she'd been sold to just one man. I could imagine what it would do to her too, having to suck men hard, twenty of them, and let them come in her face. By the time they'd finished with her she'd be so plastered with spunk she'd be barely recognisable, a thought which brought my very mixed emotions to a new peak.

It took a while to knock her down, with a lot of men determined to get in on the act, and just as long for them all to pay, but at last she was led off by the highest bidder, another of Morris' regulars. The first part of the auction was over, but there was still no sign of Sophie. I peeped into the changing area as Morris announced the second phase, but she wasn't there, and I was left with no option but to climb up on to the stage without her. Annabelle was clearly going to be busy cock sucking for quite a while, and Melody and Harmony were off for the evening. I'd left Kay where we'd been sitting, making it very plain she wasn't available and, for a moment, I was the only woman on the stage.

I was extremely glad when Patty climbed up, then Miss Barbara from the puppy show. Jean de Vrain moved her chair a little closer to the centre and there were four of us, all dominant, but with the proportion of submissive men in the audience that was no bad thing. I could cope with whipping a few, for all that it did nothing for me personally, and was wondering how to get the most for the fighting fund as Morris once more began to speak.

'Our first candidate then, Miss Patricia Whitworth, for whose services I will accept no bids beneath one hundred pounds. Anyone wishing to dominate her had better have five hundred in his pocket.'

It was nice to discover she switched, but I was more than a little surprised at the offer, especially in front of her own grandmother. It was a lot of money to ask though, and all that came up from the audience were bids to be punished by her, mostly from men wanting to be her puppy-boy. She got £275 from a young man with a face so submissive he looked scared, yet he still had the nerve to ask her to make him eat dog food in front of thousands of people.

As she took him away on a lead, I was wondering where Bitch was, as we badly needed a submissive woman to make up our numbers. Miss Barbara had stepped forwards, and she looked a good deal more comfortable as a straightforward domina than she had as a puppy mistress. Morris had already made it plain that we had the right to refuse bids we weren't comfortable with, and she turned two down: a guy offering a hundred and fifty for her to pee on him in the centre of the floor space and some complete maniac who wanted to be taken down to the marshes and buried alive with just a straw to breathe through. She accepted two hundred to drip hot wax on a man, which she did in front of everyone, first on his chest, then on his back and buttocks, and lastly on his cock and balls, which left him with a straining erection and an expression of raw agony on his face. Even I'd have taken pity on him by finishing him off by hand, but she left him to hobble away, clutching at his wax-coated genitals, presumably to masturbate in a corner. Morris stood forwards once more.

'A hot one there, boys and girls, but now for a rare treat indeed, in fact, a unique treat, an opportunity for a good old-fashioned spanking from perhaps the country's senior domina, Mrs Jean de Vrain!'

Jean stood up. Her dress and hair made her look desperately out of place in the club, as if Mary Whitehouse had wandered into a strip joint, but she did look stern. Although the audience were supposed to be able to ask for what they liked, plenty were keen, and not just the men. One woman in an immaculate and plainly expensive rubber catsuit bid two hundred, and Jean had accepted it with a gesture before Morris could see if the bidding was going to go higher. The money was for her fund, and he didn't make an issue of it, especially, I suspected, because just like me he wanted to see the woman spanked.

It was beautifully done, and my admiration for her increased as she stepped down from the stage and across the floor in a firm, no-nonsense manner. The woman was taken by the wrist the moment she'd climbed over the ropes, and led to where the chair still stood at the centre of the cleared area. Everyone had gone quiet, watching. There was a glorious look of disapproval on Jean's face as she took in the woman's perfect make-up, skintight catsuit and six-inch heels. When Jean spoke her voice was icy with disdain.

'What is your name, girl?'

'Honey.'

'Your proper name, and you will address me as Mrs de Vrain, as you are about to be put across my knee.'

The girl gave a single, frightened nod.

'Laura ... Mrs de Vrain.'

'That's better. You are a slut, Laura. Now let's have you out of this silly costume.'

Laura clearly hadn't expected to be bared, and gave a little gasp as Jean's fingers found the zip of her catsuit. Not that she tried to stop it, merely closing her eyes as it was drawn down, all the way to her fanny, revealing the sweat-slick, powder-smeared skin beneath. She was stripped, completely nude, and I could only watch in delight and fascination as it was done, the arms of her catsuit peeled off, her shoes kicked aside on instruction, the legs eased free, to leave the beautiful garment a tangled mess of sweaty, powder-stained rubber on the floor. Laura's skin was no better, and the stripping had reduced her from a poised beauty to a bedraggled ragamuffin in a few minutes. She was still cute, her high breasts and little rounded bum both delightful, and I was feeling both aroused and envious as Jean sat down on the chair.

'Over you go, my girl.'

I could see Laura shaking, but still there was no resistance, nor hesitation. She obviously needed it badly, but she had never expected to take it in the nude, and kept her legs firmly together as she draped herself across Jean's legs. I could have told her it was hopeless, but her embarrassment was turning me on even more than seeing her naked. She had another shock coming. Jean had brought her handbag with her, and it was on the ground by her chair. Holding Laura carefully in place, she reached down into it and drew out a hairbrush, small, but quite clearly a serviceable spanking implement.

Laura didn't even realise, or perhaps she was expecting to be stroked and teased before the spanking began, or at least warmed a little. Jean evidently didn't believe in frills. An old-fashioned spanking was what she had offered, and it was what Laura got, the hairbrush applied hard to her pretty little bum cheeks from the start. She was squealing immediately, and within three smacks her legs had started to kick, just below the knees, but truly frantic. Her bum was bouncing well, hinting at the dark opening between her cheeks with every smack: a delightful sight.

A moment later, Laura had lost control complete. Her thighs came wide, kicked open in her pain, to spread out the sweetest little fanny, shaved bare and absolutely soaking between her lips. She began to buck and her bumhole was showing too: a tiny pink star that opened and closed as her bottom squirmed to Jean's smacks. I was wishing I could see Laura's face as well, but Jean's was a picture, cool and composed, utterly matter-of-fact as she punished the writhing, naked girl across her lap.

It only stopped when Laura fell off Jean's lap, to sit down hard on her smacked bum. She'd shown it all, her pert breasts, every tiny detail of her shaved fanny and her bumhole, all modesty stripped away, and not just physical, but mental. The instant she'd recovered herself she was at Jean's feet, cuddling on to her, smacked bottom stuck out behind, no longer caring who saw, but only for comfort from the woman who'd spanked her. I was wishing I'd done it myself, badly, and I could have been the one to stroke her hair and back as she clung trembling to me, her head buried between my breasts, her naked body mine to do with as I pleased.

I would have done it too, probably had her lick me, maybe even with everybody watching, but not Jean. She simply spent a few moments providing the comfort Laura so obviously needed, and then gently disengaged herself, to stand up and acknowledge the applause of the audience with a slight inclination of her head. Laura hastily gathered up her things and scampered away, her little red bum bouncing behind her, and Jean was left on her own.

She was genuine, that much was clear, and more than just an old-fashioned disciplinarian. Spanking a girl is one thing, but to comfort her afterwards is quite another. I could just imagine Laura's feelings, all too easily in fact, and the episode left me feeling more muddled than ever, and more strongly aroused. I wanted Kay, and it was only with great effort that I held back from dragging her out on to the floor, stripping her naked and giving her just the same treatment.

What I didn't want was to have to dominate some man, but unless I was very lucky it was what I would get. Morris had already begun to talk, and it was impossible not to feel proud at being called up last, even after Jean. I stepped forwards, planting my feet a little apart at the centre of the stage and folding my hands across my chest. I was hot, drunk and highly aroused, but I did my best to seem cool and dominant as my announcement was made.

'. . . Miss Amber Oakley, available to answer your darkest fantasies. Put your hands deep in your wallets now.'

There were plenty of bids, including from Patty, who still had her puppy-boy on a lead. Unfortunately, she'd been trumped immediately and I didn't get a chance to accept, leaving only men in the bidding and me seething with frustration. Most of them just wanted to be dominated in one way or another, so I could hardly turn them down in favour of Patty, and I hadn't caught what she'd wanted above the chorus of offers. The bids reached £375, with a rather nondescript man in PVC shorts and a collar wanting to be put across my knee, when the crowds parted to the bulk of Mr Protheroe.

I'd forgotten all about him, and he wasn't going to be bidding for me to deal with him, just the opposite. My whole body seemed to go cold as he spoke.

'I'll put a bid in, Morris. Four hundred pounds to spank her, OTK, on the bare.'

Morris just laughed, and a surge of relief washed over me. Then he spoke.

'Amber over your knee for four hundred? You can do better than that, Mr Protheroe.'

I turned to Morris, frantically trying to make myself understood. I could turn down four hundred pounds if I could accept three hundred and seventy-five, but if Protheroe put in some huge bid, I would have to go down. They knew I switched, and if I refused I'd end up looking mean in front of just about everybody on the London SM scene, including most of my customers. I could already hear Mel calling me a coward, and I knew she'd have done it. Patty had offered too, and I knew

36

I'd lose respect from Sophie, Harmony, and others, not Kay, never Kay, but she was just about the only one. Even then I could refuse, just about, but it was going to make me feel bad, perhaps worse than I would if I accepted. One day I might find myself in the same situation as Jean, and every penny was going to count.

Protheroe was considering, or pretending to consider, stroking his second chin and shaking his head.

'Oh, I don't know, Morris. She does have a gorgeous bum, and by God she's in need of a spanking, but to go over four hundred –'

'It's in a good cause,' Morris answered him, indifferent to my unspoken pleas. 'Patty Whitworth asked five hundred, so I say you have to top that.'

'Five hundred?' Protheroe said, and made a nasty little sucking noise as he pulled some spittle back between his front teeth. 'OK, I'll go for five hundred, but that's with her knickers down and her tits hanging out.'

I thought I'd been blushing before, but it was nothing to my reaction as I imagined his fat, sweaty little hands on me, first pulling up my bra to expose my breasts, then on my knickers, to pull them down, baring me, just as Laura had been bared, fanny and bumhole on show to thousands of leering men and gloating women as I was spanked across a dirty old man's knee.

To accept was out of the question. So was to refuse. Morris was holding the microphone between the three of us so that our conversation was being broadcast to the entire warehouse. Burning with embarrassment, I began to bargain over the details of my spanking with three thousand people listening in, and I found I couldn't even remember Protheroe's Christian name, if I'd ever known it. It was going to sound horribly respectful.

'Five hundred is fair, Mr Protheroe,' I began, 'not generous, but fair. OK then, you can spank me, but just on my jodhpurs, all right?'

37

Morris shook his head.

'Come on, Amber, let the greyhound see the rabbit, yeah?'

I tried to throw him a dirty look without making it obvious. He took no notice.

'Five hundred sounds fair for bare bum and tits.'

I forced a laugh.

'I'm a dominant woman, Morris, and a lesbian. It's a lot to ask.'

'Six hundred then,' Protheroe put in. 'Tits and arse.'

'Six hundred,' I managed. 'Well ... maybe on my knickers ...'

Protheroe nodded thoughtfully before replying.

'On the knickers is good, not as good as bare, but good. I'll have to use a hairbrush on you, of course –'

'No.'

'Why not?'

'It hurts.'

'So it should, but if you must insist on keeping your panties up –'

'OK, OK! You can use the bloody hairbrush, if it means so much to you, but you're not to take my knickers down. In fact you must promise not to take them down.'

I was getting flustered, but I couldn't help myself. It was going to hurt like hell, and I knew I wouldn't be able to keep control, any more than poor Laura. I thought of how I'd enjoyed it when she started to really thrash and her thighs came apart, and bit my lip. She'd ended up on her knees, trembling, cuddling into Jean de Vrain's chest. Not me, not with Protheroe, not ever. He nodded.

'Six hundred for the hairbrush on your panty seat and your tits out?'

'Not my ti ... my breasts, no.'

He chuckled, amused by my modesty, which made my blushes hotter still.

'OK, do it, you dirty bastard, you can take my breasts out, but you leave my knickers alone.'

Again he nodded, and extended his hand.

'Deal?'

I reached down and shook. He kept his grip and made a big show of helping me down from the stage. I was boiling with emotion as I was led to the chair on which he'd sit to spank me, determined to take it well, but fighting to keep my arousal down, wishing I wasn't quite so drunk, that I didn't feel quite so helpless. We reached the chair and he sat on it, his toadlike face split into a happy grin as he patted his lap. I was pouting furiously as I laid myself over his knees, but I couldn't help it, and the sulky expression grew worse as I felt the hard bulge of his cock pressing into my side.

'Hips up,' he ordered, trying to sound stern but only managing dirty.

My hips came up and, as he begun to fiddle with my fly, I was wishing I'd had the sense to take them down myself before going over, and so rob him of one more excuse to feel me up. I felt my button pop and he was groping for the tab of my zip, his fingers pushing into my flesh to make my fanny twitch. Down it came, with a soft rasp. I felt my waistband go loose, giving me a sharp pang of vulnerability, and then his hands were in the sides, pulling. My teeth were set hard against my lower lip to stop myself sobbing as my jodhpurs began to come down, tugged off my hips, and lower . . .

Protheroe made an odd little wheezing noise in his throat as my knickers came out. They were big, and white with pink polka dots, hardly what a dominant woman is supposed to wear, and I caught laughter and giggles from among the crowd as they saw. I could feel the sobs starting in my throat, and the tears in my eyes, but I clung on, biting my lip, determined to take it with dignity. My jodhpurs were settled halfway down my thighs, the tail of my pinks and the tuck of my blouse were turned up, and the full expanse of my knickers was on show, ready for spanking. He could have done it, and it would have hurt, a real punishment, but that wasn't enough, not for him, he had to extract every last drop of humiliation I'd agreed to.

I was still on my toes and, as his hands went up under my pinks, I lifted a little more, my eyes shut tight in my shame as I prepared to have my breasts stripped. My pinks were turned up all the way, over my head, and all I could see was scarlet gloom and a little section of the floor. I was grateful because it let me sob my emotions out without making any more of a display of myself than I already was. It was still agony as his fat clammy hands pushed in under my armpits to squeeze my breasts, cupping one in each hand. His wheezing grew louder as he fondled me as did my sobbing as my nipples betrayed me by popping out under his hands. He chuckled, and spoke.

'Anyone for melons, tuppence the pound?'

Some of the audience laughed, and I biting was my lip to hold back the tears. He stopped groping. His hands went to my buttons, fumbling clumsily at the first until it came free, and then his fingers were tickling the bare flesh of my cleavage as he started on the second. He hadn't bothered with my necktie, or my top button, and with the third loose he simply pulled my blouse wide, to leave my breasts bulging from the hole, fat and heavy in my bra.

I knew it would look ridiculous, and several people laughed at the sight. It was going to get worse too, as one podgy hand pushed up beneath my blouse at the back, his fingers moist on my skin as he groped for my bra catch. He couldn't do it, pinching at my skin and making my breasts wobble in my bra cups, but failing utterly. One hook came, but he seemed puzzled and I found myself snapping at him.

'There are three hooks, you idiot!'

He gave a little grunt, then a cluck of satisfaction as my catch gave way. I felt the weight of my breasts loll down as my bra came loose, and Protheroe was speaking as his hands once more burrowed down under my armpits.

'You really are overdue, aren't you, Amber, long overdue. When were you last spanked?'

'I ... don't remember,' I answered angrily as his fingers delved for the wire rims of my bra cups, 'ages ago. Ow! You're pinching!'

'Sorry, my dear. Now, let's have those big titties out, and we'll soon have you ready.'

Even as he spoke he was tugging my cups up. My boobs fell out and I was bare, for all to see, both of them dangling naked from my chest, pink and fat and round, my nipples embarrassingly stiff. Protheroe took them in hand and began to grope again, making his odd little noises as he enjoyed my flesh. I shut my eyes, biting my lip as I struggled not to let it get to me, or to speak and show my anger and shame.

He had a really good feel, but at last he stopped and I let myself down on to his lap. His arm came around my waist, holding me in place, his cock now prodding into my side through his trousers. The way he'd opened my blouse left my boobs hanging free against his leg, showing to just about everyone. His hand settled on the seat of my knickers, then lifted, and I braced myself for punishment, only for him to let go of my waist and start to tug at my pinks instead.

'Better have your jacket off,' he remarked. 'It's so important to see a spanked girl's face, don't you think?'

I couldn't deny it, but couldn't bring myself to agree either, and stayed sullen and silent as my pinks were pulled off my arms and dumped casually on the floor beneath my face. A glance showed a great ring of people, all staring at me in my humiliation, bright eyed in pleasure at the thought of seeing me get spanked. I hung my head, unable to look. Protheroe chuckled as he took me firmly around my waist again, and his hand found the underside of my cheeks, bouncing them.

'Quite the ripest bottom I've ever had the pleasure to spank,' he remarked, 'and now, you naughty little girl, you know what happens, don't you?'

I didn't answer. He wanted me to say that naughty little girls got spanked, or something equally degenerate, but I couldn't, the lump in my throat was just too big. He spoke again, his hand now on my bum, making little circular motions on the seat of my knickers.

'Well, Amber, what happens to naughty little girls?'

Still I didn't answer, and the circular motions changed to squeezes, bunching my knickers into the crease of my bottom and spilling more of my flesh from the leg holes. If he kept doing it, he would soon have them right in my crease and my cheeks would be bare, if not my fanny. I forced myself to swallow the lump in my throat and answer him.

'They ... they get spanked,' I managed, in a sullen whisper.

'Louder,' he demanded. 'I can't hear you.'

Suddenly, the microphone was being held under my mouth. I glanced up, to find Morris grinning down at me. Protheroe was still fondling my bum, pulling my knickers further up into my crease. Most of my bottom was showing already.

'Don't,' I managed, my voice full of unshed tears. 'We said not bare.'

He merely chuckled, but began to stroke my cheeks again, now on my bare flesh. His awful, lecherous groping was bringing the heat to my fanny. I knew I had to stop it.

'What happens to naughty little girls?' he repeated.

'They get spanked,' I answered, and my voice boomed out from the loudspeakers, echoing in the huge room so that every single person got to hear.

'Yes,' he answered, still stroking me. 'They get spanked, but first, what happens first?'

'I . . . I don't know,' I blurted out. 'They . . . they get put over someone's knee . . . they . . . they get their knickers pulled down, but not me, not my knickers, you promised, Mr Protheroe, you promised.'

'So I did,' he responded, his hand moving lower, to tickle where the tuck of my bum cheeks meets my thighs, 'so I did, but the fact remains, when a man spanks a woman, her panties should come down, always.'

I'd begun to wriggle helplessly to the tickling, my head full of confusion and shame at the way he was treating me, my arousal soaring so high I could barely contain myself. I just broke.

'No. Not my knickers, you promised. Just spank me, you bastard. Get it over with.'

'Temper, temper,' he chided, 'and such language. Yes, I think those panties are definitely going to have to come down.'

'No. You promised . . . you promised, Mr Protheroe, you promised.'

'So I did,' he repeated, 'so I did. Hmm . . . Melody, darling, might I borrow you for a moment?'

'Sure, what for?' Mel answered from right behind me.

I hadn't even realised she was there, and I jerked sharply around, to find her just a few feet away, with Angel beside her, both grinning down at my discomfort.

'To pull Amber's panties down for her,' Protheroe said casually.

'No!' I squealed, my hand already groping for my waistband because I'd realised his intention an instant before he'd spoken.

As Mel stepped forwards, I was snatching at my knickers, and I caught them, my fingers locking in the cotton to spill the full volume of my bum cheeks out of my leg holes. That no longer mattered. My fanny did, and I was clinging on desperately as Mel took hold, determined not to be made to show.

'Come on, Amber, down they come,' she said, laughing. 'You're just making yourself look silly.'

I was, but not half as silly as I'd look with my fanny on show from behind, and maybe worse, my bumhole, because I knew full well I wouldn't be able to keep my cheeks together once the spanking got underway. Mel was pulling hard, and had the far edge of my knickers well down, but I fought back, hauling on them in desperation, struggling to break Protheroe's grip on my waist and screaming in protest.

'Get off! Get off! You promised, you bastard, you promised! Let go of me!'

'Prise her fingers open, Angel,' Mel grated, and her friend had joined in.

The audience was in fits of laughter, delighted by the sight of me fighting to keep my knickers up. I set my teeth, determined they would stay up, however ridiculous a display of myself I made in the process. My persecutors were no less determined, but I'd have won, because for all her boasts Angel just wasn't strong enough to force me to open my hand. Her nails were digging into my flesh, but I didn't care, and she'd even begun to give in when there was a sudden ripping noise – my knickers had parted at the crotch. Mel let go, and I jerked the ruined remains high up over my hips, exposing myself completely. Shrieks of laughter erupted from the audience, then clapping. I let go, limp and defeated, at least for a moment, but with my thighs pressed tight together.

My knickers were taken down, or at least what was left of them, and off, pulled over my lowered jodhpurs and boots by Mel, to leave me bare bottomed and ready for spanking, with a great bubble of shame welling up in my head, and the fight all but gone out of me. Protheroe blew his breath out and patted my bottom, only not with his hand, but with something cool, and hard – Jean de Vrain's hairbrush.

'Please, no,' I begged, my words coming out as a sob. 'You said not with the hairbrush, not if I was bare. Be fair, Mr Protheroe, please –'

My words broke off in a squeal of pain as he brought it down across my bum, hard. The spanking had begun and, for all the agonisingly slow exposure of my body, I just wasn't ready, not for the pain, not for the awful humiliation of being punished in public. I was kicking immediately, my knees jerking in my lowered jodhpurs, and bucking and fighting to escape the pain, but only succeeding in making a yet bigger exhibition of myself. My thighs were coming wide, and my bum cheeks too, showing off my fanny and anus to the crowd, but I just couldn't stop myself. My boobs were bouncing and slapping together under my chest, another foolish display I could do nothing to prevent. It hurt too much and, as the awful, helpless shame of it overwhelmed me, I burst into tears. Angel laughed.

'Ah, baby's crying.'

I managed to turn her a single, furious glare, but Protheroe kept right on spanking, holding me hard around the chest as he applied the hairbrush to my quivering, wobbling bottom, fast and furious, then slower, a firm, methodical beating. My squeals gave way to a broken, miserable wailing, punctuated by gasps and screams each time he caught me. The hairbrush was coming down full on the cheekiest part of my bottom, right over my fanny, and I knew exactly what it was going to do to me. I began to struggle again, fighting his grip and whimpering pitifully into the curtain of blonde curls now hanging loose around my face.

'No, not that, Mr Protheroe, please . . . ow! Not that . . . no . . . just punish me . . . ow!'

Again I heard Angel's voice, full of laughter and derision.

'Oh God, the little slut's going to come, how funny. Some dom she is.'

I tried to spit out an angry response, but Protheroe's hairbrush caught me low, smacking into my protruding fanny lips and it came out as a choking gasp of pain. Angel laughed again, Protheroe adjusted his grip in an effort to keep me still and the spanking went right on. I was going to break, I just knew it. My bottom felt hot and fat, my pussy ready for fucking, and as the first agonising sting of the slap on my fanny began to fade it was replaced with a warmth I knew would spread.

An awful sense of frustration welled up inside as my pain began to give way to pleasure. Much more and I'd be masturbating at his feet with his cock in my mouth and my red bum stuck out behind for all to see, or down on Mel and Angel, licking fanny as they took turns to whip me. It couldn't happen. I had to fight, but it was going to, with my bum warm and open to the smacks, my titties swinging to the rhythm, my eyes still streaming tears and my mouth wide, only not in shock and pain, but ecstasy.

'What a tart,' Angel crowed, and suddenly it had stopped.

My knees were together but my feet wide apart and kicked up, my bottom was up, my cheeks splayed apart to show my anus and the pouted rear lips of my thoroughly wet fanny. It was hard to imagine a more ludicrous position for a woman to be in. Protheroe spoke.

'Would you like a go?'

'No . . . not her –' I managed, but it was pretty feeble.

Angel was gorgeous, and if she hadn't been such a bitch I'd have happily switched for her. Not that my opinion mattered anyway. She gave a smug little noise that Protheroe took for assent, and both his arms locked to my waist, holding me firmly in place with my bum stuck high and cheeks well spread, showing

46

everything. I hung my head, still trying to fight my own feelings but wanting to give in, to take a good, firm spanking from her and then get down on my knees and lick her to ecstasy . . .

. . . until her dog whip cracked down across my bottom with the full force of her arm. I screamed, really screamed, and lurched violently. The tip must have hit Protheroe because he gave a cry of surprise and pain and let go. I tumbled off his lap, sprawling upside down on the floor with my legs up and fanny spread to half the audience. Angel was lifting the whip again, aiming at my exposed thighs, her face set in an expression of gleeful malice. I scrambled frantically away, but the lash caught my hip and one bum cheek as I turned, setting me squealing as I struggled to escape on all fours with the laughter of the audience ringing in my ears.

Again the lash caught me, and I went down, face first on the floor, bum up. She was on me in an instant, straddling my back, her weight pressing me down. I tried to struggle, but couldn't, and she was spanking me, by hand, as I squirmed on the floor, my tits squashed out on the dirty concrete, my bum wobbling to her slaps. She seemed to have lost her whip, and if she'd just turned me over and sat on my face I'd have been hers. Instead she called out to Melody.

'Whip her, Mel. Then Fats can fuck her up the arse.'

I lurched, with a strength rendered hysterical by the thought of submitting to buggery from Protheroe. Angel squeaked in surprise as she lost her balance and I was up, running for the changing space with my jodhpurs clutched in one hand and my bright red bottom wobbling behind me. They were still laughing, but nobody followed, and I made it through the screens, to collapse panting on a chair. Kay appeared, looking worried.

My head was full of images of my punishment, the way I'd been manoeuvred into going over his knee, having my jodhpurs pulled down, my breasts laid bare, fighting for my panties, and losing, being spanked, and whipped, and sat on, sat on to be thrashed and then buggered by Protheroe. I knew full well he wouldn't have done it, not with me screaming blue murder and three thousand people looking on as he raped me anally . . . no, not rape, because I might not have been able to help myself, and I would have been pushing my poor spanked bottom up as his fat, ugly cock was forced in up my bumhole.

Only he couldn't have done it. He didn't have the wind. I'd have had to suck him off, with him seated in comfort and me on my knees, or mount him, straddling his great flabby legs as I fed him in up my fanny, or behind, into my bottom hole with my back turned to him to show off my spanked cheeks and the junction of his bloated cock and my straining anus, with three thousand people staring as I utterly degraded myself by frigging off with his cock up my bum . . .

I had to come. My legs were open and I was kicking at my jodhpurs to get them properly down, with my hands already snatching at my fanny and tits. Kay understood, and she came to me, down between my open thighs to bury her face in my sex, and lick. I tried, briefly, to focus on her, on her beautiful, svelte body, on the way her darling bottom filled out her rubber pants, on her pretty face and the eagerness with which she was licking my fanny. It was no good. I'd been spanked, my knickers taken down and my bare bottom spanked . . . spanked like a naughty little girl . . . spanked . . .

There was as much despair in my voice as ecstasy as I cried out in orgasm. I'd tried so hard, but I couldn't help myself. They were right, I was a slut, a tart, a fat-bottomed little trollop fit only for spanking across a strong man's knee, or a truly dominant woman's. Maybe both. Maybe held tight across Mel and Angel's locked knees while Protheroe prepared me, telling me I was a naughty little girl as he bared my bottom, and more ... jacket tail up ... tits out ... jodhpurs down ... blouse tail up ... knickers down ... my fanny on show, wet and willing ... my bumhole exposed and vulnerable ... spanked until I howled ... and buggered ... my bumhole fucked and spunked in ... left masturbating my dirty little fanny as Protheroe's come bubbled out of my abused anus ...

I really screamed, again and again, with the full force of my lungs. They must have heard, all of them, but I couldn't stop myself until the last tremors of my orgasm had died away and Kay had come up into my arms, cuddling me, both of us shaking hard. It had been glorious, but I still felt bitterly ashamed of myself. Yet however much I'd wanted it, I hadn't done it. I'd come, yes, but I hadn't been buggered in public, or even made a further exhibition of myself by sucking Mr Protheroe off. Besides, it had been in a good cause.

It wasn't easy to come to terms with what Mr Protheroe had done to me. I believe that when it comes to SM sex, it's wrong to dish out what you're not prepared to take yourself, but that was not much consolation. Being spanked is one thing, being spanked by Mr Protheroe in front of a huge crowd is another. He knew how I felt too, and either refused to accept that my desires didn't extend to him, or at least not until I'd been put into a state of utter submission, or he merely enjoyed picking on me because he knew how I hated it.

Kay did her best to cheer me up, with a long cuddle before she began to play puppies, begging with her tongue lolling out until I finally gave in and began to throw a ball for her, one that another of the puppy-girls had been using to play fetch. She was so good at it, trying to snatch the ball out of the air with her teeth and rolling on the floor in delight once she caught it, that I was soon smiling despite myself. We were still playing when Patty Whitworth came in. Her face was full of concern until she saw what we were doing, and then she laughed.

'Hi, Amber, I was going to ask if you were OK, but I should have known you're tougher than that.'

I wasn't going to pretend otherwise, and threw her the ball, Kay jumping up to snap at it as it went past. We began to play puppy in the middle, laughing together at Kay's increasingly ridiculous antics, until at last Patty dropped the ball. It rolled towards Kay, who snatched it up in her mouth and squatted down, growling at us.

'Bad Patch! Bad girl! Drop!' I chided, and she obeyed, slightly to my disappointment.

'You should have entered her in the competition,' Patty said. 'You might well have won.'

'She's a bit shy,' I explained, 'especially in front of men.'

Patty nodded.

'What happened to Bitch?' I asked. 'I thought she'd be up on stage for the auction?'

'She threw a paddy,' Patty answered. 'It happens sometimes. She wants to do it, but she can't always cope with her own fantasies. I should go and find her really, but I expect she's out in the car, and she's impossible when she's sulking.'

I nodded my understanding. Kay was much the same, except in that she was taking it slowly after a couple of false starts. I picked up the ball again, intending to throw it and hopefully tease Kay into something ruder, when the drapes were pushed aside and both the gay couples who'd been in the puppy show came in, followed by Sophie. She was still in her schoolgirl outfit, but her blouse was open and she'd lost her knickers, revealing a very red bottom. She giggled as she saw me. I lifted a warning finger.

'Not a word, Sophie Cherwell, or you're in big trouble. You saw then?'

She nodded.

'You can speak, Sophie, just not about that.'

'OK,' she answered. 'I need to ask you a favour, as it goes.'

'Ask away.'

'I'm going up to Loughborough the week after next, to do a photoshoot. I've never met the guy, and he sounds OK, but I need a chaperone –'

'Of course, better safe than sorry. Doesn't Mel usually go with you?'

'It's not through Mel. I got the contact on a web group. She'd want twenty-five per cent, and I'm really broke, and . . .'

I knew what she meant. I wouldn't charge.

'Of course I'll come,' I told her. 'Who is this man, and what's he into?'

'He's called Denis Humber, and he wants to do a shoot with me in nappies.'

Two

Sophie's shoot was on a Friday afternoon, but that wasn't a problem for me. I could leave Kay in charge of the shop and drive up. Sophie was always fun, and we both knew full well that it wouldn't be Denis Humber who got the pleasure of her excitement after the shoot, but me. Kay had yet to get her head around nappies. To put a girl in one is deliciously humiliating and, with a little encouragement from Sophie, is was about time she was introduced to them. Even at the photoshoot it would also be amusing to watch Sophie pose, maybe even made to wet herself.

She was going to come up on the Thursday night and stay over, which would be an excellent opportunity to advance on Kay's training. What I didn't expect was for her to be chauffeured up by Melody in the Rolls-Royce.

'Have you changed your mind?' I asked as she helped me close the gates, leaving Mel to park.

'Uh, uh. Mel wants to talk to you.'

'I do have a telephone.'

'OK, not so much talk to you, as persuade you.'

'Into what exactly?'

'You'll see. I'm not supposed to say anything.'

I slapped her bottom for her and she scurried into the house, giggling. Mel was pulling a large bag from the boot and I walked across to her. She turned, grinning as she dumped it on the ground. She was in jeans and a skinny top, but still managed to look pretty aggressive.

'What is it you wanted to ask me?' I queried.

'About the wrestling next month. You're going to enter, aren't you?'

'So your friend Angel can spank me and pee on me in front of a couple of thousand people? No thank you.'

'Oh, come on, Amber, you love it. That's not the point. I don't want you to lose, I want you to win –'

'Yes, Mel, I believe you.'

'No, really, I mean it. She's great, but does that girl need taking down a peg or two.'

I nodded, because I understood, exactly.

'You mean she won't play with you?'

'Not sub, no, and I'm not going down for her if she won't go down for me.'

Again I nodded. I felt the same way, maybe not quite so strongly, but I could certainly understand. There are heights of pleasure you just can't reach unless you switch. Yet Angel was prepared to enter Morris' annual competition, what he called the Dirty Bitches Wrestling Extravaganza. Dirty was about right because not only was the idea to get your opponent's clothes off and thoroughly humiliate her, but it was done in a ring full of mud, or custard, or even baked beans. If Angel was prepared to enter, she was presumably prepared to lose.

'So you think she wants it really but needs to find her excuse?' I ventured. 'And that's why she's going in for the wrestling?'

'Uh, uh, she really thinks she's going to win.'

'Why do you need me then? Wouldn't you rather do it yourself?'

'Sure, I aim to, but she's good, really good. Maybe she'll take me, but if she does I want to know you're there for me.'

'You're going to fix the draw, obviously?'

'Sure. There are heats, but I'll have you seeded, so you go straight into the last sixteen.'

'Four fights? In one evening!'

'Sure. I'll make sure your first two are easy.'

'And if you beat her you meet me?'

She nodded.

'I'm not sure I trust you, Mel.'

'What's not to trust? You've taken me down before.'

I nodded. It was true, but I'd never seen her so lacking in confidence, or apparently lacking in confidence, and that was worrying. We'd always been more or less evenly matched. Possibly there was some really horrible fate in store for me, something either she or Angel were going to dish out. Then again, Angel had already threatened to spank me and pee on me.

'And if she beats me?'

'Then there's Vicky.'

'You're not taking any chances, are you? Why not just have her drawn against Vicky in the heats?'

'No good. I want it done properly. She might beat any one of us, but not all three in a row. I want whatever she does to the others done to her too. If she spanks me, you spank her. If she pisses on me, you piss on her.'

'What if I win but the moment I've got her down she starts screaming "red"?'

'Red' was the generally accepted stop word. I could happily pee on Angel, but I couldn't break her consent. With a somewhat bitter pang of self-awareness, I realised that I'd never even thought to use it while being punished by Mr Protheroe.

'Call her a baby and walk away,' Mel advised.

She was right. Angel would lose face as a domina if she lost anyway, but if she backed out and I made an issue of it she'd lose more. It was tempting, but I could almost feel the wet and heat of her piddle splashing on my skin as I knelt, stripped and defeated at her feet. Yet if I had to, I could take it. I hesitated, not at all sure about my decision, but thinking of how Angel had called me a baby when I'd burst into tears during my spanking, how she'd called me a tart and a slut, how she'd whipped me, made me crawl on the floor, suggested Mr Protheroe bugger me . . .

'I'll do it,' I answered.

The more I thought about Mel's suggestion, the more I was certain there was a catch. There has always been rivalry between us, and she delights in dominating me, but it all seemed a bit elaborate if she simply wanted to take me down, and after the auction she should have had her fill of seeing me dealt with, at least for the time being. More likely Angel wanted to finish what she'd started, and had persuaded Mel to make up the story so that I'd be ripe for the plucking at the wrestling match. Perhaps Angel really was good, and could beat me easily. It was a chance I was going to have to take because the opportunity for revenge was too good to miss.

Mel had to get back, leaving me with Kay and Sophie for the evening, which was also too good an opportunity to miss. It was a glorious day, and we ate outside, sipping well-chilled Alsace wine with a salad of cold chicken and just a few capers. Sophie was obviously ready for mischief and, when we finally went indoors with the light almost gone from the sky, I asked her to show us what she'd brought for the photoshoot. She was giggling as she unzipped her huge bag.

'There's lots,' she said gleefully. 'The guy's a fanatic. There's this mail-order company he put me on to for proper sexy ones, not the sort hospitals use, look . . .'

She pulled one out. They were big, and pink, and soft, with fat yellow teddy bears printed on them. I could tell that on a girl Sophie's size the waistband would come right up her middle, and it was obviously stretchy. So were the leg holes, while the front and the crotch were puffy and a good three inches thick. It was impossible not to giggle, and Kay's hand had gone straight to her mouth in embarrassment and delight. The thought of getting her into them was too good to resist, far too good, a superb piece of humiliation

'He wants me to get the feel of them before the shoot,' Sophie went on, turning the nappy around to show us the rear, which was even bigger and puffier than the front, 'and he's explained all about it. These are safe, and won't leak at all, so it's OK to wear them on their own, maybe under a big coat with nothing else at all, outdoors, even to let people have a peep.'

There was rising excitement in her voice, and I knew it would be her thing, to exhibit herself in such a shocking way. Kay had gone very red at the idea, and I took her hand to give her a reassuring squeeze as Sophie continued, putting the pink nappy aside and drawing out a piece of thick cream-coloured towelling.

'But these are different, old-fashioned ones made of towelling that fasten with a pin at either side. It's quite tricky to get them on properly, but they're more comfy, if maybe not quite so kinky.'

She stood up, quickly pulling the towelling between her legs to show how it went on and holding the sides in her fingers. Even over her jeans, it looked wonderfully rude, and when she was otherwise naked I could imagine the effect being even stronger than with the ready-made sort. They also had more potential.

'It would be fun to make you go in them and then wash them,' I suggested.

'No,' she responded, 'an adult baby-girl needs a mummy. You're the one who'd do the washing.'

I just laughed as she once more began to rummage in the bag, still talking.

'They're a lot cheaper though, because you can reuse them. Terries, he calls them, but there's a drawback. He wants me to wear these horrid plastic pants over them, and they're not comfy at all.'

She'd picked them up: a bizarre garment a bit like a pair of big knickers, only made of clear plastic and with a frilly elasticated waistband and leg holes. They didn't look very nice, but I could well imagine the strength of feeling of a girl who'd been put in them, so they did have an appeal. For Sophie, it would be pure exhibitionism, especially with nothing underneath; for Kay, a deep humiliation, and perhaps more so with the terry nappy on as well.

'There's other stuff too,' Sophie was saying as she began to pull out more items: a ridiculous little hat, a pink bib with a teddy bear like the ones on the nappy, a large dummy, a plastic bottle with a teat, baby powder, cream and, last of all, a suspiciously large thermometer.

'Guess where this goes,' she said happily, holding it up.

'Up your bottom,' Kay answered in horrified fascination.

'I think you should get into a nappy,' I suggested. 'After all, he wants you to practise.'

'I might,' she answered, 'but no spanking me.'

'No? I'd love to get you across my knee in that terry thing, and peel the back slowly down . . .'

She stuck her tongue out.

'Seriously, Amber, I expect he'll want to see everything before the shoot's over, and you know how men who're not into CP get about bruising.'

'OK, I promise. Get into one anyway.'

'What sort?'

'I'm not sure, but if you want to wet yourself you're to use a disposable, or put the plastic pants on.'

She giggled, and didn't answer, but her hands were already at the button of her jeans. I sat back to watch, enjoying her open enthusiasm for being rude, which she brings to just about everything. For all her experience and lack of embarrassment, she still managed to look vulnerable, with her sweet, cheeky face and shoulder-length blonde hair. It was well worth watching her strip too: peeling her top and the little sports bra she had on beneath as one to let her lovely round breasts free, then pushing her jeans and knickers down with her bum stuck out towards us just to be cheeky. As she bent to pull her shoes off I glimpsed her fanny, and caught the scent of her sex. She'd shaved, presumably because she was going to be an adult baby-girl, and her neat little lips were pink and smooth, with just a hint of the fleshy folds between.

Kay was watching too, with the nervous excitement that turned me on so much, her eyes wide and her mouth slightly open. The sexual tension between us was already high as Sophie went nude, and higher still as she bent again to choose a nappy, picking up first a disposable, then the terry, before deciding on the disposable. She was giggling with delight as she pulled it on, wiggling into it to encase her middle in the puffy pink material, from her waist down, although it left a fair bit of chubby pink bum cheek sticking out around each leg hole.

'How do I look?' she asked, craning back in an attempt to see her own bum over her shoulder.

'Very cute indeed,' I told her, and I meant it.

The nappy made her look exquisitely vulnerable, all the better for her being otherwise stark naked, with her little breasts bouncing as she scampered into the dining room to admire herself in the mirrors. She came back giggling, and gave us a twirl, then stuck her bottom out to show off the big puffy nappy seat.

'How does it feel?' Kay asked.

'Naughty,' she answered. 'I'd like to go out in the street like this, maybe down to the pub, and when I was ready I'd just do it in them, and I mean everything.'

Her face was glowing with pleasure, and I was wishing it was possible to do as she wanted: take her out in just her nappy and let her wet herself when the need came. Unfortunately, I knew full well how my neighbours would react, and it would not be positive.

'I think that's important,' she was saying, 'that I should just go when I have to, without even thinking about it.'

'How many disposables have you got?' I asked.

'Four. I bought a six pack, but I tried one last night, to sleep in. It was great. When I woke up this morning I didn't even have to get out of bed to go to the loo. I just did it, right in my nappy, then had the most gorgeous frig.'

'With the nappy still on?' Kay asked, giggling.

'Sure, all squishy and warm around my bum and pussy. It was lovely. You should try.'

'What, tonight?'

'Now, come on, Kay, it's great.'

Kay had gone pink, and shot me a nervous glance.

'I'd like you to,' I told her honestly.

She bit her lip.

'Come on, Kay,' Sophie urged. 'It's fun. It feels so naughty.'

'I ... I would like to play,' Kay admitted. 'But a nappy.'

'Come on,' Sophie urged, picking out a second disposable. 'Get in your nappy and no nonsense, my girl, or Amber will just have to spank you and then we'll put you in it anyway, only with a sore bottie.'

Kay was blushing scarlet, but she nodded and stood up. Sophie gave a delighted giggle and bent to extract a second disposable, holding it up for Kay's inspection. Kay made a face, but she'd already begun to undress, her trousers open at the front. For the second time I sat back to enjoy the sight of a pretty young woman stripping naked to put on a nappy, my own girlfriend maybe, but it was a new experience for her.

She'd undressed in front of me a thousand times, and Sophie quite a few, but she still looked unsure of herself as she pushed her trousers down, leaving her knickers. Her fingers were shaking a little as she sat down to take off her shoes and socks. The trousers followed and, after a moment's hesitation, her top. She had no bra, and her nipples were already stiff, pointing up from her firm little breasts in her excitement and agitation. Her mouth was set in a line as she lifted her bum to take down her knickers, and she kept her legs firmly together, showing only a puff from the deep golden bush of her pubic hair in the triangle where thighs closed.

Naked, she was full of nervous excitement, which grew as she stepped gingerly into the nappy, one foot at a time. Her face and chest were flushed, and she was shaking quite badly as she pulled it up her legs and wiggled her bum into it, standing as she did so. Sophie gave a little clap of appreciation, to which Kay responded with a shy smile. I was smiling too, feeling wonderfully strong and in control with two friends naked but for their nappies, and ready to play.

Sophie took Kay's hand, to lead her into the dining room, where my two tall mirrors stand at opposite ends. The idea is to let a girl watch herself during punishment, to see how rude she looks bent down over the table with her fanny showing from the rear, and as the marks of the cane or strap or crop are laid across her bottom. It worked just as well with the nappies, and they were soon posing together, giggling as they stuck their bums out to show off the big, puffy nappy seats and how the fronts went down between their legs. I fetched some hairbands and ribbons, and Sophie put Kay's hair into bunches, set high on her head, with her golden curls tumbling down over each ear. We chose royal blue ribbons to suit her hair, which left her giggling hysterically at her look, and more flushed than ever.

'I just have to come like this,' Sophie announced happily, 'but not until I've wet myself, and I want to feel I can't help it. Have you got another bottle of wine, Amber?'

'Of course, but I think we can do better than that.'

I went back to the kitchen and put another bottle of the Riesling in the fridge to chill it down quickly. I had one litre of orange juice and another of apple, and set them both out on the table, along with two glasses. Kay and Sophie had come to the door, watching me as I poured the juice.

'Me too?' Kay queried as she watched the level of orange juice rise in the second glass.

'You too,' I told her. 'Drink up, girls.'

Sophie came without hesitation, to down her glass so eagerly that she spilt some, leaving her with a trickle of juice running down between her breasts. Kay wasn't so sure, and she was looking a little sulky as she put the glass to her mouth, sipping gingerly, only to suddenly begin to gulp it down, as if she had reached a decision. I waited until she'd finished, then refilled the glasses. They drank again, more eagerly this time, exchanging glances over the rims of their glasses as they swallowed down what would shortly be coming out of their fannies.

I'd finished the orange juice, and switched to the apple, making them drink the whole litre. Both their tummies had started to bulge a little, pushing out the waistbands of the nappies. I filled the glasses with water, and that went down too, leaving Sophie with a hand on her swollen tummy and Kay looking slightly dizzy.

'No more, please,' Sophie begged. 'My tummy hurts, and I'm already starting to want to go.'

'Not yet you don't,' I instructed. 'You're to wait until you really can't help it. Now let me see, how shall I amuse myself with you until you're ready?'

I wanted to watch them do it, to enjoy their helplessness and their ecstasy, before I came myself, but that didn't mean I couldn't play with them. Sophie might need to stay pristine behind, but Kay didn't. I pulled one of the kitchen chairs out and beckoned to her.

'Over you go, Kay, and let's have that nappy down for a spanking.'

She nodded and swallowed, pushing her thumbs into the waistband of the nappy as she stepped forwards. Down it came, just far enough to leave her fleshy little bum naked, but still half up at the front, ripe for spanking. I took her wrist and pulled her close, adjusting the nappy so that her fanny showed at the front before taking her gently down across my knee. She lifted her bottom a little and I began to spank her, just pats really, to get her warm. After all, it wasn't a punishment.

Her cheeks are a little too fleshy to really show her off when she's over the knee, but there was a tiny puff of golden hair visible between her thighs, and her crease was open enough to hint at her bottom hole. I wanted more, but I kept spanking until she started to sigh and her breathing had deepened before giving the order.

'Up a little more, Kay, let's have your bottom hole showing.'

Sophie giggled as Kay lifted on her toes, spreading the deep crease between her meaty little buttocks to show off her darling little bumhole. She was brown, quite dark, a ring of coloured flesh like a tiny starburst with the actual hole a tiny wet cavity at the centre, closed by four little pieces of flesh set in a perfect cross. I'd made her look in a mirror often enough, and she knew just what she was showing.

'She is rude, isn't she?' Sophie giggled. 'Can I kiss her?'

'Kay?' I asked.

Her answer was a soft whimper, which was good enough for me, and for Sophie. Taking hold of Kay's bottom, I spread the cheeks wide, stretching her anal star for inspection. Sophie skipped over, bending with her hands on her knees, to plant a single, neat peck on Kay's anus. Kay gave a soft moan, and I began to spank again, high on her cheeks, because Sophie's head was in the way, her tongue out and lapping at the little brown bumhole.

'Make her come while I spank her,' I ordered.

Kay gave a little whimper, and began to squirm, but her resistance lasted only a moment. Sophie's tongue had begun to work its way in up her bumhole and her cheeks were well flushed, bringing her too high to let her stop herself. I reached the back of the nappy and tugged it a little further down, allowing Sophie to push her chin in over the waistband and bury her face between Kay's thighs. Kay was whimpering as I began to spank her again, harder now, to make her bum cheeks wobble and shake as the smacks landed.

I hadn't intended to bring her off so quickly, but I wasn't stopping. She just looked too good, with her nappy pulled down and Sophie's face between her thighs as I spanked her. Sophie was licking fanny, and Kay's tiny brown bumhole was on show again, now wet with saliva and a little open. I tightened my grip on her waist, spanking harder, to make her cry out in pain, just momentarily before her pleasure caught up with her. Her bumhole started to wink and she was coming, her thighs spread, tight in the lowered nappy, wriggling her smacked bum in Sophie's face as her cheeks bounced to the slaps. She was gasping, then crying out my name in broken ecstasy, and her body gave a last climatic heave before she was through.

Sophie sat back, her eyes bright with mischief, smiling broadly, her face sticky with fanny cream. She was giggling as she jumped up to clean her mouth. I was ready and, as Kay cuddled into me with her body warm and trembling in my arms, it would have been so simple to ease her down to her knees and put her face between my thighs. She hadn't pulled her nappy up, and I could feel the heat of her spanked bottom through my jeans as she sat on my knee. I gave her a pat.

'Pull your nappy up, darling, I'm not done with you yet. Sophie, could you get the wine out of the fridge.'

Both obeyed promptly. Kay rose to tug her nappy back into place, covering her so that no more than a fringe of smacked flesh was visible around the sides of her leg holes. Sophie quickly poured the wine, passing me a full glass before swallowing a good half of the contents of her own at a single gulp.

'Soon,' she said, placing a hand gently on the bulging front of her nappy, 'quite soon now.'

'Don't rush it, wait until you have to,' I told her.

She nodded and made a face, clearly already a little uneasy. Kay sat down on my lap again and we began to sip our wine, both watching Sophie as her discomfort slowly increased. Second glasses followed the first and she had begun to wriggle, squirming her thighs with her knees pressed together. She was fidgeting too, ever more nervous as the pressure in her bladder rose and she drew closer to the moment she'd just have to let go, whether she liked it or not.

We'd started on our third glasses, finishing the bottle, before her urgency finally got the better of her. She started to wiggle her toes, and closed her eyes, one hand pressed firmly to the crotch of her nappy. I could see her tummy muscles tightening, and the tension in her throat as she tried to resist. Then her eyes had come wide as she gave a little whimper and I knew she had reached the end of her tether. She gasped, then spoke.

'I'm going to do it, Amber ... I can't help it ... I –'

She broke off with a sigh, her eyes closed again and I caught the hiss of her pee as she let go. My throat felt suddenly dry and I drained the last of my wine, my arousal soaring as I watched Sophie wet her nappy in front of us. She was whimpering deep into her throat, and still pressing on her crotch, only to take her hand away and put it to her chest, stroking a nipple as the expression of strain on her face slowly gave way to bliss.

Her pee was still coming, and as she emptied her bladder into her nappy the front began to swell, then to droop, bulging thick and heavy between her legs. The moment she'd finished her hand went down the front, her eyes still closed as she began to masturbate, with her little breasts jiggling as she rubbed herself and her wet nappy still slowly expanding between her open thighs and around her bottom.

I had to come too, and pointed to the floor at my feet. Kay went down, her hands at the button of my fly immediately, to pop it open and draw down my zip. I lifted my bottom, allowing her to tug my jeans and knickers down, all the way to my ankles. Immediately, she buried her face in my fanny, licking, as Sophie's sighs rose to moans and gasps.

'Do it, Kay,' I ordered, my voice coming hoarse and breathless. 'Do it in your nappy while you lick me ... be dirty for me ...'

She didn't respond, too busy licking me, holding my bottom as her tongue flicked over my fanny lips and in my crease. Sophie cried out, and she was coming, her thighs tight together to squeeze the bulging, pee-soaked nappy material forwards into a fat, wet bump. Her eyes came wide as she finished and fixed on us, her hand still down her nappy. I took Kay's head, stroking her hair to soothe her, because I knew she'd find it hard, even with her bladder straining to the point of pain.

'Do it, Kay,' Sophie urged. 'Do it for us. I want to see you.'

Kay gave a little sob into my fanny and suddenly I caught the hiss of pee. She was doing it, wetting her nappy as she licked me, the pee squirting into her crotch. I could just imagine her feelings, the nappy swelling beneath her, growing fat and heavy with her piddle as she worked on my fanny. It was perfect: my beautiful, shy girlfriend grovelling at my feet in nothing but a sodden nappy, her pee still squirting out, her bum cheeks warm with spanking, her anus wet from Sophie's tongue, her mouth full of my taste ...

I screamed out as I came, revelling in what I'd made her do, so rude, so submissive, kneeling in her wet nappy as she licked me to ecstasy, just the way it should be.

Our little adult baby-girl session had been so much fun that by the end I wouldn't have minded being put in nappies myself, or at least, had they insisted I would have let them. After all, it was just the three of us, all girls together, and I could trust them. It wasn't really in Kay's nature, and Sophie always likes the attention to be firmly fixed on her, so I escaped, with slight regrets.

We went to bed together after cleaning up, but stuck to cuddles, the intensity of our nappy game enough to keep all three of us happy. Sophie and I were supposed to be in Loughborough by lunchtime, so we rose fairly early and got a good breakfast in, bacon and eggs then plenty of toast and marmalade to keep us going for the day. I drove up the A1 and across Rutland, not rushing, and talking as we went. I asked about Angel, as if anything suspicious was going on Sophie was very likely to have picked up on it, and as far as she knew Mel's suggestion was genuine.

Angel had appeared a few months before, and very quickly made her mark on the club. She had been full of enthusiasm and bounce from the start, and took a genuine pleasure in dominating both men and women, although she apparently tended to assume that all men were submissive or at the least wanted to submit to her. Melody had quickly befriended her, and by her third club she'd been getting free admission and had really begun to strut. Morris wasn't best pleased, but he knew the drawing power of a top-quality, beautiful young dominatrix, and had put commercial needs before his personal feelings. The tensions were building up though, hence Mel's desire to see Angel beaten in the wrestling ring.

The other major piece of news was that it seemed likely that the international puppy show would become reality. Between them, Morris and Hudson Staebler had contacts right across the States, in Europe, and even Australia, and they had been feeding off each other's enthusiasm ever since the club. Staebler apparently had fingers in all sorts of pies: internet sites, clubs, magazines and more. He seemed to have won Sophie's respect, as opposed to her mere acquiescence.

I also found out why Sophie was so keen to go on her photoshoot with me rather than Mel. She had seriously overextended herself on her credit cards and, while Morris was doing his best to help her clear the debt, she still felt she was being exploited. She'd been sent to so many men for spankings that she'd lost count, and was starting to lose her taste for it from over-exposure, not just for the punishment and the sex, but for displaying herself, and at heart she was an exhibitionist. Hence she'd jumped at the chance to be put in nappies, which was different enough to be fresh and exciting, while Denis Humber apparently paid well. Exactly what he wanted she wasn't sure.

We got to Loughborough in plenty of time, but it took us quite a while to find the place we were supposed to be going: a set of studios built into the upper storeys above a shop selling dirty magazines and sex aids, with a seedy pole-dancing club in the basement. Even when we'd found the place it proved impossible to park nearby, and I ended up in a residential street a good half-mile away. By the time we got there I was feeling not a little flustered, but Denis Humber greeted us with coffees and did his very best to make us at home, which made me feel a lot better. He was quite a small man, rather nondescript in appearance, with a nervous eagerness about him that was anything but threatening. The same was not true of the man who'd let us in and appeared to run the place, a shifty-looking individual who pinched Sophie's bum as she started up the stairs.

'Ignore Dave,' Humber advised as we reached the landing. 'He's harmless.'

I nodded in response and took a sip of my coffee as he pushed open a door.

'This is the playroom,' he stated, 'but we can use any room we like, even the club downstairs. It depends what scene you want to do.'

'What do you want me to do?' Sophie responded.

'Everything,' he answered, 'but it's always best if you're into it. I hate it when you can tell a girl's only going through the motions.'

'OK,' Sophie said gingerly, 'so let's see what we've got.'

We'd entered the room, which wasn't customised as an adult-baby girl playroom, but was at least clean and neat. The walls were plain white and the floor polished wooden boards, there were shutters on the windows and a single tall mirror between them, but Humber had spared no expense fitting it out. A cot stood in one corner, big enough for Sophie to curl up in. He'd put a big splash mat with a Little Bo Peep motif on the floor, various somewhat suggestive toys, and also a double sheepskin, which had Sophie exclaiming in pleasure as she squatted down to stroke it. A pink chest of drawers stood to one side, decorated with fluffy white sheep and with a padded plastic mat on top.

'There's plenty of everything you could want in the drawers,' Humber pointed out. 'You like the rug then?'

'I love it,' Sophie answered. 'I'll go nude on it, if you like, or any way you want me.'

'How about in just plastic pants?'

'Sure.'

Humber was starting to relax, and it would have been hard not to in the face of Sophie's open enthusiasm. I could imagine it took a fair bit of courage to ask a girl to put on nappies for a photoshoot, and that he would get a lot of rejections, but Sophie was a natural. There was an ordinary plastic chair in one corner, and I went to sit on it, sipping my coffee. Sophie began to undress, chatting away happily as she peeled off her top and sports bra as one.

'Plastic pants then, and maybe one in disposables. I like the disposables.'

Humber swallowed hard as her breasts came bare.

'Good. I bet you look great. I'd like one in the terries too, with the plastic pants over the top.'

'Fine. Do you want me to wet?'

He'd started to go red, and no surprise. Sophie had kicked her shoes off and bent to do her socks, still talking.

'Because if so I'll need plenty of water.'

'In the bottom drawer,' Humber said weakly.

Sophie nodded and stood up to undo her jeans, then she pushed them down, knickers and all, stepped free and was stark naked, pushing out her tummy to show off her bare pubic mound. She'd depilated that morning, leaving her fanny pink and baby smooth, while her natural colouring made her seem fresher still. Humber nodded, and Sophie went on as she began to gather up her clothes, giving us both a peep at the rear of her fanny as she did so.

'So what else have you got for me?' she asked as she stood up.

'The room across the landing is a dungeon,' he explained, 'but I'm not really into leather and that sort of stuff, unless you'd –'

'Not in nappies, no,' Sophie answered, 'but you can punish me if you like. I don't mind a spanking, although it would be extra. You'll take the photos, won't you, Amber?'

He gave me a slightly doubtful look. I shrugged. It looked like being a long afternoon, and it was going to be more fun taking rude photos of Sophie than just sitting there drinking coffee and watching. It would also be more fun to have her punished.

'Maybe, yes,' he went on. 'There's a bedroom upstairs too, and the bathroom, both of which we could use, an office set too, but I don't suppose that's much use.'

'I don't know,' Sophie answered him. 'Maybe I could play your secretary, made to wear nappies as a punishment, and spanked too.'

'Good idea,' I put in, keen for anything that involved a bit of humiliation for Sophie rather than simple nappy play.

Humber turned to me.

'Would you want to do the spanking?'

'Um . . . maybe. I'm not really dressed the part.'

'No, maybe not, but you'd make a great mum, for a nappy-changing scene? I'd pay you, of course, the same as Sophie.'

'I don't need your money, thanks.'

'I do,' Sophie put in. 'Come on, Amber, please . . . pretty please?'

'What happens to the pictures?' I asked.

'They're for my website –,' Humber began, but Sophie cut him off.

'– which is a paysite, and if anyone's paid to look at pics of girls in nappies, then they're in no position to complain about who's in the pictures.'

I nodded. It was true, but I wasn't one hundred per cent happy about it.

'Let's see how I feel,' I told them.

Sophie nodded, knowing better than to press the issue, and went to her bag. Humber evidently understood because didn't say anything either, but began to fiddle with his camera, an expensive digital with a zoom. He had a good tripod too, and with the bright but diffuse ceiling lights I could see he'd made the effort to produce some worthwhile pictures. Sophie had gone to the chest of drawers, and was drinking water from a two litre-bottle.

'Which do you want me to wet in?' she asked. 'I'll do the others first.'

Humber thought for moment, evidently struggling with a difficult decision.

'Or a little bit in all three?' she suggested.

He shook his head.

'No, just the plastic pants, and as much as you can.'

Sophie nodded, took another deep swallow of water and went to her bag. Pulling out one of the remaining pink disposables, she put them on, tugging the elasticated waistband high and settling them into place around her bum. She went to the mirror, admiring herself from several different angles, as Humber began to take photos. I sat back, enjoying the show but nothing like as much as I had the previous night. Sophie looked cute, especially once she'd put a dummy in her mouth and begun to pose, but it was nothing like as intimate.

They worked well together because Sophie was a natural show-off and had a knack for knowing what was wanted. Humber only gave her the occasional instruction as she moved from pose to pose, kneeling, crawling, curled up on her side, lying on her tummy, all judged to make the best of her pretty face and the bulging pink nappy around her hips and midriff. She was genuinely getting into it to, adding details such as sucking her thumb and taking the baby bottle in her mouth without having to be told.

By the time Humber had his fill he was obviously getting flustered, and I wasn't entirely unaffected either. Sophie just oozed sex, and submissive, playful sex at that. With maybe three or even four hundred shots of her in the disposable taken, she peeled it off and put the terry on, with Humber photographing her as she pinned up the sides and pulled on the plastic pants over the top. In just the terry she looked even sweeter and more vulnerable than in the disposable, and the plastic pants actually added to it, to my surprise, tight around her thighs and waist to trap the thick folds of towelling within, and the huge nappy pins at her hips making her condition absolutely, blatantly obvious.

He asked her to dress and undress again, and she went all the way, even managing to get her jeans on over the top of her nappy. Even fully dressed she looked impossibly rude, with her tight blue jeans bulging at the back and front and the waistband of her plastic pants on show, so that there was no question that she had a nappy on underneath. She even suggested going on the street to be photographed as passers-by realised she had a nappy on under her clothes, but the idea alarmed Humber so much I began to wonder if he wasn't some well-known local dignitary.

When she began to strip it got better still. First her jeans came off, but she kept her socks and put her shoes back on, creating a deliciously rude impression, as if she'd been put in a nappy instead of her lower garments as a punishment, or because she was likely to wet herself. Humber was in ecstasies, photographing her from every possible angle, and in pose after pose after pose, although nearly every one involved having her bum stuck out. He also concentrated on her face, which raised my opinion of him. So many men don't seem to care as long as they get plenty of boobs and bum and fanny.

She took off her shoes and socks for a few that concentrated on her bare legs and feet, then her top and she was back to square one, in just her nappy and plastic pants. He had another four hundred odd shots on his memory card, and two excellent shoots. Humber was in heaven, full of praise for her, and shaking so hard I had to help him change the card in his camera while Sophie peeled the plastic pants down to remove her terry from underneath.

He was nearly ready to go on by the time she'd pulled her pants back up, and if the effect was a little less cute, it was a great deal ruder. The plastic pants hid nothing, leaving every detail of her bum and fanny on show, yet in a way that was far, far naughtier than had she been stark naked. She'd been taking sips from the water bottle between pictures, and I could tell she was ready, with her tummy a hard little ball and the muscles of her thighs twitching slightly.

She got down on the sheepskin rug, first just showing off before getting into more babyish poses, sucking her thumb and curling up with her knees high so that the transparent plastic was pulled tight over her shaved fanny-lips. When she got up into a crawling position I knew she was going to do it, her face slack and one leg twitching slightly as she pulled her back in, lifting and spreading her bottom with her thighs set well apart to show her fanny off from the rear. I could hear her breathing, deep and even, and Humber began to circle her, snapping away, picture after picture after picture, until at last she gave a little moan and turned her head to look up at him.

'I can't hold it . . . not any longer –'

Her voice broke to a low gasp and she started to pee, a little golden fountain erupting out from between her fanny lips and into the plastic pants, to trickle down the groove of her sex. Piddle had quickly begun to pool beneath her mound, making a rounded yellow bulge in the plastic. The pants filled quickly, and she was panting with emotion as pee began to well up around her fanny and higher still, into her bottom crease, wetting her anus and swelling out the back of her pants, until I was sure something must give way.

It did, one leg hole, pee trickling out of the side to run down her thigh and onto the sheepskin. Humber didn't even try to stop her, but let her do it, snapping away frenziedly as the bulge in her plastic pants fattened and the piddle ran down her thighs. I wanted to masturbate, just watching her, and if Humber hadn't been there my knickers would have been down in an instant. As it was

I couldn't resist stroking the crotch of my jeans, to feel the swell of my fanny lips beneath, thinking how it would feel to have Sophie lick me with her plastic pants bulging with pee, or to do my own all over her, or to just let go into my knickers . . .

I was feeling dizzy with arousal as she finally jumped up and ran giggling from the room, leaving spots and splashes of pee on the bare stairs as she went. Humber looked thoroughly pleased with himself, grinning and shaking his head as he checked the settings on his camera. I was more than ready to photograph him punishing Sophie, and helped him gather up what was needed, taking the water, her terry and a fresh pair of plastic pants so that he could deal with the electronic equipment safely.

Sophie was still in the bathroom, with the door wide open, hosing her bum and legs down in the bath. I'd brought her towel up, and she gave me a big grin as she climbed out and wrapped it around her middle. Humber had been taking photos from the door, which was bit cheeky, but Sophie didn't seem to care so I didn't comment. After all, he'd seen everything she had to show.

'How are we going to do this then?' she asked. 'I've only got my street clothes, and I'd really need a skirt, wouldn't I, if I'm going to be your secretary.'

'Start with just the nappy, top, sock and shoes,' I suggested. 'Isn't that what you'd do if you wanted to humiliate your secretary, so everyone can see?'

'Sounds good to me,' Sophie answered, and started back down the stairs.

Humber wasn't really dressed the part, in casual clothes chosen for comfort and not look. I took a couple of him sitting at the desk looking official while we waited for Sophie, and decided he'd pass, perhaps as the boss of a small fruit and veg wholesalers or something. Sophie came back up, as before in her terry with the plastic pants over the top, no jeans, but otherwise fully dressed. It was the best look, for me anyway: not an adult baby-girl in a role, but a fully grown woman made to wear a nappy to humiliate her, as a punishment, for the amusement of her boss and her co-workers.

Sophie had it down pat, looking sulky and crestfallen as she posed, first standing in front of his desk as if being lectured after he'd first made her get in the nappy. The camera was easy enough, and I was soon getting into the stride of things, giving them both instructions as I took photo after photo. I had him make Sophie put her hands on her head and turn around slowly, showing off the nappy. Her face was set in utter misery, at least in some shots, because she was enjoying herself hugely and struggling not to smile.

A few secretarial tasks seemed a good idea, so I had her taking dictation, in the classic style, sat with her legs neatly crossed and a notepad on her knee, only with her hips encased by plastic pants bulging with nappy material. I had her fetch coffee from the machine downstairs, which really did fluster her, because while she was OK with Humber, Dave the proprietor was just too sleazy for comfort. Not that he saw, but she knew that all he had to do was step into the passage. I had her stand smartly to attention while Humber began to drink the coffee, then called a halt.

'OK, Denis, stop right there. Have you ever spanked a girl before?'

'No,' he admitted.

'Then just do as I say. The coffee's revolting, make a face.'

'It's not that bad.'

'No, no, pretend.'

He nodded and made a disgusted face.

'Great. Now put the coffee down and look at Sophie. You're angry. Wag a finger at her if you like. Say something too, to get your expression right.'

'Er . . . this coffee's repulsive,' he tried. 'If you've peed in it again, young lady –'

Sophie burst out giggling.

'Try again,' I instructed, 'and this time don't make her laugh. Sophie, you're supposed to be feeling scared and ashamed.'

'I know, sorry.'

'Once again, then.'

'Er . . . this coffee's repulsive,' he repeated.

'Yes, sir, sorry, sir,' she answered, looking at her feet.

I had both of them in shot, and it looked great, with the seat of Sophie's plastic pants at just the right angle, showing the sweet tuck of her bottom and the full rear bulge.

'Sorry's not good enough!' he barked.

'Good line,' I put in. 'Now tell her she's overdue a spanking.'

It was Protheroe's line, and I felt a pang for my own recent humiliation as I said it, and again as Humber responded with his own.

'Not nearly good enough. You're obviously overdue a spanking.'

'No!' Sophie squealed, backing a step.

'Oh, yes,' he answered her, starting to rise. 'Get on my desk.'

He was really getting the hang of it, his face like thunder and the order snapped out in a voice that brooked no disobedience, a real little Hitler. I kept quiet, sure I would get the best results if I just let the scene run. Sophie scrambled onto the desk in what really did look like fear, kneeling with her hips lifted to bring the seat of her plastic pants into prominence, with the nappy beneath now tight over her bum. Humber was standing, his knuckles on the desk.

'Not like that, you stupid girl,' he shouted. 'On your back, the way I told you.'

Sophie obeyed, rolling over immediately, so that she was lying flat with her legs dangling down over the edge

76

of the desk, not at all an easy position to spank a girl in, unless . . .

'Legs up, right up,' he yelled. 'Hold your ankles.'

Sure enough, and no surprise really, as it was him, he was going to do her in nappy-changing position. I felt my stomach tighten as Sophie's legs came up and she grabbed hold of her ankles, leaving herself in the one position that is perhaps even more humiliating than being held helpless over the knee: on your back, legs rolled high, fanny flaunted to the world, bum cheeks spread wide, everything showing and everything vulnerable, to slaps, to fingers, to a man's cock . . .

Humber stepped around the desk, looking down on her with a wonderful expression of amusement blended with lust. I both in shot, perfectly, with the broad seat of Sophie's nappy showing in detail and him beyond. My own desire was rising, among a flood of mixed emotions – embarrassment and sympathy for her, anticipation for what was about to happen, feelings of humiliation at the thought that any woman, ever, should be obliged to adopt such a lewd position, and be physically punished.

He began to spank, on the seat of her nappy, which can't have hurt, but still sent her into a frenzy, sobbing and shaking her head, squirming on the desk and wriggling her bum in a futile effort to avoid the slaps. She let go of her ankles and he immediately caught on, holding her by one leg with the other kicking wildly as he spanked her, with her blonde hair flying wildly. His fingertips were catching her thighs, leaving little red imprints, maybe not even intentionally, but I was hoping he'd pull her nappy up her legs, to expose her, then make a proper job of it. Finally, I spoke.

'She can take quite a lot, Denis. Bare her if you like.'

Sophie gave a little mew, which might have meant anything. Denis paused, and then he was reaching under her bum, to grip the plastic pants and haul them up her legs. He left them inverted around her thighs, a tangle of plastic above the terry nappy. Again his hands went down, and her nappy was tugged up to join the plastic pants, exposing her bottom, her fanny, her anus. She squealed for real as her nappy came down, and went on squealing as the spanking began again, now on her bare flesh with her thighs pumping in the lower nappy.

It was no longer put on, but real pain, and real excitement, with her fanny open and juicy, clearly ready for entry. Her little pink bumhole was winking too, and how he held himself back from stuffing his cock up one hole or the other I couldn't imagine. He was certainly ready, his cock making a big bulge in his trousers front, and I realised that it was probably only my presence that prevented her from getting a fucking then and there, whether she liked it or not. I let him plant a few more hard smacks, and then called a halt.

'Enough, that's great. Stop, Denis, and pull her up, by her ear.'

He gave her a last, resounding smack, full across her spread bottom, and stopped, hauling her upright as I had suggested. She squeaked in pain as her ear was taken in a firm pinch, and the expression on her face as she was forced into a standing position was wonderful to see, full of pain and contrition.

'Lecture her,' I instructed. 'Sophie, leave your nappy down, but take hold of the sides.'

She did it, giving me a last few wonderful shots of her rear view, bare red bum to the camera, plastic pants and terry nappy held well down so that nothing was concealed and yet the full extent of her humiliation was evident. He kept a firm hold of her ear, talking right into her face from a few inches, their bodies so close the lump of material made by his cock was poking against her flesh.

'Let go,' I told him. 'Sophie, step back. Keep that lovely pout, yes ... now pull up your nappy, as quick as you can ... wiggle your bum into the seat ... yes, perfect, and we're done.'

I took over twenty pictures as she went through the motions and they stood apart. Denis was red faced, a bead of sweat had formed on his forehead, and he looked as if he was about to burst. His mouth had begun to work, struggling to form the words before they at last spilt out.

'Could I ... might I ...'

Sophie glanced at me. I shrugged. It was obvious what he wanted, and not my place to stop it if she was willing. The bulge in the front of his trousers was huge, his cock sticking up underneath, almost straight out. Sophie just giggled and reached out to draw down his zip, looking him right in the eyes. His cock popped out as the zip came down, a hard, thick rod encased in bright purple cotton. Sophie began to stroke it and he swallowed hard, his eyes fixed on her plastic pants and the nappy within. I thought he was going to come in his pants, but somehow he managed to hold back, even as Sophie squatted down to pull his cock free of his underpants and take him in her mouth.

He was not that long, but thick, with a fleshy shaft and fat glossy helmet; virile enough and ugly enough to set my stomach fluttering as I watched Sophie suck. After a moment she pulled her top and sports bra up, freeing her breasts, and he gave a moan of pleasure. Again I thought he would come, but he was made of sterner stuff, gently fucking her mouth and mumbling under his breath as she worked, until at last the muttered noises became words.

'... just to do it ... just to fuck you in your nappy ... please, Sophie ...'

Sophie shook her head, still sucking cock, and his face set into such misery I really thought he was going to cry.

'Please,' he went on, 'I've ... I've never ... and I've always wanted to ... and ... and ... you're so lovely, and ...'

Still Sophie sucked, working diligently on his cock but not responding to his words as he went on, pleading to be allowed to fuck her while she had the nappy on. I was going to speak, to tell him not to harass her, but she pulled her head up.

'OK, you bad boy, if it means that much to you.'

He was babbling immediately.

'Thank you . . . oh, thank you, Sophie . . . you are an angel, a true angel . . . bent over the desk, please, and stick your bum well up.'

She gave him what I suppose was meant to be a look of admonition, but it didn't really work with his erect cock just inches from her face and still wet with her saliva. He took hold of it as she scrambled up, wanking himself with his eyes glued to her as she got into position, bent low over the table with her back pulled up to round out her bottom, stretching the terry towelling and the plastic taut over the globe of her bum.

He got behind her, his cock still in his hand as he spent a moment caressing the seat of her plastic pants. Then he was behind her, his hands on her hips, rubbing himself in her crease with the plastic against his cock and the nappy pushed in between her cheeks. There was sheer rapture on his face and, for the third time, I thought he'd come, but yet again he held himself back. Stepping away, he put one shaking hand to her nappy, urgently pulling the seat of her plastic pants aside, the terry towelling too, to show off her fanny, the mouth wet and ready for his cock. He pushed close, entering her, and she moaned, but he couldn't get it in properly, with the thick towelling in the way. For a while he tried anyway, grunting and gasping as he fucked her, with his hands locked in the top of her nappy.

Only his helmet was up, and I could see it popping in and out of her hole as he fucked her, until he changed his mind, suddenly tugging her nappy hard down over her bum, exposing her fully to his erection. One of the pins had sprung open, and she gave a squeak of pain as it dug into the soft flesh of her thigh, but he was too far gone to care, driving his cock deep up into her sopping fanny. Her nappy was only just down, his balls rubbing on the plastic as he fucked her, grunting and puffing with effort, his face scarlet. Sophie's bottom was wobbling to his thrusts, her smacked cheeks squashing out wide every time he pushed into her.

She gripped on to the table, her mouth wide in ecstasy, her whole body shaking. Then he was out, his cock in his hand, jerking frantically at the shaft as he grabbed her nappy, tugging it out, his cock over the gap between her waistband and her bum flesh. He came, ejaculating wad after wad of thick white semen over her bottom and down into the pouch of her drooping nappy.

I was staring, my fingers frozen on the camera, and I wasn't completely sure that I hadn't taken a picture at the crucial moment. Sophie gave a long sigh as he milked the last of his spunk out into her nappy seat, perhaps a little of resignation, but mainly of pleasure. She'd been punished and fucked quite hard, so had to want to come, but she contented herself with an arch look for Denis Humber as she stood up. Holding her nappy at half-mast, with the soggy pouch swinging between her legs, she scuttled off into the bathroom. As her red, come-spattered bottom disappeared, I turned to Denis.

'Is that enough for you?'

He nodded, then glanced at his watch and spoke.

'We can fit another set in, if Sophie's up for it.'

'I'll ask. What did you have in mind?'

'Nothing too heavy. Would you mind changing her?'

I didn't, not at all. For somewhat more than three hours I'd been watching Sophie pose and play, which had left me in need of something more tactile. I didn't mind the pictures either because, as Sophie so rightly said, anyone paying to look at pictures of girls in nappies had no right whatever to criticise me for appearing in them. So long as I remained in a dominant role it was fine. It meant she would get extra too.

'Are you ready to pee again yet, Sophie?' I asked, poking my head around the bathroom door.

She was standing in the bath, her neck craned back over her shoulder as she inspected her bottom, the shower hose in one hand.

'Give me ten minutes,' she answered. 'Am I clean?'

As she spoke she pushed out her bottom, her cheeks wet and glistening, still rich pink from spanking. There was no spunk, and I nodded, wishing I was bare myself, and sitting on her face with her tongue well up my bottom as I masturbated. She smiled and I turned back to tell Denis we were up for it, then went downstairs to fetch myself a badly needed coffee. I felt flushed, so aroused my fingers were shaking as I put the cup to my mouth, with ideas for what I could do with Sophie going round and round in my head.

Changing her would be fun, and then with luck I'd have a few minutes alone, to take my own pleasure with her before the long drive back to Hertfordshire. Just possibly I'd even do it in front of Denis, who was OK, but I knew the climax wouldn't be as good. He was ready in the playroom when I went back upstairs, with the chest of drawers pulled out from the wall so that he could get a decent angle. Sophie appeared a moment later, in just her towel.

We had two disposables left, and she climbed into one, tugging it up around her waist and wiggling her bum to get comfortable as if wearing a nappy was something she did every day. Denis gave her an appreciative glance and stood back, aiming the camera at us. I heard it click and felt the tension in my stomach grow a little at the realisation that this time I was in the set, doing something thoroughly rude, even if it didn't mean going bare.

'I'm not wet yet,' Sophie pointed out.

'Climb into the cot,' I suggested. 'Pretend to be asleep. Aren't you going to put your top on?'

'No,' she answered firmly. 'After all, what's an adult baby-girl got to hide?'

She had plenty, and she bounced them in her hands to prove it before climbing into the cot, pausing only to grab the dummy she'd been posing with and pop it into her mouth. I stood away as she curled up, her nappy-clad bottom stuck out so that the pink material was pressed to the bars, sucking away happily on her dummy. Denis moved in, taking pictures of her from several angles before going back to where he could get a wide shot with both of us in it. For a while she stayed still and silent, then spoke.

'Ready? I'm going to wet.'

I heard the hiss of pee and watched as her nappy started to swell, with Denis clicking away frantically. By the time she'd finished the material around her bum had a fat, heavy look, sagging slightly with the weight of what she'd done in it. I waited until he'd taken a few more shots in close-up before approaching the cot, moving slowly to let him get plenty of pictures but already in role.

Reaching down into the cot, I gave the seat of Sophie's nappy a thoughtful pinch, then nodded. She was wet, and needed to be changed. I shook her shoulder, just gently, and she turned her face to me, sleepy and a little puzzled. She reached up, her arms open for a cuddle, and I took her in, to hug her, then slipped one arm in under her knees and lifted her from the cot. It was not easy, but I managed, even swinging her around so that her bum was towards Denis, with the soggy bulge of her nappy sticking out at the camera. She clung on to my neck, which helped, until I'd laid her down on the changing mat.

She was almost limp, and completely unresisting, quite without shame as I carefully tore the sides of her nappy and rolled her legs up to pull it out from between. It was heavy with pee, and landed on the plastic play mat with a squashy noise as I dropped it. She was soaking, her hairless fanny and pink bum cheeks glistening wet with her own piddle and also plenty of juice. I took her ankles, rolling her high to leave her sex and bumhole blatantly flaunted to the camera, as I began to pull the drawers open in search of baby wipes.

I struck lucky on the third, by which time Denis had taken maybe a dozen close-up photos of Sophie's pee-wet fanny and bumhole. She suddenly let go, a tiny fountain of pee erupting from her open sex to splash on the changing mat and trickle down between her bum cheeks. I slapped her leg for her, and Denis was moving back again as I began to apply the wipes, rubbing down her smooth fanny mound, the tuck of bottom cheeks, and between them, pushing my finger a little way in up her anus. She gave a low moan as she was penetrated, and another as I used a fresh wipe to clean her fanny, rubbing right between her lips.

She'd begun to squirm a little in my grip, and the muscles of her tummy and bum cheeks were moving to a slow rhythm as I finished her off. There was cream in the drawer, and I applied a little to the crease of her fanny and her bumhole, this time slipping my finger in up to the first joint, not for the sake of the pictures, but because I wanted to. Her response was a moan of appreciation and I pushed in deeper still, buggering her briefly before pulling free.

Again I held her fixed in her rude pose as I searched out the powder and applied it liberally to her still moist skin. A few gentle smacks cleared away the excess before I rolled her higher still to make her fanny open and spread out her bumhole. More powder, more smacks, and her whole underside was pink and powdered and clean, also dry, save in the crease of her fanny and at the very centre of her bumhole, which had opened a little, and stayed moist and glistening with cream.

One more exquisite touch remained. Still holding her ankles, I put my hand to her forehead, held a frown just long enough for Denis to get his pictures, and bent to take the big anal thermometer from her bag. The tip was huge, for a thermometer, maybe half-an-inch across, but her bumhole was slippery with cream. She opened easily, her tiny pink ring spreading to accommodate the bulb as I eased it up. I held it like that for a moment, to let Denis get the shot, and to enjoy the way her bumhole kept trying to contract on the bulb in her excitement, then slid it deep up into her rectum.

Her anal ring was pulsing on the thermometer shaft, and her vagina had opened a little, making a bubble in her fanny cream. I decided she had to come, like that: powdered and creamed with a thermometer up her bum. Tightening my grip on her ankles, I put one knuckle to her clitty and began to rub. She moaned and began to squirm in my grip, maybe unsure if being brought to orgasm for Denis' camera wasn't too much. I paused, but she didn't speak out, just whimpered softly with the muscles of her whole lower body still in soft, even contraction.

Again I began to rub her clitty, more firmly, to set her wriggling and moaning. Her breathing picked up; the gentle pulsing of her fanny and bumhole grew faster. I rubbed harder still and she cried out in ecstasy, once, then again as she tipped over the edge into orgasm, her vagina opening, her bumhole in frantic contraction, her cheeks squeezing tight. I held her tight, still rubbing, until it was over, and continued, as if bringing her to orgasm was as much part of her changing routine as powdering her fanny.

What I wanted to do was strip down my jeans and knickers, climb up on the changing mat, straddle her face and masturbate myself to ecstasy as she licked my bottom. What I did was calmly extract the thermometer from her rectum, read off the temperature, which was normal, and put it aside before selecting a fresh terry nappy, lifting her to slide it under her bum. There were pins in the drawer, even bigger than the ones she'd used earlier, with pink plastic safety heads, and I used two of them to fasten the nappy around her hips.

In the background Denis was saying 'plastic pants, plastic pants' over and over with increasing urgency, so I went through the drawers until I found some and pulled them up Sophie's legs and into place around her hips, to leave her clean and fresh in her new nappy. All that remained was to lift her down from the changing mat, set her on her feet, give her a gentle pat on the bottom to send her on her way and I was done. Only I wasn't. He'd come, and so had she, but I hadn't, and I needed it very badly indeed.

'That was superb,' Denis said as he extracted the memory card from his camera. 'Thank you so much, both of you.'

'Are we done then?' Sophie asked.

Denis glanced at his watch.

'Maybe something quick.'

'OK. What do you want?'

He hesitated, then spoke, stammering out his words.

'I . . . I . . . w . . . what I'd really like is both of you in nappies, p . . . playing, if you get what I mean? There's extra, I could go to . . . to . . . maybe eight hundred?'

Sophie gave me a worried glance, but she was pleading with her eyes.

'Not me,' I told him. 'Sorry, Sophie.'

'But, Amber –'

'No, I can't, not in front of a camera.'

'The camera's full,' Denis pointed out, 'all six cards. I meant just . . . just for me.'

I found myself with my mouth open but out of words. Sophie was looking at me, pleading with her eyes. Denis looked as if he was about to cry again. I wanted to come, to come with Sophie as my plaything, but then again the thought of being put in a nappy had my tummy fluttering, so strong. There would be no pictures, so nobody need know, save Sophie, who I could trust . . .

'OK,' I managed, 'but . . . but I . . . I'm not really that comfortable in front of men, so I may need a little time –'

'I understand,' he broke in, 'of course.'

I was blushing so hot I couldn't even look him in the eye as I began to undress. My emotions were a jumble, but I did want to do it, with Sophie, and in front of him, maybe just a little. It was only fair anyway, if he was paying her extra, but even as I pulled up my top I was promising myself I'd have my revenge on Sophie, long and slow. I always feel uncomfortable being bare in front of men, and this was no exception; my fingers trembled and my skin flushed and pricked with goosebumps as I stripped, the awkward way, keeping the embarrassing bits to last.

Sophie was smiling as I peeled off my top, my shoes and socks, my jeans, my bra, and, at last, my knickers. Showing my chest had put a tight knot in my stomach, and it grew tighter still as my knickers came down, and off, with both of them watching me appreciatively. As I stood, Denis' eyes were on my chest, but moved quickly down, over the swell of my belly to my fanny. His tongue flicked out to wet his lips.

'A terry, please,' he said, 'and the plastic pants.'

I responded with a weak nod, and suddenly being in the nude was nothing, not when I was about to put a nappy on. He'd said there was everything we could possibly need in the drawers, and he'd meant it. There were enough terries to put a nursery's worth of adult baby-girls in nappies, and the plastic pants to go with them. Unfortunately they were all the same size and, at five foot ten with a full figure, it was not mine. The terry nappy was quite baggy on Sophie's petite figure, especially around her bum, with a big puff of material at either hip where the pins were fastened. I could only just get mine on, with the sides stretched taut and the back not quite covering the top of my bum crease.

Trying to get into a nappy was bad enough, but the discovery that I was really too big for it had me seriously flustered. I just managed it, with two of the big pink-headed nappy pins at either hip and the back pulled well up into my bottom crease. Being in it was more humiliating than I could possibly have imagined, bringing out my submissive side in moments. The plastic pants made it worse, every bit as uncomfortable as I'd expected, and they were stretched taut around my thighs and waist.

By the time I was ready I wanted to melt; to wet myself; to be changed, with the whole routine of being creamed and powdered; to be spanked as a punishment; to have the rectal thermometer pushed deep in up my bum; to be brought off under Sophie's fingers while I sucked on Denis' stout, ugly cock . . .

He had it out, lying fat and limp in his hand. I wasn't going to stop him. I wasn't going to ask either, but as Sophie came into my arms I was wondering just how bold he would be. Sophie's mouth met mine, her lips opened, and we were kissing, even as her hands came around me to take hold of my bottom through my nappy, stroking and kneading at my cheeks. I began to touch her neck and back, moving slowly down as our tongues entwined in a kiss that might have been giving a man pleasure, but was in no way false.

I could hear the thick slapping noise of him pulling at his cock to bring it to erection, but I ignored it, concentrating on Sophie's smooth, resilient flesh. My hand had reached the waistband of her plastic pants, and I slid my fingers under and down the nappy beneath, to tickle the top of her bottom crease. I felt her trembling in my arms and her kisses grew more passionate, her eager fondling of my bottom more intense.

Our mouths broke apart and she moved lower, kissing my neck, my chest, my breasts, taking one nipple in her mouth and then the other. I closed my eyes in bliss, letting her explore me, kissing and caressing, stroking my nappy-clad bottom to keep me firmly in mind that I was in a terry nappy and plastic pants. When she reached my tummy I started to shake, and wondered if she'd simply tug my nappy down a little and bring me off under her tongue, with him watching.

If she had I wouldn't have tried to stop her. I couldn't. All I could manage was to respond as she eased me gently down onto the floor and climbed on top of me, between my open thighs, her mouth moving up. I was stroking her hair as her mouth worked on my belly, my breasts and my neck once more before we began to kiss again, now with her between my legs, fanny to fanny through the thick towelling of our nappies.

I was getting too close to stop myself, and began to rub on her. She responded, squirming herself against me, to make the folds of my nappy rub in the groove of my fanny. It was good, glorious, but not enough to get me there, not quite. I needed her tongue, and began to push her down. She let our kiss break, but clung on, giggling as she began to kiss my breasts again, and to suckle me, drawing one nipple deep into her mouth to wring a cry of pleasure from my lips.

It was too much. She squeaked in surprise as I rolled her over on to her back and swung around, mounting her head to tail, my nappy-clad bum right in her face. Her thighs were wide, the crotch of her plastic pants taut over the folds of towelling beneath. I pulled it all aside and buried my face in her sex, licking eagerly. She'd begun to feel my bottom, squeezing my cheeks through the nappy, then spanking me and telling me off.

'Slut! Bad girl! Imagine going in a nappy. Now I'm going to have to spank you, and finger you –'

She broke off. I kept licking, enjoying her fanny, and gave my bottom a wiggle to show that I was willing. For a long moment nothing happened, before I felt the leg hole of my plastic pants pulled open and her hand slide into the rear pouch of my nappy. I felt the cream, cool and greasy on my skin, between my cheeks, on my bumhole, and Sophie was giggling as she slipped a finger inside. A second finger found my fanny hole and she was working both, pushing deep up me.

All it needed was a touch to my clitty and I'd be there, penetrated and rubbed off. It was glorious, still in my nappy with Sophie's fingers in me, and not only my fanny, but my bumhole too, deep in, opening me, maybe opening me for Denis' thick ugly cock, to have it slid up my fanny from behind, for a good hard fucking with my nappy seat pulled aside and his balls dangling in Sophie's face. Worse, he could bugger me, forcing my slippery, creamy bumhole without so much as a by-your-leave and spunking in my rectum while Sophie sucked on his big, wrinkly scrotum . . .

I heard him grunt and looked around, to find that he'd come, his hand closed tight around his erect cock shaft with a dribble of spunk running down over his fingers. A twinge of disappointment caught me, but it was my own fault, because I could perfectly well have asked him to ram it hard up my well-creamed bumhole. He stood, reaching for the wipes.

'Do you want your private moment?'

His cock was deflating slowly. Sophie eased her fingers out of my fanny and bottom.

'Please, yes,' I managed.

'Fine, that's no problem at all. Look, I have to get to the building society before it closes if you want your eight hundred in cash.'

'You do that,' Sophie answered. 'We'll wait.'

'I'll give you a bit of time then, but it might be better if you went down to the club, where you can lock the door, or Dave might catch you. You'll be safe there. It doesn't open until nine.'

I nodded, grateful for the advice. Just a little attention to my clitty and I'd have come. The orgasm would have been special, the culmination of hours of rising excitement, and I was not going to miss it. As Denis tidied himself up I climbed off Sophie, my head still spinning with lust as I smoothed out my nappy. Having it on now felt good, bringing me an exquisite sense of erotic humiliation and defining me as what I was, if only for the moment: an adult baby-girl, naked but for my nappy, with no right or reason to cover my chest, or to hold back, anything . . .

Denis disappeared down the stairs and we followed. I took my bag, but we left our gear, giggling together as we scampered along in nothing but our nappies. The door to the shop was ajar, just a little, but the sleazy proprietor, Dave, wasn't visible, to my relief. The bottom of the stairs opened out to the rear of the pole-dancing club, which was absolutely dark until Sophie managed to find the lights. It was small, and quite shabby, with an odd animal smell. Two rows of seats upholstered in worn crimson plush faced a stage with a single central pole for the girls to dance on.

It was all too easy to imagine the double rank of dirty old men gaping lustfully as a girl went through her routine on stage, pouting and posing as she stripped, moving her body into teasing or blatant positions, concealing and revealing, shaking her boobs and waggling her bottom, until she was nude and spreadeagled and they'd come in their sweaty little hands. No doubt plenty of rude things had happened in the little room, but nothing compared to what was about to.

Sophie already had the door locked behind us, with a big bolt that was presumably meant to stop people sneaking in without paying. I took her hand and led her up to the stage, imagining how it would be if the club was full, and she and I were obliged to perform in front of a house full of men, in our nappies. She went to the pole, playfully sliding around it with her fanny pressed hard to the metal and her legs wide open.

'Imagine,' she said, 'dozens of them, all watching us.'

'Exactly what I was thinking.'

'I'd do it too. Maybe we should stick around until they open?'

I shook my head, and I meant it.

'Maybe not,' she agreed, 'but what if we were made to?'

I nodded. 'Go on.'

She began to dance, talking as she wriggled against the pole and posed her body, as if showing off her nappies to the audience. I put my hand to the front of my own, pressing my fanny through the plastic and towelling.

'Imagine,' Sophie said. 'Made to perform like this, not nude, not striptease, but in our nappies, maybe chained to the pole and told we wouldn't be let go until all the men had come . . .'

'They wouldn't just watch either,' I added, massaging myself through the nappy. 'They'd get themselves hard watching us dance, then come up on the stage . . .'

'. . . and take turns with us . . .'

'. . . making us suck them off . . .'

'. . . and spunking in our faces.'

'Like they did to Annabelle, only worse, because they wouldn't want to wait their turns.'

'They'd fuck us . . .'

'. . . both of us . . .'

'. . . on our knees, side by side . . .'

'. . . with cocks in our mouths and cocks up our fannies.'

'Maybe even up our bums. My bumhole's all creamy . . .'

'. . . mine too. I thought Denis might try to put it up my bum.'

'Would you have stopped him?'

'I don't know, maybe not, not if you'd cuddled me while he did it.'

'I'd have cuddled you, tight, and licked you too, with your nappy pulled aside.'

'He had trouble like that, that's why he pulled yours down. I liked that, but I was wishing he could get in me properly, so you could suck his balls . . .'

'. . . and lick his arsehole.'

'Sophie, you dirty bitch!'

'I lick yours.'

'That's different, and that's just what I want you to do.'

'Yes, please!'

We came together, cuddling into each other's arms with even more passion than before. I was still imagining being chained to the pole and used by the audience as we went down on the floor together, Sophie beneath me as I straddled her face.

'They'd make us do this,' I breathed. 'Lick each other's bottoms for their amusement, turn and turn about.'

My nappy was in Sophie's face, and her answer was too muffled to make out. I lifted up a little as she spread her thighs and slid a hand into the front of her nappy.

'When . . . when they'd finished with us they'd make us wet ourselves in front of them,' she gasped. 'Do it, Amber, right in my face.'

'Yes.'

My bladder was quite full, and it was going to be a relief. I settled my bum in Sophie's face and let my muscles go loose, thinking how it would be, the two of us kneeling, side by side, our faces covered in spunk, well buggered, our nappies pulled back up so that we could wet in them. Or as I was, sat in Sophie's face as I peed in my nappy . . .

I let go, my mouth wide as my piddle exploded into the soft towelling folds encasing my fanny. Sophie gave a little shiver beneath me and she started to masturbate, rubbing her fanny with one hand down her nappy and the other on her titties. I knew she could feel it, the towelling swelling against her face, until it could take no more, overflowing, the warmth of my pee as the plastic pants began to fill, sagging and bulging between my open thighs.

She was masturbating hard, and my pee was still coming, bubbling out into my nappy with the level in my plastic pants slowly rising, to wet my bum and the mound of my sex. I sat down more firmly, and felt the wet bag of pee squash in Sophie's face. Another shiver passed through her and she was coming, her feet thumping on the floor and her body bucking up and down as she writhed in orgasm. My leg holes gave way and I felt the pee start to trickle out, down my legs and into her face. Her whole body locked tight in ectsasy, she'd come, again, and I still hadn't.

'Greedy little bitch,' I gasped, and reached down, to snatch the bulging underside of my nappy aside, emptying the contents of my plastic pants into her face as I sat firmly down.

It hurt, the nappy pins pulled tight against one hip, really digging in, but I didn't care. As my bottom spread in Sophie's face her tongue found my bumhole, pushing up into the creamy, sensitive cavity, and she was licking me, my bottom in her face, her tongue up my hole where it belonged. I took my boobs in my hands, stroking them and feeling their weight, my fingers brushing over my nipples.

My mind was a muddle, a dozen dirty images and sensations, competing for my attention. I was going to come anyway and, as I pushed my hand down into the soggy towelling around my fanny, I knew it would be in moments. Sophie's tongue was pushed deep up my bottom hole, doing wonderful things. I had my fantasy, chained to a pole in a sleazy club and used by dozens of men to pay for my release. I had my memories, hours of nappy play, Sophie's pretty face and sweet body in a hundred lewd poses ... her wetting herself ... her getting her spanking ... the thermometer up her bum ... her sucking cock ... Denis fucking her with his fat balls rubbing on her lower nappy ... a finger sliding up into my creamy bumhole ...

It all came together, nappies and pee and creamy, penetrated bumholes. I wanted to be buggered, with a fat, ugly cock forced up deep into my rectum through a hole cut in the seat of my nappy. I wanted it done to me as I knelt, my boobs hanging heavy and naked under my chest, swinging to the rhythm of my bum fucking. I wanted it done when I was so full of pee I couldn't hold it, and went in my nappy, helpless to prevent it as the hot piddle squirted backwards from my fanny. I wanted my bottom spunked up, filled with thick sticky white stuff as my soggy nappy squelched to the pressure of his balls ...

I wanted it all and, as I screamed out my ecstasy to the empty club, one last awful, glorious thought hit me: me chained to the pole, creamed and buggered in my wet nappy, then left there, left until I could no longer hold what had been pumped up my bottom, in agony as I struggled to keep it in, but failing, and filling the pouch of my nappy with spunk and mess in front of two full rows of leering, wanking dirty old men.

The thought stayed in my head as I came, a perfect mental image, before it finally began to fade. At last it went, and I collapsed sideways, weak and dizzy, to slump on the stage. Sophie sat up, gasping, her face sopping wet. I managed a smile, which she returned before speaking.

'You're so noisy! What if that Dave heard?'

I'd been far too far gone to think of Dave, but she was right. We froze, listening, Sophie's face set in such a comic expression I finally burst out laughing. Nothing happened and, after a while, we made our way back upstairs to clean up, trying not to giggle as we passed his door, now shut. Denis wasn't back, and we took our nappies off and got into the shower together, teasing each other as we washed. The towels Sophie had used were still wet, and there were no others, so we went downstairs to use some of the terry-towelling nappies from the chest of drawers, to find Sophie's bag gone, along with every last item of our clothing. Only one person could have taken them.

'Dave, it has to be,' Sophie said firmly.

'What for?'

'Who knows? Probably thinks he can squeeze a blow job out of us, but he's got another thought coming.'

'Absolutely.'

We wrapped the damp towels around ourselves, and made straight for the stairs, intent on teaching Dave a few home truths, only he wasn't there. The shop was empty, the metal shutter down outside, and there was no sign of our stuff. He'd gone, taking our clothes with him. We looked at each other.

'Shit!' Sophie swore.

'What about Denis?'

'How's he going to get in?'

'He could fetch Dave. Do you know his number?'

'No. We did everything on the net.'

'Maybe there's a computer?'

'I don't think so.'

There wasn't, but while we were searching somebody banged on the shutters. We were upstairs. Sophie ran down and went to the window, which I got open just in time to see Denis disappear around the corner. I also got quite a few funny looks from passers-by, leaning out in just a wet towel from a window above a sex shop. I was not calling for help, not when our choice of clothing consisted of either soggy towels or nappies. I did at least have my keys, and my mobile, but it looked like we were stuck until the club opened, which was going to be highly embarrassing. Even if we could get out it was half a mile back to the car, half a mile of streets busy with late-afternoon shoppers and people coming out of work.

Sophie's voice sounded from the stairs as she came back up.

'It's OK, the door to the club's on a latch.'

'It's not OK! How are we supposed to get to the car, and even if we could there's the drive back.'

'There must be something we can wear.'

There was, nappies, a choice of terry towelling and two sorts of disposables, pull-ups or ones that fastened at the side, that and see-through plastic pants. Even the towels were no good, too small to cover me properly, and even pinned around Sophie's hips and chest far from decent. It also left me nude and, at the very least, I'd have to run from the club door in the basement to the car. We'd get arrested.

'I can do it,' Sophie insisted, peering at herself in the mirror.

I shook my head.

'No. We'll have to ring somebody.'

'Who? We're in fucking Loughborough!'

'Patty Whitworth, she lives in Lincoln.'

I rang the number, praying she'd answer. On the eighth ring she did and I was talking immediately.

'Hi, Patty. This is Amber ... yes, from Morris' club. I've got a little problem ...'

Three

Patty found our situation extremely amusing, and I couldn't blame her. Other than being unable to keep a straight face, she behaved like an angel. She drove over, and arrived long before the club was due to open, bringing clothes down to the basement door. She was halfway between Sophie and me in size, but she'd brought dresses and I managed to squeeze into one, then ran to the car. Sophie was determined not to leave without her money, so I sat in Patty's car while they went to an internet café in the hope of contacting Denis. There was a long and apologetic email in Sophie's box, explaining everything.

Dave, it turned out, was not the sleaze we had taken him for. He had genuinely thought we'd left, and had gathered up our clothes thinking we'd left them, not knowing we had nothing to change into, so that he could take them to Denis. It took an hour for Denis to respond to Sophie's email asking for his phone number, and the best part of another to find his house. By the time I was back in my own clothes it was nearly ten o'clock. Denis was full of apologies, but I felt pretty foolish and didn't feel he was to blame, or even Dave. The four of us ate together at a local Chinese, with Denis listening in fascination to our discussions of puppy-girls and strip wrestling.

As Patty jokingly pointed out, I owed her a big favour, but by the end of the evening she was too tired to want to call it in, and Sophie and I had to get back. It was long gone midnight before we arrived at my house, to find Kay still up and waiting for us. I'd called her to explain and say we'd be late. Like Patty, she thought it was hilarious, but I was too exhausted even to spank her, and the three of us just collapsed into bed.

We took the Saturday very easy, minding the shop in a half-hearted fashion and going to bed early. Morris had called to ask if we wanted to watch the first of the heats for the wrestling, but it was more than I could face. The next one was in a week's time anyway, and I knew the formula, with mainly girls who wanted to lose up against each other, along with a few serious newcomers. As the draw was fixed I didn't need to worry about watching my opponents, while if some psychotic super-heavyweight entered then there wouldn't be much I could do about it anyway.

Mel rang on the Monday to report on the event. Four girls had been chosen, only one of whom I knew: Naomi, a tough young woman from Belfast whom I'd beaten before. She was apparently the best of them. I was beginning to get the feel for it, the thrill of competition and the apprehension of what would happen to me if I lost – a heady cocktail. We decided to attend the second heat, a small event at an old Victorian school scheduled for demolition.

The legality of venues had never particularly bothered Morris, but this one turned out to be a dive even by his standards. It was invitation only, five pounds a ticket and bring your own drink. When Kay and I arrived it was to find a bouncer lurking beside a blocked-up gate, and we were let in by having a piece of corrugated iron pulled aside. Inside was little better, with the ring in what had once been the assembly hall, film spotlights rigged up to a generator for illumination and precious little seating.

Kay and I climbed up to one of the window ledges to watch, which gave us a good view if not a lot of comfort. As usual, most of the competitors actually wanted to lose, making it difficult for Morris to make effective pairings. The first fight was between June, a voluptuous Indian girl I'd met a couple of times, and a tiny redhead, so timid she was stripped out of her school uniform, upended and spanked within just a few minutes. June was hardly a serious contestant, but went through anyway.

The next pair I didn't know at all, and they were so hopeless Melody eventually had to climb into the ring and box their ears for them, selecting the one who squealed the least as the winner. So it went, until eight were left to make the selection for the finals.

My interest was increasing. So far all the girls had fought in either schoolgirl kit or bikinis, both quite easy to get off, but Morris switched to a sort of parody of a call girl outfit: PVC micro skirts fastened with big belts, tight tops, fishnets, thongs and high heels. It was hard to fight in and harder to get off.

The first bout was between a well-built, aggressive lesbian called Sam and a girl I didn't know. Sam had been waived through, and made short work of her opponent, holding her face down on the mat in an armlock as she was stripped before making her lick, which brought the first serious applause of the evening. It was getting to me, and to Kay, who had snuggled into me and was making little purring noises as we watched the naked, defeated girl bring Sam to orgasm under her tongue.

Next up was Miss Barbara from the puppy show, who had beaten her first opponent quite easily and obviously thought a lot of herself. Unfortunately for her, she was drawn against another of the little group of dykes, a solidly built Chinese girl. It was a good fight, with Miss Barbara stripped from the waist down by the end of the second round, but fighting to keep her top until the fourth. Eventually she got sat on, her top ripped open to expose her big, silicon-assisted breasts and her bottom spanked for her before she was released, which she was not happy about. I put the Chinese girl, who turned out to be called Xiang, down as a serious opponent.

She wasn't the only one. In the next heat was a huge woman with a shaved head, Angie, who did the door for various women-only clubs around London. Not only was she strong and heavy, but she knew what she was doing. Her unfortunate opponent had been put in an unbreakable hold in just seconds, and was slowly and methodically stripped nude before being put on her knees and made to kiss Angie's bottom hole. I could see myself going the same way, and was wondering if Melody hadn't been rather too optimistic.

The last bout was between June and the last of the dyke contingent: a small but tough woman whose name I didn't know. Something was obviously going on because before June had fought giggling and showing off, even pulling up her own blouse and bra when her opponent couldn't do it. This time was very different. She seemed angry, and made the best of her weight, preventing the lesbian girl from getting at her clothes. It took seven rounds, with the unfortunate lesbian growing more and more chagrined as her clothes were pulled off, until at last, in just her thong and the ruined remains of her fishnets, she called out the stop word, which counted as a submission.

I felt good, and took Kay into one of the old classrooms for a spanking, across my knee with her knickers down, before going down to lick me to ecstasy.

Angel wasn't there, so Melody and I ran through what was supposed to happen again and she also promised to make sure I avoided Xiang in the draw. My excitement was running high as we drove home, both from the prospect of having free rein with anyone I beat, and in apprehension for my own possible fate. At home I queened Kay – sat bare on her face as she tongued my bottom – and I masturbated to the thought of giving Angel the same treatment.

I had to accept that I was likely to lose, and the consequences, which were likely to be thoroughly humiliating. It would at least be with another woman, and in the ring, so whatever happened to me it would be nothing like as bad as being spanked by Mr Protheroe. He'd be there, inevitably, along with the rest of Morris' paying customers, but that I was prepared to put up with in return for a chance to beat Angel.

Unlike the heats, the finals were to be done in style. We were back in the warehouse in Barking Creek, with a crowd even larger than for the puppy show and a proper mud-wrestling ring in place of the roped-off mat used at the old school. There was even raised seating. I learnt from Harmony that each stage would be distinctive, with opponents, costumes and what we were to wrestle in chosen by lot. Patty and Jean de Vrain were there, so we went to talk to them, and were soon joined by Hudson Staebler.

I was a bit surprised to find that Hudson was making the draw, as I knew from Mel that Morris was keen to keep him in blissful ignorance of their more dubious practices. He was in his white leathers as before, and had got well in with Morris, talking about the international puppy show and the odds on the wrestling as if he was the main organiser. Only after I'd spoken to him did Mel take me aside.

'Slight change of plan, Amber.'

'What's that?'

'Hudson's doing the draw, so it's going to be straight.'

'Straight? But –'

'He wanted to do it. He said because he was American and so completely unbiased everybody would know it was fair.'

'That's true, I suppose, but what's going to happen?'

'We'll just have to take our chances. If you're drawn against Angel, do your best.'

I nodded, unsure whether to believe her and feeling more apprehensive than ever. Hudson was walking towards the stage, where Morris was already standing, and there was nothing I could do but hand Kay's lead to Patty for safe keeping and follow Mel through the crowd. As I climbed up onto the stage, I found myself scanning the audience. Sure enough, Mr Protheroe was there, his flabby bulk entirely obscuring the chair on which he was seated, and next to him was Denis Humber. I felt my stomach go tight, imagining their conversation, swapping stories of how I looked in terry nappies and plastic pants with ones of how I behaved during a spanking.

Just having Mr Protheroe there was humiliating, yet after what had happened, to defeat Angel in front of him would be immensely satisfying. He'd given me to her to spank, as if he had the right to dispose of me as he saw fit, and she'd treated me with an arrogant dominance that might have turned me on, but left me hot with indignation every time I thought about it. He needed to see that I was not so easily pushed down.

Unfortunately, with an honest draw, it seemed quite likely that I would never come up against her at all. There were the eight seeds, and Mel had ranked me number eight so that it looked as if I was just a makeweight. Vicky, who had to be favourite for anyone who knew anything, was seeded third for some reason, behind Mel herself and Angel. Fourth was Topsy, a big, frankly fat, girl whom I'd beaten before but was no pushover. Fifth was Harmony, as big and as strong as her sister if less aggressive. Sixth was a girl called Diane I'd only ever met briefly, and seventh, Cassie Smith, another black girl and not really in the same class as the others.

103

Against us would be the eight who'd come through the heats, Angie the bouncer, Xiang, Sam and June from the one I'd attended, Naomi, Annabelle and two girls I didn't know at all, Emma and Nikki. Annabelle was tall and lithe, but really only there to be shown off, while both Emma and Nikki were average sized and pretty, perhaps fit, but really only there to be stripped and humiliated. Morris had stepped up to the microphone and the music died down as he launched into a preamble, introducing all sixteen of us, and then Hudson Staebler.

I'd known Morris to have Harmony tied upside down and to draw numbered balls from her fanny, which ensured he could cheat. This time they simply had Sophie, naked but for a collar and hobbled boots, with a large bowl chained to her wrists. Hudson picked the first ball, for what we wrestled in, and got number two, which was proper wrestling mud. Three of the male slaves Morris had signed up as helpers began to mix it by the ring as Hudson chose the second ball, for costume. He got five, which meant bikinis, and my heart sank. Short of plain underwear, nothing comes off more easily, which means that chance really comes into play.

I crossed my fingers behind my back as Hudson prepared to draw the pairings, praying I wouldn't get Xiang or Angie. Mel came first, as top seed, and drew number three, Emma, making me wonder if it was rigged after all. For Angel he drew Sam and my doubts faded a little. Sam was no pushover. Vicky got Xiang, which could well have been a final, and Topsy drew Naomi, which also looked tough.

My fingers were crossed more tightly than ever, with big Angie still in the draw, but to my immense relief she came out next, against Harmony, which at the very least would leave her tired. It also left me with an easy first round. Diane got Nikki and it looked easier still, Cassie was paired with Annabelle and I had June, the smallest

104

and probably the least fit of all. I'd seen her against the little lesbian girl, but she'd won by using her weight and making her opponent angry. That wasn't going to work with me.

A row of seats had been put on the stage, and I took mine, accepting a welcome cold beer. We were on in random order, and Diane and Nikki were chosen first, allowing me to relax a little and ready myself for what was ahead. Angel came to sit beside me and I greeted her with a measured nod.

'Didn't think you'd be here,' she said, 'not after we had to spank you last time.'

I shrugged. She went on.

'I just want you to know, if we meet, and you chicken out, I'm going to take you in the loo and give you the same treatment anyhow.'

'What treatment?'

'Spank you and piss on your hot bootie,' she answered, laughing. She got up, and walked away with a taunting sway of her hips.'

'Let's see you get past Sam first,' I called after her, but all I got was a derisive laugh.

She was plainly out to needle, but it made no difference. I already knew what I could expect if I lost, and it could have been worse. I certainly wasn't going to be calling out my stop word in any case, which means a bigger loss of pride than anything an opponent can do, or at least, anything an opponent has yet done to me. As the slaves began to pour wrestling mud into the ring, I was wondering what she would find most humiliating if I did meet her and win.

June and I had been called out sixth, so I settled down to watch the others. Diane and Nikki came out from the changing area, now in bikinis supplied by Morris, which didn't cover a lot anyway, with most of their bottoms on show. They were tied with bows too, at either hip and between the breasts, so the winner was likely to be whoever could protect herself more effectively, and not who was stronger or the better wrestler.

Diane was in red, maybe an inch shorter than me, slim, with lean, muscular legs and arms. Nikki was a little shorter but fleshier and probably heavier, and her blue bikini was straining a bit over good-sized boobs and a chubby bottom. As they climbed up into the ring it was hard to judge who was better, but the moment they began to fight it was obvious. Nikki didn't want to get dirty, which is a really bad move. Twice she disengaged rather than risk going down in the mud, and the second time she slipped and sat down on her bottom with a heavy squelch. She'd tried to save herself and, before she could recover, her bikini top had been twitched open and her boobs were out.

She covered them by instinct, leaving a muddy handprint on each when she pushed at Diane, who went down, slithering in the mud. Nikki snatched forwards, one side of Diane's bikini bottoms came loose, and then she slipped, landing face down to come up gasping and spitting mud, her face a filthy mask. Diane responded instantly, both remaining bikini ties were tugged open as one, and Nikki was nude, her bare bum marked by a neat pink triangle in sticky brown mud.

Nikki was still trying to get the mud out of her face as Diane stood, triumphantly holding the blue bikini aloft to show she'd won, at which point her own gave way, the single tied side dropping around her ankles to leave her with her bum and fanny bare to the audience, who were laughing and clapping in delight. She was entitled to take out her victory on Nikki, but seemed more concerned with concealing her fanny and left it at that.

Harmony and Angie were to follow: a much tougher match and, with bikinis to fight for, by no means a foregone conclusion. Angie knew what she was doing and had the weight, but Harmony had been in every competition since the first and knew all the tricks. Harmony was in yellow, her bikini tight over her ample breasts and big, muscular bottom. Angie, in green, was still at a disadvantage there, her back so broad and her hips so big she'd barely been able to do up her ties.

I knew what I'd have done, and Harmony did the same, avoiding a grapple and going straight into the mud, so that her body was slippery and her agility would count. Angie's response was simply to grab out, and after just moments she had caught Harmony by the ankle, keeping the hold, mud or no mud. I thought it was the end as Harmony was dragged in and Angie's fingers clutched for her bikini bottoms. It wasn't. Harmony twisted her whole body at the last second, snatching at Angie's top. The tie came loose, Angie's massive breasts fell out, but Harmony's bikini pants were already halfway down her legs.

Harmony spread her thighs, determined to keep her pants from being pulled off her legs, and giving the crowd a fine view of the moist pink crease of her fanny and the jet-black spot of her anus. Her hands were grappling for Angie's bikini bottoms even as her own were forced slowly down her legs. A tug of war developed, with both girls clinging on to the other's bikini pants and hauling with all their strength. Both gave way at the same time, Angie's badly tied bow going just as Harmony gave in and closed her legs. Both were bare from the waist down, but Harmony had her top on, and so she'd won.

Angie knelt up, grinning, mud running slowly down around her shaved head and over her huge breasts. She extended a hand, which Harmony accepted, a wise move. A defeated girl might be expected to take whatever punishment or humiliation was dished out, but there was nothing to say she couldn't get her own back later. The crowd were not impressed, two bouts having ended without the loser being dealt with, and there were even one or two boos mixed in with the applause.

They got what they wanted with the next bout: Melody against Emma. It was a foregone conclusion, even in bikinis, with Mel half a head taller and maybe half as heavy again. In green, her bikini was tied even tighter than her sister's, so that it looked as if her boobs would spill out at any moment, while the back was pulled tight up between her heavy, dark bottom cheeks. She looked like an Amazon from a kitsch 50s thriller. Emma, a pretty blonde with freckles and a snub nose, looked as if she'd just come in from a day on the beach, in her neatly fitting blue bikini.

They bell went, they closed, Mel feinted, snatched out to grab Emma's wrist and spun her around, twisting her arm and pushing a knee up into her back in one smooth motion. Emma merely squeaked in shock and surprise, as she was caught, as her bikini top was stripped off with a single tug and as her bottoms followed with two more. Now stark naked, she was held, her body flaunted to the audience. Mel made a slow turn to show her victim off before Emma was pushed down, forced on to all fours in the mud, so that Mel could mount her. I could see the humiliation in Emma's eyes as she was ridden around the ring, three times, all the while with Mel urging her own with slaps to her bottom and steering her by her hair. The crowd thought it was hilarious and cheered her to the echo, and again as Mel scooped up a handful of mud and plastered it into Emma's pretty face.

Emma did not look happy or, at least, so far as I could see through the mask of mud, and she had to be led away to wash by one of the helpers. She hadn't backed down though, and the crowd gave her a good clap as she left. Vicky and Xiang were next and, as they stood out, it was quite clear we'd moved up a whole notch. Vicky had the height, and she looked sleek and strong, but Xiang was more compact and heavier, with a hard look on her face. Vicky was smiling, evidently enjoying herself, because for all her power she preferred to be dominated. In a sense, she couldn't lose, but that didn't mean she wouldn't try.

They were very wary of each other, circling carefully for nearly a minute before coming together. When they did, both tried to grapple but neither could exert her strength over the other. Xiang lashed out a foot, trying to trip Vicky, but lost her own balance. Both went down, Vicky on top, with a splash that sent flecks of mud spraying over the crowd They had each other's arms, and their legs were twisted together, struggling and sliding in the mess. In moments both were plastered in mud from head to toe, and it seemed that neither could get an advantage, only for Vicky to suddenly squirm away, with Xiang's bikini top in her teeth.

The bell went, and they paused for water and to wipe the mud away from their eyes. Xiang was topless, her hard, wide breasts on show, but it didn't seem to bother her as she spoke to the tall, leather-clad butch dyke in her corner. She came out grinning, and rushed to the attack the instant the bell went, but her attempt at a feinted failed, Vicky simply skipping back at exactly the right moment. They began to circle again, came together, and this time Xiang's feint worked. A dart for Vicky's bottoms, a change of direction and it was done, both girls topless. The only problem was that instead of protecting herself, Vicky had made a calculated sacrifice and, as they came apart, both held a garment in her hands. Xiang hadn't even realised, and was astonished to find her in the nude. She gave a single grunt of annoyance and climbed from the ring, indifferent to her nakedness and not waiting for her punishment. Vicky didn't press the point.

It was about time I got ready, but I wanted to watch Angel wrestle with Sam. They'd come out, in red and

109

blue, both toned and muscular, both tall, and if Angel looked supremely arrogant in her confidence, then Sam wasn't far behind. They squared up, and went in hard, both grappling for the other's bikinis without much thought for protection. Sam's top came free at the same instant she was tripped, and she went down hard in the mud, but bounced back before Angel could take advantage, both now spattered with mud.

Angel had some in one eye, and took a step back to brush it away, only to dart forwards, snatch at one of Sam's bows and tug it loose. Sam gave an angry hiss, snatched forwards, but too late, her fingers missing Angel's top even as her bottoms were pulled free and she was naked. Angel stood back, crowing in delight as she raised Sam's bikini pieces in her hands. Sam stayed where she was, looking somewhat bemused for a moment, with one hand placed half-heartedly over her bare fanny, then recovered and reached out to offer her hand. Angel shook her head and pointed at the mud.

I saw Sam say something, but Angel shook her head again, and this time snapped her fingers as she again pointed at her feet. Sam hesitated, glanced around, then got down, kneeling, looking up at Angel, who stepped close, pushed her hips forwards and quite casually began to urinate over Sam's head. Sam had thought she was going to be made to kiss Angel's fanny, and realised the truth only just in time to avoid a mouthful of pee. As it was she took it, gasping and spluttering as the piddle ran down over her head and back and arms, turning her beautiful if slightly muddy hair to so many pee-sodden rat-tails.

The moment Angel was done she turned away, lifting her trophies once more as she made a brief lap of honour, with Sam still kneeling in the middle of the ring, dripping piddle and not daring to open her eyes. At last Xiang climbed in to give her a cloth, and I left them to sort it out as I went in to change.

Morris had the area well rigged up, with a long shower against the back wall. Vicky was still washing, rinsing shampoo from her long black hair, and she gave me a friendly grin. Angel appeared as I began to undress, walking with a confident swagger as she went to the shower. She pointed a finger at me and made some sign I didn't understand, but I ignored her. June was there too, frowning slightly as she realised just how little of her big, coffee-coloured breasts the red bikini top she'd chosen covered. I smiled.

'I have the same problem. Morris does it on purpose. At least yours does up at the back easily.'

She adjusted one of the little triangles of red material before replying.

'You're going to slaughter me, aren't you?'

'I'm going to try,' I told her.

'What do you do to the girls you beat?'

'That depends what they deserve,' I answered, and threw a meaningful look towards Angel, who unfortunately had her back turned.

'You can if you want,' June said, which presumably was an open invitation to pee on her head.

'I'm saving it,' I told her, 'but you can expect a spanking.'

She giggled, and there was an appraising look in her eyes as I stepped out of my knickers. I straightened up and stretched, letting her see, before going to the box of multi-coloured bikinis in one corner. Sam came in, still dripping pee and mud, and went to the opposite end of the showers from Angel. I wanted to speak to her, and promise revenge if I could, but with Angel still there it seemed best to hold my peace.

I chose a blue bikini to suit my tawny hair. As I'd expected, I could only manage small bows, but it was at least on properly, unlike Angie's, and while I would have drawn quite a few glances on any British beach, it was not actually indecent.

'Cute,' June said, extending her hand. 'Do you like to spank other girls then?'

'Very much.'

'Oh right, it's ... it's just that I saw you getting it from that old guy last time, and –'

'That was for charity.'

'Oh.'

I took her hand and we walked out together, to clapping and wolf-whistles from the audience. Unless something went badly wrong, I'd won. She'd been aggressive at the heats, but that was gone. I climbed up into the ring, stepping down into the mud, which was cool and felt pleasantly squishy between my toes. June had immediately knelt down, to scoop up a big double handful and drop it into her cleavage, sighing as she moulded her filthy hands over her breasts and belly. She squatted lower, and wiggled her bottom in it, then stood, looking pleased with herself and full of mischief as we faced each other.

The bell went and I moved forwards, cautious despite my advantages. She moved in, tried to grab for one of the ties at my hip and I'd got her wrist, quickly twisting her hand up behind her back. She squealed in pain, but her hand was still groping for my ties, even as I caught hers. Her top came open, one hip, and she'd just got my bow loose. I tugged the second one on her pants away, grabbed both halves of her bikini, pulled and she was nude, and giggling in delight at being so rudely and quickly stripped. My own bikini pants were half down, but I didn't bother to do them up, instead making a knee and pulling June down over it, with her lovely cheeky bottom stuck high.

She was giggling, and obviously enjoying the treatment, so I took hold of her big cheeks and hauled them wide, spreading out her bumhole to the audience, to their delight, and hers. Her cheeks were filthy, but her crease and fanny were clean, so I took a good-sized

112

handful of mud and slapped it between them, rubbing it well into her sex before I began to spank her. She took it squirming and wriggling, with her meaty cheeks bouncing to the slaps and spattering mud over both of us.

June was fun to spank, and I was in no rush, making sure she had a nice warm rear glow and that the audience had enjoyed a good stare before I stopped. I got covered in mud, and when I stood up my bikini pants fell down, much to the crowd's amusement. One of my nipples was half out of my top too, and my front was slimy with mud, which was how Angel saw me as she stepped out from the changing rooms, half naked and filthy, presumably after a hard won victory. She turned me a sneer of pure contempt, and I didn't bother to disabuse her about what had happened. If she thought I'd had trouble beating June, all the better.

I went in to wash, leaving Topsy and Naomi to the ring. Like Angie, Topsy didn't have a hope of getting her bikini on properly, and Naomi was no pushover either. It took them three rounds to sort themselves out while I was in the shower, and both came in naked and muddy, but what showed of Naomi's neatly formed bottom was a cheerful pink. She'd been spanked, plainly, but both looked happy, and we chatted as we washed.

Outside, Annabelle and Cassie were in the ring, a contest everyone assumed could have only one victor. To my surprise it was Annabelle who came in grinning, topless and plastered with mud, but plainly the winner. Sure enough, Cassie was naked and didn't look best pleased, as she seemed to have had her face pushed in the mud. I was dressed by then, in knickers and bra under one of the robes Morris provided, because I knew I'd be back in costume soon enough.

When I came out, Hudson was already doing the draw, holding up a ball from Sophie's bowl to announce that the next round would be in baked beans and dressed in ball gowns. That meant smart shoes, stockings, suspenders, knickers but no bras, and would be a great deal harder to get off than the bikinis. I went to join Kay and Patty, taking another bottle of beer from Morris' private cold box on the way. Angel was with Mel, holding a pint of lager in one hand and a litre bottle of mineral water in the other.

'. . . and for our quarter final draw,' Hudson was saying, 'we have, let us see now . . . Amber, against . . . Annabelle!'

I drew a sigh of relief. For the second time I'd got the easiest opponent in the draw, although I couldn't help but feel I was being set up for a fall. Perhaps Hudson Staebler wasn't the straight-talking, honest guy he pretended to be, but was in on some complicated plot with Melody and Angel. I knew I was being paranoid, but the punishments always got tougher as the competition went on, and if I was beaten by Angel in the final I could really expect no mercy.

'I'd better get changed,' I said, and kissed Kay before leaving them.

'. . . next pair,' Hudson was saying. 'We have . . . Melody, against . . . Harmony.'

Her own sister, surely a fix.

'And for our third pair . . . Vicky, against . . . Topsy, which leaves us Angel and Diane for the last heat. If you'd care to get dressed, girls, and you boys down there can make work with the baked beans, we can get it rolling.'

I was already in the changing area, sorting through the ball gowns, all second-hand, but actually quite nice. Some it was a shame to spoil, but both Mel and Harmony would be looking for the same size as me, so I wanted first choice, and I wasn't being vain. There was one in blue velvet that looked about right held up to my front; the bodice was low cut and ruffled, but the waist was tight and heavily pleated, while the back fastened with hooks. It was heavy too, lined, with boning at the waist.

The others were piling in as I went off to change in a corner, all eager to get a good choice. Vicky joined me, and we dressed together, discussing our prospects. Like me, she was sure it had been fixed for Angel, because she'd had Xiang and now had Topsy, both big girls who could be relied on to put up a fight and leave her tired. Angel had a far easier run, but then again, so did I.

It felt odd to be in comfy knickers, stockings and suspenders, a ball gown and court shoes, as if I really was going to a respectable ball rather than wrestling another woman in a pit full of baked beans. I knew Morris, and they'd be deep. The only consolation was that I was first and wouldn't be in a mixture of the beans and Angel's pee.

Annabelle was ready before me, looking very sweet and demure in a white silk gown. Outside, the crowd were getting into party mood, drinking heavily and placing bets on the outcome, either money, or the pleasure of their partners. I had no idea what my odds were, but I was sure they'd be lower than Annabelle's. I climbed up, and into the ring, my shoes sinking deep into the baked beans, which popped unpleasantly as I let my weight settle. They were about six inches deep, well over my ankles, and the hem of my gown was immediately sodden with tomato sauce. I quickly kicked my shoes off under the surface and, as the bell went, moved forwards.

There were plenty of cheers and dirty suggestions as we moved close, mainly aimed at me, demanding that I make Annabelle lick, even sit on her face, but a few supporting her. I blanked it all out, waiting my moment, then darting in, to grapple Annabelle's waist and throw her down, face first in the beans. She went down hard, and a great wave of beans and sauce washed over the sides of the ring and onto the floor, drawing complaints from those foolish enough to stand near.

I barely heard. Already I was on top of Annabelle, straddling her back. She was having trouble keeping her face above the baked beans to breathe, and I simply grabbed the collar of her gown and heaved, tearing it wide all the way down her back. She began to fight back as I struggled to pull her arms out of the sleeves, but I took her head and pushed it well down in the baked beans, holding her under until she had begun to squirm and thump her fists in the mess. I let go and she came up, gasping for breath, but still fighting as I struggled with her sleeve.

She was writhing like an eel underneath me, but she couldn't get me off. I couldn't get her any further either, and had to change tactics, jumping up and back to grab her skirts and haul them high, over her head. She fought back, gripping the inside of her dress with furious strength as I dragged her through the slippery mess of baked beans, with her body leaving a broad wake behind. Her legs were waving wildly and her knickers were full of baked beans, sending the crowd into delighted laughter, but still she clung. Again I changed tactics, dropping her and quickly straddling her body to deal with her knickers and stockings, but I'd only got one off before the bell went to mark the end of the round.

We separated, moving back to our corners. Patty and Kay were waiting for me with water. Annabelle was in a fine state, filthy with baked beans and sauce from the top of her head to the tips of her toes. Her gown was ruined, torn and soiled and half off, one stocking gone, her knickers packed with baked beans and slippery with sauce. She wasn't allowed to do her gown up, while she'd barely touched me, and I knew it was only a matter of time before I had her nude.

The bell went after what seemed just seconds, and we came together again. I got a hold on her, meaning to throw her down and straddle her again, but my foot slipped in the baked beans, which had begun to turn to a thick slurry where we'd been fighting in them. Both of us went down, and she managed to get on top of me. Her hands clawed at my bodice as I grappled her. One hard jerk and my boobs were out, setting the crowd baying in delight, but I already had her dress. Up it came, hauled over her head, and she realised her mistake too late. Her arms were trapped and, as I threw her off me, I twisted the material, trapping her arms and shoulders and head in the sauce-smeared material.

Her whole lower body was naked, her long legs kicking frantically, her little tits bare and quivering, the muscles of her belly squirming. I threw a leg over her, to sit down squarely on her neck, and grabbed her by her knickers. Up they came, tugged high in a shower of baked beans, baring her fanny to the world. She tried to spread to stop me getting them off, but she was too slow. Her knickers were off, and a moment's struggle with a leg had her remaining stocking too.

Only her gown remained and, as I lifted, I grabbed it, only to slip and sit down hard in the baked beans. She was still trapped, her naked, filthy body thrashing crazily in the baked beans as I wrenched on her gown, forcing it up, and off. It came with a jerk and I went backwards, sprawling in the beans, but she was nude, defeated. I spent a moment catching my breath and then stood, with the crowd cheering and clapping.

My boobs were out and I wasn't allowed to cover up, but that was it, my victory, and Annabelle had put up quite a fight. She was now mine – Mel's playmate – and I didn't intend to let the opportunity go to waste. I picked up her ruined gown and the soggy knickers and held them aloft in triumph. She stayed down, her slim, pale body half submerged in baked-bean pulp, her eyes wide as she looked up at me. I could do anything, spank her, piss on her, make her lick me out, anything. I put one foot out and rolled her over.

'Up, on your knees.'

She went into a kneeling position, orange mess dripping from her body, her neat little bum lifted to the audience, her face turned up to look at me. I dropped the gown and took her knickers, holding the waistband wide to scoop up some baked beans, filling the pouch so that it hung fat and heavy, like a peed-in nappy. I brought them to her, holding them open as I pulled the waistband over her head, with her face right in the heavy mess of squashed beans. A twist of the waistband and her head was trapped in her own filthy knickers, her mouth well in the mess, although quite a bit was oozing from the leg holes.

'Eat up,' I ordered.

One sauce-encrusted eye looked up at me from a leg hole, pleading, but I shook my head and she began to eat, feeding on the mass of squashed baked beans in her knickers. The audience thought it was hilarious, clapping and cheering and calling for more. They were going to get it. I went behind Annabelle and knelt down in the beans, to take her around the waist. Every inch of her skin was filthy, but her neat, shaved fanny and trim little bum cheeks were on plain view, nothing hidden.

I hauled her cheeks wide, showing off her bumhole to the audience, her fanny too, with Mel's tattoo just visible on the low bulge of her mound through the sauce and her hole open and moist. She was still eating as I began to amuse myself with her pretty bottom, slapping her cheeks and tickling her anus to make it twitch. Her open fanny hole was just too good to resist, so I scooped up a big handful of baked-bean pulp and slapped it on, pushing as much as I could up the hole. It went quite easily, and I tried a second handful, then a third, packing her hole with mess until it was stretched wide around a fat plug of crushed baked beans, which began to ooze out the moment I let go. I stood up.

'Now, Annabelle, you're to masturbate, as you are, so everybody can see.'

Her response was a muffled sob, but she did it, reaching her hands back to her fanny. It left her face well in the beans, and she was forced to turn her head just to breathe. Her sauce-smeared face protruded from one of the leg holes of her soiled knickers, slack with submissive ecstasy as she began to rub herself. The crowd were clapping in rhythm and stamping their feet, and I glanced around to take in the scene of my triumph. Just about every single person was rapt in attention as they watched Annabelle masturbate, her fingers now working fast in the slippery crease of her fanny, with the baked beans oozing from her hole bit by bit, to fall onto the mat with squashy plops.

I leant down and began to spank her, sending shivers through her flesh. Her thighs went tight, her bumhole began to pulse, more mess squeezed from her fanny and she was coming. I wanted to do it myself as I watched, or make her lick me, but it was enough. I was hot, scratched and filthy, my boobs were bare and smeared with baked-bean sauce, and I decided to leave it at that, contenting myself with waiting until Annabelle had reached the very peak of her orgasm before extending a foot and pushing her over into the mess.

The audience broke into wild cheering as I turned to them, curtseying as best I could. Most of them were on their feet, but there were exceptions, including Protheroe who was counting out notes to a man in a blue suit. Morris' announcement of my victory boomed out over the PA and I gave a second curtsey before climbing somewhat unsteadily from the ring. Melody and Harmony were on next and, even as I dragged myself into the changing area, I could hear the buzz of excitement at the prospect of watching the twin sisters fight.

All the other girls were changed and ready, and only Kay had followed me in. I stepped into the shower, fully clothed, and turned it on. She watched, her face set in a faint, shy smile, as I stripped under the gloriously refreshing cascade of water. She took my discarded clothes to the bin provided, and I stepped naked from the shower to inspect my body. My breasts were scratched where Annabelle had clawed my bodice down, and my muscles had begun to ache here and there, but I was basically all right, also high on victory.

I could see what Kay wanted, and I was too high to refuse. Still wet, I went to sit on a chair, my thighs spread in invitation. She came straight to me and got down on her knees, immediately burying her face in my fanny, as nervous as she was eager. I was going to come in moments, and I didn't hear Angel until it was too late. She laughed, and Kay scrambled hastily up, blushing.

'Two bitches together, huh?' Angel said, laughing. 'How about you both go down on me while I wait to take Diane?'

Kay shook her head, seriously flustered, because however much she didn't want to do it, the desire was there and she knew it. So did Angel, who simply laughed as she walked over to where she'd laid her dress, an ankle-length sheath of a golden material that looked like satin. She went on talking as she began to dress.

'You should lighten up a little, Amber, drop the pose. How about you two as my dogs for the international puppy show?'

'I thought you were showing Rubba Dobie?' I answered, refusing to let her bait me.

'I am,' she told me, 'but there's no reason I can't have three. A dog and two bitches, it would be great. You ought to be something little and fluffy, Kay, a spaniel maybe, and Amber, a big, fat Old English sheepdog, like that guy last time.'

I'd put a robe on, and walked out, not answering, but the image had stuck in my mind, of myself in the great hairy grey-and-white dog suit, my haunches lifted in the ridiculous pose he'd adopted, and next to Kay on Angel's lead. She was trying to needle me, and she was succeeding.

In the ring, Melody and Harmony were still going strong. Both had managed to pull the other's front down, exposing two pairs of identically big and meaty black breasts, both well smeared with sauce. Otherwise, Harmony had clearly been getting the worst of it, with her face and hair plastered with muck and her gown badly torn at the hem. As Kay and I settled down to watch they came together again, grappling briefly before Harmony slipped and went down with a splash. We just about avoided the shower of baked beans, and I moved my chair a little further away.

Mel was on top, pinning Harmony down, bum to face, and rummaging under her sister's skirt. Harmony fought back, and managed to unseat Mel, but a moment too late as her knickers were hauled free of her legs and she'd lost her first garment. The bell went and they separated, both panting and running with sweat, as they moved to their corners. Kay snuggled up to me, bringing my desire for her back, but I was not about to put her to my fanny in front of the huge crowd.

The moment the bell went Mel stood up, with Harmony a little slower, and reluctant to close. Mel caught her anyway, clutching at the ripped dress in an effort to tear it off, but Harmony tripped her and they went down in the beans. They clung together, fighting to get on top in a writhing mass of strong brown limbs, bare boobs and sauce-smeared cloth. It was impossible to see what was happening, but when they did break apart Harmony was clutching the side of her gown, which was split wide from the hem to her waist. She already looked beaten, and I knew it was only a matter of time.

She made the end of the round, just, but the fight had gone out of her. In the next, she was quickly pinned down, with her sister straddling her chest as her stockings were pulled off, then the remains of her dress. She was naked, and that was that, but Mel stayed seated, holding the remains of Harmony's gown in triumph before quite casually pulling up her own gown, easing her knickers down at the back and sitting her naked bottom in her sister's face. Kay and I had a fine view: the heavy, naked brown orbs of Melody's bottom well spread to show the jet-black wrinkle of her anus.

The crowd went wild as they realised that Harmony was to be made to kiss her own sister's bottom hole, cheering and stamping with perverted glee, then suddenly quiet as Mel gave the order. Harmony puckered up immediately, full red lips pushed out, to plant a single, gentle peck, right on her sister's anus. For a moment I saw the pink of her tongue flick out, to caress the tight knot of Melody's anal ring, and it was done, a kiss of submission to a bumhole, and between twin sisters. The crowd stayed quiet for a long moment before erupting in noise once more, and my own stomach was tight with reaction.

Mel took a bow and they climbed out of the ring together, arms around each other as they disappeared into the changing area. I was shaking slightly as I accepted another beer and Morris stepped forward to announce Vicky's fight against Topsy. I could see a lot of betting going on among the crowd, and Protheroe and Denis Humber were discussing something urgently together, two other men also, hunched close so that their neighbours couldn't hear them. Something was definitely going on, and I wondered if Angel, or Mel, was planning to invite Protheroe up into the ring when I'd been beaten, to make me suck his cock . . . to have him fuck me . . . to let him put it up my bum . . .

It was right on the edge of the rules, and I could always refuse and face their derision, yet once I'd been beaten, maybe spanked, maybe pissed on, I might accept. That was what it would be. They'd wait until I'd been defeated and brought low in some girlish humiliation I could cope with, then invite the men in to use me properly. In a semi-final it would be accepted, certainly by Morris. In fact, Morris was likely to be the first one up me.

My stomach was fluttering badly as I took Kay by the hand and started towards the back entrance. I needed to come down from the erotic high building in my head. I know myself only too well. Too excited and put into submission and I'll take just about anything. It wasn't going to happen, not this time, not with the huge crowd watching.

The big service bay was deserted and lit gloomy orange by the security lights, with pools of shadow here and there, where Morris' Rolls-Royce was parked, behind stacked pallets and a pair of containers. I led Kay in among the pallets and sat down, the wooden slats hard against my bottom through the robe. She went down as my thighs came apart and she was licking me, her tongue flicking over my fanny lips and the curve of my bottom to bring me quickly up towards ecstasy.

I closed my eyes and thought of her bottom, so cheeky on her tiny figure, and the lovely way she was always shy about her exposure and punishment. Just that morning I'd put her across the breakfast table for an impromptu spanking, with her jeans and knickers well down and her bottom lifted, her cheeks open to show the tiny, dark-brown rosebud of her anus and her sweetly pouted fanny lips. I'd spanked her well and made her kiss my bumhole, just Harmony had been made to kiss her own sister's . . .

My mouth came wide as I started to come, with my mind full of the glorious image of one woman putting her mouth to another's anus, an act so wonderfully improper, so exquisitely rude. Kay loved to kiss mine, and lick it, with my bottom in her pretty face, just as Mel had sat on Harmony, bum to face, anus to mouth, in utter submission, just as Angel would undoubtedly make me kiss hers, with my lips pressed to her tight black ring in front of thousands of gawping spectators . . .

I let out my breath in a long, heartfelt sigh. Kay had her hand down her knickers and was frigging, her tongue on my fanny, then lower, burrowing between my cheeks as I slid forwards to let her get at my bumhole. I felt her tongue push in, wet and firm, and she was whimpering with pleasure as she licked. My own orgasm had barely faded, and I put my fingers to my clitty, bringing myself up to a second peak as Kay came, this time over her, pure and simple.

She was still coming, and I let her lick for a while, her tongue well in up my bottom hole. I felt a lot better afterwards, and we sat and talked for a while, enjoying the cool night air and letting the tensions of the wrestling fade away. When I felt sure I could cope we walked back in, to find that Vicky had managed to defeat Topsy over five rounds. Both were in the showers, and Diane and Angel were already in the ring. There was really no contest. Angel was already astride Diane's back, one hand twisted hard in her victim's hair to hold her helpless while she was stripped.

Diane struggled, squirming in what by now was a mere filthy mess of squashed beans and sauce, but every time she tried to unseat Angel she got her face pushed into the beans and was held down until she was forced to put everything she had into breathing. I watched in mingled pity and sadistic delight as her ball gown was pulled up, her knickers removed and her bottom spanked, all in a leisurely fashion. Her stockings followed, Angel briefly adjusted her seat to get the zip, and Diane was nude, stripped in the first round and left gasping for breath in the muck.

Angel stood up, her face set in amused contempt. As Diane twisted around, Angel spat, catching Diane right in the eye. I thought she'd pee, as she had on Sam, but either she was saving it or she didn't think it was worthwhile for such a poor opponent. Instead she simply took hold of Diane's hair again, pulled her head up and forced her to take her own filthy panties in her mouth, leaving her lying exhausted in the mess with a little tab of orange and white cotton hanging out from between her lips.

The crowd were less exalted than they had been for Annabelle and me, or for Mel and Harmony, but they were betting furiously, with several people passing among them with little note books to take the money. The ring needed cleaning for the next round, so there was bound to be a pause, and I nipped around to the rear of the stands to see what odds were being offered on me. Not that I was going to risk any money, but it was nice to know. The man in the blue suit who'd been talking to Protheroe was there, and I went to him.

Five minutes later I was back, and feeling thoroughly chagrined. Angel was favourite, at 2/1, and people were still putting money on her. Vicky and Melody were both 5/1, while I was being offered at 20/1 with very few takers. Despite my reservations, I sent Kay to put twenty pounds on Vicky and ten on Mel, but it was hard not to sulk, and not to feel angry. New determination welled up in me, to at the very least hold out for several rounds, maybe even force a decision, but my confidence had started to wane.

The male slaves were dragging the canvas full of baked-bean sludge away, and Morris and Hudson were on their feet, with Sophie holding out her bowl. The music died once more and Morris began to talk, going over the previous round before Hudson drew a ball for what we would be wrestling in. It came out as vegetables in cooking oil, and I sunk my head into my hands. I knew exactly what sort of vegetables there would be: courgettes, carrots, parsnips, cucumbers, anything of a

125

convenient shape to push up a girl's fanny. My bumhole wouldn't be safe either, not with the ring swimming in cooking oil.

Hudson drew again, for costume. I was hoping for something simple, knickers and bras maybe, which would give me my best chance against a stronger opponent. What I got was full dom gear, which was just as bad as it could possibly have been. Every buckle, every piece of lacing, every catch had to be undone, which was hard enough at the best of times, never mind when smothered in cooking oil. Worse still, Angel and Mel had plenty of gear with them. I didn't, and nor did Vicky.

My head went back in my hands and, as I did so, I caught a glimpse of Protheroe, chuckling as he nudged Denis Humber. I'd had it. Unless I drew Vicky I was going to be stripped in minutes, have an assortment of phallic vegetables stuffed into me, then Protheroe's cock, probably up my bum, and finally pissed on. I glanced towards the doors, wondering if I should just quit, but I couldn't bring myself to do it.

'And our pairs for the semi-finals,' Morris was saying. 'Mr Staebler?'

Hudson drew a ball, nodded and spoke.

'Angel . . . and she is against . . . Amber.'

My heart sank. I was doomed. What had she said she'd do if I backed out: take me in the loos, spank me and pee all over my hot bottom. It was better than what would happen to me if I didn't, but it was also disgrace. I stood up with a sigh as Morris pointed out that the other match would therefore be between Vicky and Melody. I needed to borrow some armour, and I knew the stuff in the changing area wouldn't be the best, as surely as I knew that whatever they said, the draw had been fixed.

I took Kay to Patty, who was talking with her grandmother. She was in black, not leather, but a boned corset, that covered her breasts and hips, sealing her

126

body from chest to thighs in smooth satin. It was fully laced, and had pegs at the front, almost impossible to get off, especially when slippery. She greeted me with a big smile.

'You go get her, girl.'

'I aim to try,' I assured her, 'but I haven't any decent gear. I know I already owe you a big favour for rescuing me, but could I borrow your corset, please?'

'My corset? Amber, it cost a hundred and fifty quid, and that was second-hand. It'll get wrecked.'

'I'll make you another one, any style you like, free.'

'Now that's tempting –'

'Please?'

'OK, but you really do owe me, Amber, big time.'

'Thanks, Patty, you're a darling.'

They were already pouring out the oil on to a new canvas, and I hurried her into the changing room, leaving Kay with Jean de Vrain. Morris had provided some leathers, old stuff of Mel's, but nearly all of it did up with poppers and would tug away far too easily. Sophie was there, helping Angel into what looked like medieval battle armour. She was out of her hobble and wrist cuffs, which matched, both of heavy duty leather with locks. I pinched both, feeling a little guilty as I forced the slim chains with a buckle, then began to dress with Patty's help.

I knew her corset would be too small for me, and it was, far too small. My boobs barely fitted into the cups and, even loose, I had great bulges of flesh sticking out over the top, while the back wouldn't close, leaving a four-inch gap that showed the middle of my back and my bum crease. It was also too short, leaving the tuck of my cheeks bare, while I couldn't find any black knickers at all. I added the cuffs, buckling them tight to my wrists and ankles, and a black studded collar.

Angel was already laughing and, looking in the mirror, I could see why. On Patty it had looked cool

127

and dominant, giving her slender figure a languid yet commanding poise. On me, with my boobs spilling out at the front and my bum showing at the back, it looked completely and utterly submissive, and silly. The cuffs and collar just made it worse, giving the impression that I was just waiting for the chains and a stern owner before being put in bondage, or turned across somebody's knee for a thorough spanking.

I would have gone for something else, so that I could at least start with a bit of dignity, but it was too late. Morris was already calling for us. Patty was still doing up my corset laces as Angel strode over to me, her face full of amusement and contempt. I was barefoot and, in her huge stack boots, she topped me by a good two inches. She was looking down at me as she spoke.

'Nice gear, Amber, suits you, especially the way it shows off your big fat arse, and there is nothing I like to spank more than a big . . . fat . . . white . . . arse.'

'You have to win first,' I managed.

'Yeah,' she drawled, 'and this is what happens. You can last the first, but you go down in the second and let me get on your back, OK?'

'No, if you want to win, you win fairly.'

'I thought you might say that. Here's what happens. You do it my way and I spank you and piss on your hot arse, like I said. You put up a fight, and when I've got you I'm going to sit on your face, and drop a log, right in your mouth.'

She lifted a finger, and tapped me gently on the tip of my nose with the last word. As she turned on her heel, I was left gaping, scarcely able to believe what she'd threatened to do to me. Yet I was sure she meant it, and had a nasty suspicion that if it did happen, my stop word would count for nothing. Suddenly, I was swallowing down sick fear in my stomach, but Morris was calling for us.

Even the sway of Angel's hips as she left seemed full of disdain and menace, and there was nothing I could do but follow meekly behind. She'd looked alarming before, but with what she'd threatened she now looked terrifying. Each boot had six huge buckles rising from her ankles to her knees. Her tiny hard bottom was encased in a pair of minuscule leather shorts, but there was nothing submissive about the way it displayed her. Her corset matched her boots, heavy black leather fastened with a half-dozen solid buckles, and her upper chest was encased in layered and studded black leather, sculpted over her pert breasts with fake nipples pointing almost skywards and rising over her shoulders to meet across her back. Long leather gloves completed her armour.

As I made for the ring, I caught the voice of the man in the blue suit as he spoke to Annabelle, and the words 'fifty to one'. I knew exactly what the figures meant, the new odds on my victory, and probably not even absolute victory, but just beating Angel. She climbed up into the ring, raising her clasped hands as if she were a professional and turning her body for the admiration of the audience. They clapped and cheered, then broke in a great uneven gust of laughter as I followed her.

The ring was awash with green-gold vegetable oil, several inches deep in the middle, along with all the varieties of vegetable I had suspected would be used, and several I hadn't. There were even radishes, and carrots with the foliage still on, for both of which I could think of deeply humiliating uses, and a single marrow with a girth which would have daunted a twenty-stone mother of six. Even having that forced up me was nothing compared with what Angel had threatened.

I glanced around the audience: a ring of leering, expectant faces, alight with joy at what was about to happen to me. Protheroe gave me a little wave and I managed to find enough spirit to stick my tongue out at him. Morris was still talking, running over Angel's past victories, and when he suddenly stopped and the bell went it caught me by surprise. Angel had her back to me, and I was just staring at her bottom, picturing her above me, pinning me down, squatting over my face, pushing her shorts down, spreading her tight brown bottom cheeks, the little black hole between starting to push out . . .

There was simply no way I could let her do it to me. I stepped forward gingerly, my bare feet planted well apart in the oil. Angel stayed put, beckoning for me to come on. I hesitated, wondering if I should play her game, lose on purpose and let her spank me and pee all over my bottom. Something inside me rebelled at the idea, for all that I knew it was the only sensible choice, and yet I stopped, waiting for her. The expression on her face changed, from smug superiority to surprise, and suddenly she was striding forwards, one hand stretching out for my hair, and she slipped, head over heels, and landed in the mess of oil and vegetables, right at my feet.

I reacted by instinct, hurling myself on top of her and grabbing for her wrists. She snarled in anger, twisting her body beneath me, one of her corset buckles right on my bare fanny. I was forced to move back, straddling her hips even as she gave another violent twist, and she was free. Free, only I'd caught her shorts, and I wrenched at them with every last ounce of my strength as she snatched out at my corset. My top catch broke, my boobs flopped out, and I heard the delighted roar of the crowd even as the catch of her shorts parted in my hands.

She had me by the corset, and I couldn't get her shorts down, but her zip was gone, broken and useless. I felt sharp pain, her fingernails digging into the flesh of my cleavage as she fought to get at the pegs of my corset, but it was too tight, and too slippery. My fingers found hers and I wrenched them free, hurling myself back with the same movement. We broke apart, both sprawling in the oil, our hands and feet slipping as we struggled to rise. I caught the ropes, hauling myself up and making a fine display of my bottom as I did so. Angel had come up to her knees, glaring at me, and made to rise, but the bell went, although I'd have sworn just seconds had passed since we began. Angel pointed at me as she tried to get up, slipped and had to use the ropes.

'You better not fuck with me, bitch!' she spat as she reached her corner.

I shook my head and collapsed down into my seat, reaching for the water bottle held out by Kay. She'd scratched me quite badly, with a bead of blood in my cleavage, and I was in a fine state: filthy with oil and running sweat, my boobs already out and my corset up at the back so that my bottom showed. As I fought I'd be showing everything, and Angel was still fully covered, for all that her shorts were ruined. She wanted me down in the next round, and I had to make my decision.

'You can do it, Amber,' Kay urged from beside me. 'You're stronger than her, and she can't stand up in those boots anyway. I've put twenty on as well, at fifty to one. Everyone reckons it's a fix.'

'It is,' I breathed.

'You're not going to lose are you? Amber! Not to her!'

The bell went before I could answer. I stood carefully, but not as carefully as Angel, whose boots were giving her serious trouble. Neither of us were going to be able to stand up, and all I needed to do was go down first so she could get on top of me and give in, pretending I couldn't get her off me. I couldn't do it, not with Kay's voice in my head, full of disbelief that I would give in. Whatever happened, I was going to fight.

I came forwards slowly, hoping she'd slip. She did the same, both of us crouched low, our feet sliding under the oil. Her eyes were locked on mine, watching to see if I'd move, both of us circling, until her back was to the majority of the audience, when she winked. I knew exactly what it meant, and I responded with downcast eyes and a weak nod, hurled myself forwards, on my knees, to slam into her, catching her midriff with my shoulder and sending her sprawling against the ropes, off guard and off balance as I grappled her, my fingers locking in the leather of her shorts, hauling, and they were down. Her fingers clawed out to catch them, missed as I gave a frantic jerk, and they were tangled in her boots, the leather snagged on a buckle.

She was bare, her bottom sat nude in the oil, and she was screaming abuse as I fought to get her shorts off, holding her legs as she clawed at my arm and back, her nails raking my skin. I felt the shorts rip, the leather parting on the buckle spike, as her fingers tightened in my hair and I was being pulled back, squealing in pain as she dragged me down and quickly straddled me, struggling to force me over and get my face in the oil. I'd seen what she did to Diane, but I was too heavy. She couldn't roll me, but only climb over my waist, riding me as I bucked and thrashed beneath her and she clawed at the front of my corset and wrenched at my hair.

I grabbed her waist, pulling her on to me, indifferent to the hard leather and harder steel against my naked breasts and face. She was bum up, bare and spread to the audience, fanny showing and bumhole too, and I grappled her to me with all my strength, one armed, the other out in the oil. I found what I wanted, a fat slippery carrot, which went straight between her legs. She gasped as she felt it prod at her, and tried to break my grip, only she couldn't and, with a truly exquisite feeling of triumph, I jammed the tip of the carrot up into her fanny hole and slid it home.

Her scream of outrage drowned the music out, and also the roar of delight and surprise that went up from the crowd. She let go of my hair, snatching back to pull the carrot out in blind fury, and I rolled away, leaving her sprawling in oil, her shorts now gone, naked from belly to boot tops and red faced with fury, spitting her words out as she rounded on me, trying to rise.

'You fucking bitch! I'll fucking take you! I'm going to make you fucking eat it, you bitch, eat –'

She broke off in a squeal of surprise as her boots shot out from under her. The crowd roared with laughter, and she turned on them, screaming abuse. For one moment, she wasn't looking, and I snatched forwards, catching her ankle and twisting hard even as I pulled. She came, slithering face down in the oil, with her other leg kicking wildly. I hauled her in, to mount her leg, straddled on her thighs with the other held up, her fanny spread to me. She was clawing at me as I hugged her leg to my body, struggling with her boot buckles, but I barely felt it. One came, a second, and I was jerking at her boot, knowing only the lower ones would matter.

It came, suddenly, and I lost my balance, going down on my back in the oil. Angel was on top of me immediately, tearing at my corset again, one handed. Too late I realised why, and she was laughing as something fat and round and hard was forced in up my fanny. Just like her, I screamed, but unlike her I didn't bother to pull it out. She was fucking me with it as I grappled with her shoulder pads, and the urge to just spread my thighs and let it happen was oh so strong, but my anger and determination were stronger. The buckle at her back gave, the pads were coming up, and she was forced to let go to stop me pulling it right up over her head.

She was between my legs, forcing them up, to spread my penetrated fanny to the audience, but I had her, and I didn't care. Nor did she, even with her bare bottom stuck in the air, everything forgotten except beating me. Both of us had a good grip on the shoulder pads, muscle against muscle, but Kay was right, I was stronger, and up they came, over her head, and she let go, grabbing at my wrist cuffs to pull the tab free before I could react. I had the pads though, the buckle loose, then open, and even as I hurled her off me the bell was being rung.

I was gasping as I collapsed into my corner, pausing only to extract the fat courgette Angel had been fucking me with. My skin was covered with her claw marks, bleeding in places, but I couldn't feel them, or anything else but the hot power of my muscles. Angel was glaring, but there was no longer contempt in her eyes, only determination and anger. I'd done two rounds and not surrendered, so it was too late to back down anyway and, after emptying most of Kay's water bottle down my throat, I pulled myself up, ready to take whatever Angel could give, or to dish it out.

With one boot gone she could barely stand, and we went straight to our knees, and straight together, Angel snatching for my hair. I let her, grabbing for her body to slam her down into the oil, and coming with her, on top of her, sat astride her hips. She let go of my hair, pulling furiously at my corset catches, even as I struggled to get her buckles. One buckle came, a second, but she had my top peg out, and another, grunting with effort as she hauled the sides of my corset together. I heard more pegs pop, but I had the third buckle loose, and open. Her nails were raking my tummy as I jerked the fourth buckle free, and suddenly my corset was wide, my body nude but for my collar and cuffs, and her corset still fastened with two big buckles.

I still had her pinned, her body squirming in the oil as she struggled to break free, but my weight was on her. She snatched at my fingers, fighting my grip as I forced the fifth buckle wide, but it came and her corset was open to the last one, her breasts naked. I grabbed it, hauled it high, to trap her arms, leaving her near helpless. I swung around, straddling her, my full weight on her chest, and I had her. She thrashed crazily, kicking and screaming, but her arms were trapped and

134

she could do nothing. One boot buckle came, a second, and I'd hauled it off, just as she finally managed to get her corset up over her head and we'd broken apart.

We were both near nude, our bodies scratched and filthy, slippery with oil and sweat and bits of crushed marrow and carrot leaves. I had my four cuffs and collar, Angel just her cuffs, and for the first time I saw uncertainty in her eyes. She knew I had her, and she glanced to her corner, backing away. I came forwards, and she turned, slipping on her hands and knees as she struggled to get away. She wanted the bell. I didn't. I caught her leg, hauling her in, screaming, then pleading, as I climbed on her back, my hands to her collar. As I forced the little catch open she was close to hysterics, calling me a bitch and begging me to let her up, but I was thinking of what she'd said she was going to do to me. Off it came, and she was in the nude, and suddenly limp beneath my body.

I raised my hands in triumph, but there was no roar of applause, only a few ragged cheers and the thump of the music. They were staring, every one of them, maybe in delight to see Angel brought low, maybe horrified to see their queen naked and begging for mercy. I didn't care, but I wasn't letting her off, not after what she'd threatened. I lifted a little, on to my knees, my thighs spread across her waist. Most of them could see my fanny as I let my bladder go, hot pee spurting out to splash on Angel's smooth brown skin, wetting her belly and breasts and, as I rose higher, her face . . .

. . . which screwed up, eyes and mouth tight shut in utter misery as my piddle splashed down on her, but she'd done it to Sam, and threatened me with worse. It had to be done, and done well. I tensed my pussy, stopping the flow, and spoke to her, just as the music died.

'Open it, Mistress Angel, or you get what you were going to give me.'

She shook her head, but her mouth came open, her lower lip trembling. I waited just a moment and let go and, as the stream of my pee erupted full into her open mouth, I was laughing, in pure sadistic joy. She was trying to swallow, gulping down my piddle even as it bubbled from the sides of her mouth, and she was mine, well and truly mine. I moved up, straddling her face as my stream died. Her mouth was on my fanny and she was licking, without having to be told. I moved forwards and her tongue was up my bumhole, probing and licking, as her hands came up to hold my bottom.

I shut my eyes and took my breasts in my hands, riding her face as she licked my oily bottom hole. The crowd didn't matter, or anything else, just that I had Angel under my bottom, licking my anus. I had to come, queened on her, and the moment I was sure she would well and truly have got the taste of my bottom in her mouth I slipped back a little, ordering her to lick my clitty. She obeyed without so much as a murmur, lapping at my fanny and, in just moments, I was coming, long and tight in her face.

Any other girl and I'd have left it. Not Angel. I stayed mounted up, moving her beneath me to turn her bottom to the bulk of the audience. She was limp, defeated, sliding easily around in the oil without resistance. As I sat back down on her back, maybe two thousand people had a full view of her bottom, including many men to whom she was a worshipful, untouchable mistress.

I couldn't keep from grinning as I pulled her thighs wide to show off the rear of her fanny. Her neat brown lips were swollen, her hole wet, for all of them to see how excited she was over being beaten, peed on, made to lick my bottom hole. There was a courgette nearby, fatter even than the one she'd put in me. I held it up, showing them the rounded end, with oil running down over the shiny green skin. A few gasps went up as they realised where it was going, but Angel merely whim-

136

pered as she felt it touch her fanny, and moaned as her hole filled with courgette.

With a good half the courgette up her well-stretched fanny and the rest sticking out, I hauled her bum cheeks apart to show off her little black anus. She gave a little shudder as she realised her bumhole was not to be spared, but stayed down, and silent. I took a carrot, one of the ones with the foliage still on, a good inch thick at the top, but tapering to a long yellowish root. Again I held it up, to show just what was going up Angel's bottom, then put the tip to her slippery little ring. Her sob as her bumhole was penetrated was wonderful to hear, and I watched in glee as the tiny black ring came slowly open, spreading on the carrot stem, then pushing in around the thicker part. She began to gasp and squirm as she was buggered, and I wondered if she was anally virgin, or rather, had been.

I put the whole carrot up, forcing the full bulk into her rectum to let her anus close around the foliage, which was left sprouting from her bumhole in truly ridiculous fashion. She'd begun to sob, little broken gasps of humiliation and reaction to her fucking. I still wasn't done, and began to spank her, hard at first, a hand to each cheek, then more gently, playing pat-a-cake on her naked bottom and singing out the words to really humiliate her.

For her final disgrace she had to come, stripped and penetrated in front of all her worshipful slaves, to show beyond question that she too could be brought to the ecstasy of submission. Still spanking, one handed, I began to fuck her with the courgette, easing it in and out, then all the way, withdrawing it to penetrate her sopping fanny hole again and again. In no time she began to moan and whimper, fighting her own feelings, and losing. She was going to come, no question, with her little bottom spanked and a courgette up her fanny ... her cunt: a rude word for a rude girl.

Her muscles had started to tense, contracting in her helpless ecstasy. I pushed the courgette as deep in as it would go and paused in the spanking to kneel up. She thought it was over, and began to rise, but I'd already reached for her wrist, to feed her arm in under her belly to her sex. She gave a moan of despair as she realised what I wanted her to do – like Annabelle, to masturbate in front of all of them. I caught her voice, hoarse and urgent as she tried to pull away.

'No . . . if I have to come , you do it.'

'Oh, no, you don't,' I answered. 'You do it. Show them, go on –'

'No, Amber, I –'

'Do it!'

'But Amber –'

'Do it, you little bitch, or –'

She gave a single, broken gasp and she was doing it, her fingers flicking in the moist folds of her sex, and I was laughing as once more I began to spank her. Her bum was already hot, her tight, hard cheeks flushed purple and her skin goosepimpled. She'd said she'd spank me and pee on my hot bottom, and that was just what she was going to get herself. I knelt up, still spanking, hard now, to make her cheeks quiver and shake as she frigged herself. Her bumhole had begun to squeeze on the carrot tops, her thighs were tightening and she was there, in orgasm, as I spoke to her, telling her I was going to pee on her bottom even as I squeezed out what was left in my bladder. Piddle sprayed out over her spanked cheeks, and between, wetting her buggered anus and her fucked fanny, to dribble down over her fingers, so that as she gasped and shook in orgasm she was masturbating in my urine. As she realised she was being peed on she screamed, a long cry of ecstasy, but also of utter despair, disgust and, above all, defeat.

I'd done it, beaten her, and made her bring herself off in front of the crowd, naked and oily, bumhole and fanny penetrated, spanked, her bottom piddled on, and after licking me to ecstasy. As I climbed to my feet in triumph she stayed down, her hand still on her fanny, toying with the courgette in her hole, completely broken to submission. The crowd didn't seem too happy, with their queen defeated, but that was just funny. Quite a few were cheering and clapping, and Kay was jumping up and down on her toes in excitement as she waited for me to climb from the ring.

Various heated conversations seemed to be going on, but I really couldn't be bothered with anything but getting into the shower. The adrenaline which had carried me through the fight was fading, leaving me sick at the stomach, and so weak kneed that Kay had to help me into the showers. With the cool water running down over my body, I began to come round again, but I could feel my exhaustion welling up.

I'd won, but was a major problem. My victory left me in the finals, against Vicky or Mel, both fit and strong. My whole body was covered in scratches and bruises, and every single muscle ached. They still had to fight, which at least left me time to recover and, as soon as I was dry, I lay down on a pile of schoolgirl uniforms to rest. Angel came in, supported by Harmony, and I gave her a friendly grin, happy to be friends now I'd – hopefully – improved her attitude. She wouldn't even meet my eyes, but I was in no mood for heavy discussions or arguments, and didn't make an issue of it.

Kay had gone to try to find me something to eat, but when she came back she was empty handed and looked seriously worried. I could hear raised voices outside, and the music had stopped.

'What's the matter?' I asked.

'I think there's going to be a riot,' she answered. 'We'd better go.'

'A riot, why?'

Harmony swore under her breath and made a hasty

exit, leaving Angel glaring sulkily at me from the corner of the shower. Kay was searching out my clothes as she went on, and I stood up, worried by her sheer urgency.

'Morris had some sort of betting scam going,' she explained hurriedly, 'to get as much money as possible on Angel. Annabelle told me.'

'But how did he know I'd win?' I demanded. 'That wasn't fixed. Was it, Angel?'

Angel shook her head, looking at her feet. Annabelle appeared, now dressed and looking flustered.

'We're going,' she announced. 'If anyone calls the police, you don't know who the organisers are, OK?'

'What's been happening?' I demanded.

'You really don't want to know,' she answered, shaking her head as she began to gather up Mel's clothes. 'Come out the back if you like, Morris can open the gates to the next units.'

I nodded, scrambling into my knickers. The last thing I wanted was to be answering questions to nosy police officers. Kay was near panic, grabbing our stuff as she urged me to hurry up, and Angel was out of the shower, struggling to pull a tight skirt up her still wet legs. I threw my top on, not bothering with my bra, or my socks, just jeans and shoes, still unlaced as we ran for the back exit. There was chaos in the warehouse, with people shouting and the bouncers trying to drag troublemakers to the door. A group of men were on the stage, looking angry and determined, but there was no sign of Morris, or Mel. Just as we reached the door, the lights went down, and there was a chorus of screams and yells as we fled for where the Rolls-Royce was parked in a puddle of light. One door was open, with Mel and Harmony hauling on a pair of tall, wide gates in the fence.

We ran for the car, Annabelle calling out and waving desperately. They saw, and waited, just long enough for us to pile in, any old how. Morris was at the wheel,

Hudson Staebler beside him, with Sophie on his lap. Somebody was yelling at us from behind and, as I climbed in, I saw Angel, barefoot and topless, dripping wet, with a school blouse clutched in one hand and her bag in the other. She scrambled in behind us and I pulled Kay on to my lap as we piled up, with Harmony on her sister's lap and Angel on Annabelle's. The gates were shut behind us, we were moving, and as we came out on to a brightly lit road Morris began to laugh.

Four

What had happened was not particularly flattering for me, but it was a good deal worse for Angel. Betting on the wrestling matches had been becoming serious, and Morris had known that there would be a lot of money floating around on the night of the main competition. Being Morris, he'd been unable to resist getting his grubby little hands on as much of it as possible, and so had set up the betting scam, over months.

First he'd boosted Angel up as the new sensation, giving her easy opponents to inflate her reputation and her ego. She'd gone for it, and so had the crowd, while every submissive man and most of the submissive women who attended had wanted to play with her. By the evening of the main event, she'd come to be regarded as pretty well invincible, with Mel the only person who had a chance against her. Meanwhile, Morris had arranged things so that Vicky was only ever seen in a submissive role, pulling a pony-cart in leather harness and not a lot else, used as a model in bondage demonstrations and frequently spanked, including by Angel.

Never one to do things by halves, he'd had Annabelle persuade Sam, Xiang and their lesbian friends to join in the competition, none of whom were regulars at the club or had fought before. After the puppy show he'd decided to try to get me along as well, and succeeded. Only a handful of the people there had ever seen me fight, but just about all of them had seen me get my ignominious spanking from Protheroe, bare bottomed and grovelling on the floor to Angel's whip, and so had fallen for the old mistake that submissive equates with weak. As a final touch, Morris had circulated a rumour during the match, a rumour that Angel was to be given an easy passage to the final but would lose to Mel. I'd merely been the third of her sacrificial victims, in a fight fixed for me to lose and make Angel look better than she was. Or so they'd thought.

It was a clever double bluff, and it had worked, too well. A lot of people had put large sums on Angel to beat me, thinking they had inside knowledge. They'd come badly unstuck, and a few hadn't been prepared to accept their losses, a problem which had rapidly been escalating as we'd left. I had no sympathy because they'd have been more than happy to pocket their winnings if it had gone the other way, and were really just greedy. Morris just thought it was funny. He didn't even care about the money, as such, but only that it was his rather than somebody else's. I at least had my half of the money Kay had won on my victory.

We were invited back to the Rathwells' house in Hampstead, but the chances of being stopped with nine people in one car, even a Rolls-Royce, had to be high, so I had Morris drop us at the side of the estate. Four had to come with me, and I'd expected Sophie, and maybe Hudson, whom she seemed well attached to. I was more than a little surprised when Angel got out and insisted on coming with us, but I was still hoping to make a friend of her and said she should come.

The party was breaking up, and there was a single police car parked by the door, but nobody took any notice of us as we made our way casually to my car. I couldn't face driving, and was too drunk anyway, so let Kay take over. Nobody had said much as we made our way to the car, but Angel spoke the moment we were moving.

'What a fucking bitch.'

Thinking she was talking about me, I turned around sharply.

'Oh, come on, Angel, after what you said you were going to do to me.'

'Not you,' she answered, 'fucking Melody. Anyway, I was only needling you, I told you what I'd do before.'

'Why Mel, why not Morris?' Sophie asked. 'He set it all up.'

'Because she's supposed to be my fucking friend, that's why,' Angel answered. 'Bitch.'

She sounded as if she was about to cry, and I suddenly felt guilty. In nothing but a school blouse and short skirt, with her hair wet and no make-up, she didn't seem anything like as fierce as before, even allowing for what I'd done to her. She also seemed a lot younger.

'How old are you?' I asked. 'If you don't mind me –'

'Nineteen,' she answered and I felt a great deal guiltier.

'Sorry if I took you too far,' I told her. 'I . . . I just got a bit carried away.'

'Don't be,' she answered. 'You only did what you were supposed to. I knew I might lose anyway, deep down. Not to you maybe, but to Mel.'

'More likely to Vicky,' I told her.

'Vicky? She's big, but –'

'Submissive, yes,' I interrupted, 'but she usually wins. I think this was the thirteenth contest, and she's won something like eight or nine.'

'You're joking.'

'Try her sometime,' I advised, and Angel went quiet.

'Did you want to want to lose to Mel?' I asked gently after a while.

She didn't answer, and I didn't press the point. Kay was getting confused and wanted me to read the map, and I'd managed to get her on to the A13 before Angel suddenly spoke again.

'Yes, I did, in a way . . . I suppose so . . . I'd thought about it, and yes, it was a turn on when you . . . had me, and . . . and made me do it, you know, in front of everyone, but –'

'I know how you feel, Angel,' Kay put in. 'It's not easy, especially the first time.'

'It's a lot for any woman to take, however much you enjoy it when it happens,' I added.

'I never had any trouble,' Sophie chipped in happily, 'well, not much. So how are you two going to revenge yourselves on Mel?'

We never did get to the Rathwells'. Kay turned up the East End motorway, but we just drove on, up to the M25 and around to my house. I'd had my fill, and even Sophie was too tired to want to play, so we gave her and Angel the spare bed and just collapsed. When I woke up it was mid-morning, with Kay shaking my shoulder to offer me a cup of steaming tea. My whole body ached, and Angel's nails had drawn blood in several places, mainly on my breasts and back, while I was covered with bruises and lesser scratches, so I really did look as if I'd been dragged through a hedge backwards.

The others were still asleep, curled into each other, Angel in Sophie's lap with her thumb in her mouth: an image as far from the sadistic, regal domina so many men had come to worship as it was possible to imagine. It was easier to imagine her posing for Denis Humber because she was naked, with the covers half down, and all she needed was a nappy. I brought them tea after I'd showered and we gathered together in my kitchen, eating toast and talking over what had happened the night before, and the run up to it.

It was obvious Morris would have to take a break with the club, at least in London, but that wasn't a problem as the next event was to be the international puppy show, and it was in Belfast. Angel had agreed to be mistress for Rubba Dobbie, and I knew Patty would be there too, with Bitch to show, while apparently there were people coming from as far afield as San Francisco, Sydney and Tokyo both to compete and to attend. The wrestling match would also have to be finished, and with Sophie egging us on and Angel still seething at the way she'd been treated, it wasn't long before we were plotting revenge.

Once either of us had Mel down in the ring we could do as we pleased, but there were two problems. First, we had to beat her, which was not easy at all, and if we failed we'd probably get more or less what we'd been planning to dish out. Second, when she wrestled she knew the risks, so unless we did something really awful, she wouldn't get anything she hadn't been more or less expecting anyway. Anything too horrible, she'd back out and it just wouldn't be satisfying. Before long we'd reached an impasse.

Angel was also keen to do well in the puppy show, and the conversation turned to what our competition was likely to be like and how good they'd be. After a while, we gathered around my computer, to search for any information we could get. Nearly all of what came up was irrelevant, just plain porn sites using key words without showing any appropriate content at all. Most of what was relevant was poor – photos done purely for pay, mistresses offering to make men into puppy-boys as a service, men and women on leads or with ears and tails – but one or two of the things we came up with were good, very good. Sophie recognised two of the names from conversations with Hudson Staebler.

There was Mistress Leash, a New York professional domina who specialised in puppy-boys and did it in style, with extensive kennels. She even had an announcement up on her site offering the trip to Belfast as one of her dogs as a special, the price 'on application only'. There were pictures of her with men on leads, sometimes as many as nine, and most of them in quite fancy suits. All of them had masks, not doglike creations of the sort Rubba Dobie and Bitch had, but grotesque cartoon dog faces, with huge ears, great heavy dewlaps and large, half-lidded eyes. If she was even half-competent when it came to training she would be serious competition, even a winner.

The other one was a Japanese male dom and his puppy-girl. As their site was almost entirely in Japanese none of us knew what it said, but the pictures told their own story. She was tiny, and extremely pretty, also sexy, and not unlike Bitch in style, with most of her face, her breasts and her bottom showing through a well-crafted suit with ears, a nose, a tail and even paws. It was hard to see what breed she was supposed to be, if any, but she was enough to set any man and any woman with even a hint of lesbianism drooling, and certainly stiff competition for Patty and Bitch.

We emailed the pictures and links to Patty and to Greg Hendricks, otherwise known as Rubba Dobie, whose address Angel had on her phone, and sat down to a cold lunch and a bottle of wine, discussing the puppy show and what to do about Mel all the while. Angel wanted to get her in a suit and make her eat dog food, but there was no obvious way of going about it, as it was really too elaborate to use for an after-wrestling-match humiliation. Sophie suggested somehow getting her into nappies at a club, but again there was the same stumbling block.

After lunch we went back to the computer. The email to Greg Hendricks had triggered an automatic 'out of office' response, which had Angel giggling guiltily with her hand over her mouth. Patty had replied, and was suggesting all four of us come up to Lincolnshire the following weekend for some training, an offer too good to resist.

* * *

Patty herself lived in a flat in Lincoln, but we'd arranged to meet up at her grandmother's – a detached house in a village some miles to the south, which apparently had a secluded garden at the rear. Being there was a little delicate because while Jean de Vrain had come to view corporal punishment as something that required tolerance, and was therefore prepared to extend tolerance to what Patty got up to, her background was very different. *Slap Happy* had worked on the premise that domestic discipline was an important part of a marriage, with the stronger, dominant partner doing the spanking, usually the male partner, but not always. She apparently resented the idea that spanking was in any way kinky, but found it impossible to accept that turning another girl into a human dog was anything but kinky. As had been explained in a series of emails, while the approaching court case was extremely worrying, it had only been that which increased Jean's sympathy and understanding enough for Patty to admit what she was really into.

We closed the shop up early the following Saturday and drove north, with Sophie and Angel as well. We'd tried to invite Greg Hendricks, but he'd been booked up for some corporate team-building exercise organised by the bank he worked for. Bitch was going to be there, but it took me a moment to realise that the petite, curly-haired young woman with the nervous smile and little round glasses was the same person I'd seen done up as a spaniel with just about everything showing and her face well down in a bowl of dog food.

She was called Gemma, and took to Kay immediately, the two of them soon giggling together as they helped Patty prepare dinner. Jean wasn't going to be back until later, and would apparently be visiting friends the next day, which Patty obviously found a relief. I had to agree, as I couldn't even begin to get my head around the idea of playing with my own grandmother around. Before long Patty had the pictures of Mistress Leash with her dogs, and of the Japanese puppy-girl, Sakura, spread out on the table. She'd opened a bottle of red wine, despite the warm summer evening, and we were drinking and nibbling peanuts as we talked.

'I'm really not sure we can hold our own,' Patty said doubtfully.

'Gemma's every bit as cute as Sakura,' Kay put in, 'and making her eat dog food, well –'

'The Japanese are into some pretty heavy stuff,' Angel warned, 'like putting girls in bondage for enemas –'

'– so they expel in their panties,' Sophie added with a classic mixture of disgust and relish.

'Not in a puppy show, surely?' I queried. 'But you're right. At the very least we have to assume they can be as dirty, and that Sakura is as capable of submission just as deep as Gemma. What we need is something spectacular, something they can't do, or won't think of. First off, what have we got that they haven't?'

'Nothing,' Gemma answered me, 'because if I can do it, so can she. Maybe if Morris Rathwell will put them on first, then I can try and top whatever she does? But what about Mistress Leash? She's got nine of them, and those masks.'

'I doubt we can manage nine puppy-girls,' Patty said doubtfully.

'We could manage nine puppy-boys,' Angel put in, 'twenty maybe, even thirty, and Greg could make masks just as good.'

'In three weeks?' I asked.

'I don't know.'

'Find out, but I don't think we gain much by sheer volume. Anyway, if we're only allowed two teams, you'd have to have Rubba Dobie in with the rest, and he'd look out of place, while you can't not have him at all. His outfit's too good to waste. I say we go for quality over quantity.'

Patty nodded, and Angel too after a moment, then she spoke again.

'One thing, he's changed the cock. There's a tube down the middle and the balls are hollow. You fill it with milk, right, and when you squeeze it goes everywhere, seriously gross!'

'That should help,' I admitted, exchanging a disgusted glance with Kay, 'but only so long as you get the right judges. Both Jean and Mr Protheroe marked Rubba Dobie down for his cock, and you must admit it's pretty gross.'

'Completely,' Angel agreed, 'but it's clever.'

'I gave you a nine for costume,' I told her, 'but it's risky. Who are the judges?'

'Morris and Hudson are having a bit of trouble agreeing on that,' Sophie replied. 'Unbiased experts are a bit thin on the ground.'

'It's a risk anyway,' Patty pointed out, 'but they'll probably be men, who are always going to favour the cute girls, so I don't really think Mistress Leash is that much of a problem. Any professional can get nine men, easily, and the masks probably come from a joke shop.'

'Men, yes, but maybe submissive men,' I pointed out, 'who'd mark her high if she had one man naked on a lead.'

'They'd vote Angel high too,' Kay pointed out.

'We'll have to hedge our bets,' I suggested. 'Angel, you're going to get the submissive men's votes, so you go in full dom gear, with plenty of black rubber so you match Dobie. Patty, go for a smart look.'

'We still need something special for me,' Gemma put in.

'If only you could have puppies,' Sophie remarked.

'Very funny, Sophie,' I answered her, 'but maybe, if it's OK with you, Gemma, Angel could have you get covered by Rubba Dobie.'

'Covered, as in fucked?' Gemma demanded, now staring with her mouth wide open.

'Not if you don't want to, of course,' I said hastily.

'It would be great,' Angel put in. 'I'd like to see them top that.'

'If you're not up for it, Gemma,' Sophie added, 'he can drag me out of the audience, maybe by the seat of my panties, like in that poster, where the dog's got a girl by the waistband of her panties, and you can see her bum, only he'd mount me too. I don't mind.'

'I didn't say I wouldn't do it,' Gemma said. 'It's just ... it's just ... that awful cock, inside me. It wouldn't fit for one thing.'

'You don't need to get it all in,' Sophie pointed out, 'or you could always take it up the bum.'

Gemma gave a shiver that went through her whole body, making her little round breasts quiver under her top. I found myself picturing Rubba Dobie on her back, humping away with his grotesque rubber cock in her body, either with half its length plunged up her fanny, or the whole fat pink tube in her rectum, pumping milk into her guts as she was buggered in public. It was a lot to ask, and far more than I could have handled.

'Maybe we could hold that in reserve?' Patty suggested cautiously, reaching out to put one hand on top of Gemma's.

'I ... I can do it,' Gemma said suddenly. 'I can.'

She didn't look at all certain, but it was her choice.

I thought we might all play together that evening, but Jean de Vrain came back early than expected, while we were still eating dinner, and it just didn't happen. She was perfectly friendly, and quite open, passing around old issues of *Slap Happy* and discussing how attitudes to corporal punishment had changed across her lifetime. Inevitably, she thought it was all for the worse, which started a lively discussion between her and Patty on the one side, both of whom felt that there would always be occasions when a woman, or a man, should submit to physical discipline without necessarily wanting it as

151

something sexual. Sophie disagreed strongly, although I could tell the idea of being spanked against her will held an awful fascination for her, while Gemma held her peace, watching shyly through her little round glasses as the debate swung one way and another. I could see both sides of the argument, and made only the occasional contribution to support the ultimate right of the one being punished to refuse discipline. Kay simply took it all in, snuggled next to me on a two-seater sofa, while Angel was evidently new to the whole argument and only asked the occasional question.

By the time they'd got to judicial birching I'd switched off and picked up one of the old copies of *Slap Happy*: Issue No 12 according to the cover. It was well done, for a one-horse publication from the 50s, and before long my head was swimming with images of elegantly dressed young women bent across their men-folk's knees to receive spankings, first on the seat of their knickers and then bare before being sent into the corner, smacked bum to the room. Jean evidently believe in the classic ritual, over the knee, gradual exposure to let the shame sink in, hard disciplinary spanking with no warm-up, then into the corner to think on your crime and the consequences. The letters were interesting, recounting experiences, stating opin-ions or asking advice, much of it in a way that would have been unthinkable in modern society, such as a woman who fully accepted her husband's right to spank her, but wanted to know if there was any way to make it hurt less. Jean's answer, predictably, had been that it was supposed to hurt.

It was gone midnight before we made our way to bed, and I was pleased, and amused, to find that Jean had put Kay and me in a double bed and the others in singles. I wasn't exactly sure how the relationship between Patty and Gemma worked, but they seemed to be playmates rather than partners, and Jean had evidently decided that Kay and I living together gave us some sort of precedence. In true old English fashion, not a word had been said about our lesbian relationship, it had just been accepted.

Kay knew she was going to get spanked, and was delightfully embarrassed at the thought of Jean hearing us, which was bound to happen because our rooms were next door. I knew she quite liked the idea of Jean doing it, underneath, and I was teasing her about taking her in and having her dealt with formally. She was absolutely squirming by the time I took her across my knee, and I gave her the punishment very formally, in the same style as in the magazine: held firmly across my knee, her jeans taken down to get at the seat of her knickers, a few hard swats and then bare bottom for the proper spanking. It left her shaking, and we knew that Jean would have heard, and probably the others too. As she licked me to ecstasy, I was imagining how it would have been to give it to her with all five of them looking on.

I slept well, and woke to the smell of frying bacon and coffee. Jean and Patty were already up and dressed, dealing with breakfast, and by the time I'd showered it was ready. Patty gave me a knowing look as she handed me a plate, but nothing was said, triggering the pleasant thought that I was in a household where the fact that girls got spanked was taken entirely for granted.

If Jean's attitudes were old fashioned, so was the breakfast: bacon, black pudding, eggs and tomatoes, a plate for each of us, generous and delicious, but with no question of choice. Jean, I was sure, ate what was put in front of her and expected others to do the same. Certainly Patty did, along with being exceptionally polite and well behaved. Kay joined us while I was still drinking my coffee, then Gemma, Sophie and Angel only when Jean was in her coat and ready to go. She knew what we were going to be up to, more or less, and accepted it, despite a slight air of long-suffering. As she took her car keys from a hook by the door she spoke to Patty.

'Have a nice day, dear, and do enjoy yourselves. I very doubt there'll be any callers, but keep the front door locked just in case. All the modesty curtains are properly drawn, I checked.'

'We'll probably just go in the garden,' Patty answered.

Jean shook her head.

'I'd rather you stayed indoors. The Biltons' house overlooks most of the lawn.'

'We'll stay at the back, Granny, I promise, and I'll lay the hosepipe out or something to show where people aren't to go.'

'No, Patricia, please, just stay indoors, and preferably upstairs.'

'But, Granny –'

'Indoors, Patricia. There's quite enough trouble as it is without you and your friends being seen playing puppies.'

'OK, Granny.'

She said it with a sigh, but Jean accepted the argument as closed, and gave her a peck on the cheek before saying goodbye to the rest of us. The moment she was gone the atmosphere changed, with an element of naughtiness stealing in. Gemma and Kay went to get their puppy-girl outfits without even bothering to finish their breakfasts, but Sophie was looking distinctly downcast as she turned to me.

'What am I going to do?'

'Anything you like.'

'I want to play to. I can be Angel's puppy, can't I? Angel?'

'Sure,' Angel answered her. 'What about gear?'

'We'll make you into a French poodle,' Patty promised. 'That's what Gemma and I used to do before we made the spaniel outfit. It's simple, but it's fun. Hang on.'

She disappeared upstairs, passing Kay and Gemma on their way down. They were giggling together, and holding up their suits as they came into the kitchen: Kay with her big rubber pants and top, Gemma with the spaniel outfit. They were both in their robes, and peeled off without hesitation. Both looked lovely, the way I like my girlfriends, petite but with full bottoms. Kay was a little slimmer, and maybe just an inch taller, but every bit as meaty behind, with her lovely firm, jutting cheeks. Gemma was more like Sophie: compact, chubbier behind, her thighs too. Just looking at them stripped I could have put either of them straight over my knee, and then between my thighs.

There was plenty of time, and I sat back, sipping my second coffee of the morning as they dressed: Kay wriggling into her tight rubber puppy pants and the little top, while Gemma had to have Angel help her with the fastenings. The moment Gemma was done she was transformed, her face all but hidden, her body encased in curly black fur with the little spiral tail sticking up over her bottom. Yet with her breasts hanging naked from her chest and her fanny on show from the rear there was no doubt as to her humanity, or her sex: she was no dog, but a puppy-girl – Bitch.

Kay was less doglike, and less exposed, but still ever so cute, with her glorious bottom sheathed in tight black rubber with her tail wagging above. With her thighs and midriff white, her face white, but with the two uneven bands of black at hips and chest, her markings were certainly those of a dog, my own Patch.

Sophie was looking more than a little jealous, sitting with her robe casually open at the front and a sulky expression on her pretty face. Even when Patty came back she only cheered up a little, looking doubtfully at the pieces of thick-pile brown carpet that were supposed to be her puppy suit. Patty also had a pair of heavy cloth shears, a curved sacking needle and a reel of extra-strong cotton.

'You have to be sewn into it,' she explained. 'Let's clear away and you can climb up on the table. Put collars on those two dogs would you, Amber? Mine's in my case.'

I went for the collars, leaving the others to tidy up, or, in the case of Patch and Bitch, to snuffle at each other's faces and rub their cheeks and necks together. Both were fully in role, and so was I, with a pleasant sense of being in charge as I collected the collars and leads from out bedrooms and brought them down-stairs. Patch accepted hers meekly, hanging her head to let me collar her and allowing herself to be led to the kitchen door, where I attached her lead to the handle. Bitch was less helpful, running and hiding under the table, so I was forced to drag her out by the scruff of her neck and stand over her with her body clamped between my legs as I fixed the collar to her neck. Having subdued her, I took her by the collar and pulled her out into the passage, fixing her lead to a banister before planting a dozen well-placed smacks on her furry black bottom.

Back in the kitchen, Sophie was on the table, stark naked and on all fours. Anyone who had come to the window would have had a fine view, right up her fanny from behind. I was hoping Jean and Patty were right about our privacy, but with the court case pending it seemed likely that they were. There would be no unexpected visitors.

Patty had laid out the bits of carpet, and I realised what she was doing. Sophie was not merely to be a French poodle, but in the old-fashioned style, with parts of her body bare, as if shaved, and parts furry. I was already smiling as I pictured the design in my mind, how she would look with her bottom and hips, her chest, her knees and elbows, and the crown of her head, all with puffs of thick brown fur, but the rest bare. Patty was already sewing one elbow piece into place, with Sophie holding very still as the big sacking needle was run through the carpet over her skin.

156

I began to help, cutting the remaining strips for her elbows and knees, then a round piece for the top of her head. Patty sewed each one into place as I finished, working with deft fingers as Sophie was slowly transformed from girl to puppy-girl. I did the chest piece so that the lower part could be sewn up across her rib-cage but below her breasts, to leave them bare and dangling, a fine little pair of udders, maybe a C-cup, but big against her petite figure. The pants were hardest, but I'd made enough leather and rubber ones in my time, and we soon had her ready, her hips and tummy and bottom encased in thick brown fur but with an elongated teardrop-shaped hole at the back to leave her fanny peeping out behind and to hint at the crease of her bottom. We used hairpins to attach the round piece to her hair before adding the final touch: a pompom of wool on a rolled piece of fabric to make her tail. She was done.

'What's she called?' I asked Angel, who'd sat and watched in mounting delight.

'Fifi,' Angel said firmly. 'That's what a French girl would call her poodle, isn't it?'

'It suits her,' Patty agreed. 'Come on, Fifi, down girl, off the table!'

'Bad girl!' Angel added, and slapped Sophie's furry bottom.

Sophie jumped down, only not Sophie, but Fifi, as much a puppy-girl as Patch and Bitch, both of whom had stayed squatting patiently on their haunches as we worked. Patty managed to dig out a real collar and lead from a cupboard under the stairs, and Fifi was quickly put on it and attached to the kitchen door alongside Patch. Patty began to tidy up and Angel and I sat down.

'Training then?' she suggested.

'We should go over what we're going to do in the show,' I suggested. 'Are you going to do an obedience routine, Patty?'

'Yes,' she answered, 'that and the dog food.'

'We should do a competition,' Angel suggested, 'only it's not the one who wins who gets the prize, it's the one who loses.'

'How's that?' Patty asked.

'The prize is the bowl of dog food,' Angel answered.

I laughed, but the suggestion had set my tummy tight. To make a girl eat dog food, down on all fours in her puppy outfit, her face in the bowl, pushed in if she didn't behave herself, and made to eat the contents, slippery, lumpy mush . . .

'Let's do it,' Patty said, laughing. 'I've got a tin, economy size, but if we're going to do it properly, we'll have to go outside.'

'What about the neighbours, the Biltons?' I asked.

'Easy, I'll check to see if they're in. If they're not we can play to our heart's content, and we're sure to hear their car on the gravel if they come back.'

She spread her hands and shrugged, smiling, and skipped off towards the door. Outside was better, no question, with a beautifully manicured lawn to play on and warm sunshine with just a touch of breeze ruffling the trees. I went out to check just how overlooked it was, and found that Jean had been exaggerating. Only one gable-end window of what was presumably the Biltons' house could be seen, and their view covered the front and side, but very little of the back. We could play, safely, but just in case they did come back and we failed to hear the car, I put the hosepipe out, making a boundary well short of the danger area.

Patty was soon back, and as she had both Patch and Bitch on their leads it was obvious the Biltons were out. Angel followed, holding Fifi's lead, a rubber ball, a bowl, a spoon, and a large colourful can of cheap dog food. They let the puppies loose, and the three of them began to gambol, chasing each other and rolling on the warm grass as I walked across to the others.

'I was thinking of an obedience trial,' Patty suggested. 'Perhaps running out to fetch the ball only on command.'

'I think it's a bit easy,' Angel responded. 'Something tells me they're going to be genuinely keen not to lose, so it has to be something they find really difficult.'

'Catch?' I put in, taking the soft rubber ball from Angel.

'Catch is good,' Patty agreed. 'We can make them catch, wait with the ball in their mouths or fetch if they drop it, and bring it back on command.'

I glanced at Angel, who nodded. Across the lawn, Patch and Bitch were rubbing noses. Fifi was behind Bitch, investigating her bottom, her face burrowed into the crease, sniffing, then starting to lick. Bitch gave a little whimper and let her back dip, pushing her bottom into Fifi's face.

'Stop that! Dirty!' Angel snapped, and hauled on Fifi's lead.

Fifi growled, and came only reluctantly, pulling on her collar, until Angel delivered a few hard slaps to her rump. I took Patch's collar and Patty took Bitch's, pulling the three of them together to the far side of the lawn, where a stand of delphiniums bordered the wall.

'Sit!' I ordered, and Patch squatted down on her haunches, looking up at me from big soft eyes.

She wiggled her bottom, to make her little rubber tail wag, and I was struggling not to smile. Patty and Angel both had their puppies in the same position, ready for command. I tossed the ball up in my hand and took a few steps back, then held it out, as if about to throw underhand.

'Catch, Patch, catch!'

I threw, and she did try, jumping up to snap at the ball, but missing.

'Fetch!' I ordered, as the ball rolled over the lip of the flower bed.

She scrambled after it, dipping to take it in her mouth and coming up with a smut of soil on her nose and the ball in her open jaws.

'Good girl. Now come to Amber, come on, girl.'

She came crawling towards me as fast as she could, to drop the ball at my feet and go down, chest to the ground, paws extended, bottom up and wiggling to make her tail wag. I reached down to pet her, stroking her head and tickling her under the chin before picking up the ball and throwing it to Angel.

'Try yours.'

Angel caught the ball and Fifi was put through the same routine, trying to catch, retrieving the ball when she failed and bringing it back to her mistress. Instead of petting her, Angel took her firmly by the collar and delivered a salvo of hard swats to Fifi's bottom.

'You have to be firm,' she explained as Fifi grovelled down whimpering on the grass. 'Otherwise they never learn. Patty?'

She threw the ball towards Patty, who managed to drop it and had to run after it before she could throw for Bitch. Like Patch and Fifi, Bitch failed to catch the ball in her mouth, but mainly because it went well wide of her head and in among the delphiniums behind. Bitch went after it without having to be told, burrowing in among the foliage with just her bottom sticking out before emerging muddy but triumphant, with the ball in her teeth.

I shook my head and Patty shrugged as Bitch came forwards to drop the ball at her feet. Like me she petted her puppy's head rather than smacking her, only to have Bitch refuse to let go of the ball, holding it firmly in her teeth and pulling back with her paws set firmly against the grass, until Patty was obliged to smack her anyway. Bitch let go and Patty threw me the ball, now wet and somewhat grubby.

'Best of ten?' I suggested.

'I'm not sure,' Angel answered me. 'If you try this in the show, Patty, you'll just get laughed at.'

'Maybe something smaller,' I put in. 'Have you got any doggie treats?'

'No, but they'll be great for the show,' Patty said, laughing. 'There are some grapes we can use for now.'

'Grapes are good,' Angel agreed. 'Back you go, Fifi, go on, back!'

Fifi went and, as Patty ran in to fetch the grapes, we got the puppy-girls lined up again, all three sitting. We put the tin of dog food and the bowl to one side, and I caught all three of them giving it nervous glances as we waited. As Angel had suggested, they would be trying their best, and I knew that if my Patch lost, I'd be taking Kay right to her limits. Patty was quickly back, holding a large bunch of seedless green grapes, which she began to pick from the stems.

'Ten each, OK? We throw at the same time too, to see if they distract each other, just as the crowd might at the show.'

'Good idea.'

I took my ten grapes, waiting until Patty had distributed them before addressing myself to my puppy. She was bolt upright, her tongue hanging out, eager, alert, and very determined to do her best.

'Wait for it, girl,' I told her, 'wait for it ... and, catch!'

Patty and Angel snapped out the same order and we threw our grapes together. Fifi jumped up, catching hers and quickly chewing it up, but Patch had missed, the grape bouncing off her face and into the grass. She nuzzled it up quickly, but it was still a miss, no better than Bitch's, which had gone in among the delphiniums. I shook my finger at her and selected a second grape, once more giving my command just as the others did.

She got it, a perfect catch, right in her mouth, and she was looking thoroughly pleased with herself, pushing it forwards between her teeth to show me how clever she was before she munched it up and swallowed. Fifi had caught hers as well, but Bitch had missed completely and was in among the delphiniums again, just her tail, the curve of her bum and her feet sticking out from among the big ragged leaves.

As soon as she was ready I took my third grape, gave the order, and threw. Patch missed, but so did the others. She had one, Fifi had two, and Bitch none.

She caught the fourth and Fifi missed, but Bitch caught hers. Two and two and one.

She missed the fifth completely and had to go bum up in the delphiniums to get it. Both the others caught theirs. Two and three and two.

She caught the sixth, just leaping right up to snap it out of the air and throwing me an accusing look for my bad throw as she munched it down. Fifi had missed, but Bitch hadn't. Three and three and three.

She caught the seventh, which I'd thrown very carefully at her mouth, but both the other caught theirs too. Four and four and four.

She caught the eighth easily, Fifi and Bitch both missed, and I began to relax a little. Five and four and four.

She missed the ninth completely, even though it was a perfectly good throw, while both the others caught theirs. Five and five and five.

I took the tenth, pausing to study her face to see if she truly wanted to win or to lose. She looked eager, and I threw the grape carefully, watching it rise and fall in a gentle arc, to hit her lip as she jumped up, bounce, come down on the tip of her nose, bounce again, sideways, and into the delphiniums. Next to her Fifi was proudly holding her grape between her teeth. Bitch was chewing. Five, six, six and time Patch had her dog food.

She looked aghast, absolutely horror stricken, and I could see her lips trembling as she got down on all fours,

162

crawling over to me. I tousled her head as she began to rub on my leg, but there was no backing out, not unless she chose to use her stop word, which we all knew would spoil the whole game. I clipped her lead on to her collar and made my way towards where the tin and bowl stood on the lawn. Patty and Angel followed, each leading her puppy, to form a ring, with the dog bowl at the centre.

Patch had hung her head as I picked up the big gaudy can. To my amusement it showed a picture of a puppy not unlike her, a real puppy obviously, but with the same black and white markings and big, soulful eyes. Hearing me laugh she looked up, more accusing than ever, then in sudden disgust as I pulled the tab and caught the sudden meaty tang of the food, mixed with that odd, doggie smell that always makes my stomach turn.

I was really wondering if I could make her do it as I scooped the thick greyish brown paste out from the can into the bowl. Everything I ever do to her I've taken myself – the spankings, the cane and strap and whip, kissing and licking at other girls' bottoms, being peed on, being stripped and tied and humiliated in a hundred subtle ways, pony play and piggy play, puppy play too – but I'd never been made to eat dog food. Yet if she wanted to stop, she had to say.

She was whimpering, and kept making big soppy eyes at me as I emptied the tin, scraping out every last bit of the foul-smelling pulp. I took her lead and twisted my hand into it, just gently, to pull her forwards. She was reluctant, hesitant, pulling back and whimpering badly, her whole body trembling. A single tiny sob escaped her lips as her face was brought over the bowl, just an inch or two above the dog food, and I gave her order.

'Eat up, Patch, there's a good girl.'

I sank down on my haunches because I just had to watch. She'd dipped down, her lips almost touching the top of the lumpy brown pile beneath her face. I could see the strain in her expression as she struggled with her feelings, and then suddenly she was doing it, gobbling at the dog food with tears of raw emotion running down her cheeks and her body shaking violently. I began to stroke her hair, soothing her as she humiliated herself.

In just a few mouthfuls her cheeks were bulging, and then she'd swallowed, gulping it down, and there was no going back at all. She was eating dog food, not just putting it in her mouth but swallowing. Like sucking cock for the first time, like losing your virginity, like letting a man up your bottom, it was done, and there was no going back. She was streaming tears as she ate, but I knew she wasn't going to stop, and what she wanted, what she needed.

Still stroking her hair, I slid a hand over the straining rubber seat of her puppy pants, feeling the contours of her bottom and the swell of her fanny lips. The seam had caught between them, a fold of rubber holding them open and right on her clitty. I began to rub it, her flesh moving beneath the thin rubber, masturbating her as she gulped down her dog food.

I wanted to come myself, weak with reaction for what I'd done to her, but it was her privilege, when she was so far down. Already I could feel the little shivers running through her body, replacing the trembling of her first submission. I hugged her to me, whispering in her ear, to call her a good dog and to tell her to eat up her food, and all the while rubbing at her fanny through the skintight rubber of her puppy pants. She was going to come, to come as she gobbled on dog food, swallowing it down, mouthful after mouthful, filling out her stomach, to feed her, to become part of her body, a beautiful, perfect degradation she was never, ever going to forget.

Her body went tight in my arms, she swallowed one last time and she was coming, sobbing and gasping out

164

her ecstasy with her face well down in the bowl. Even as she shook and shivered in orgasm she'd begun to eat it again, filling her mouth and gulping down the reeking pulp in near-demented urgency, again and again, and even as she finally went limp her face was still in the bowl, licking.

She was crying bitterly, and I held her for a long time while the others stood around us in silence. Patty was trying to look calm and poised, but her breathing was deep and her fingers clenched tight around Bitch's lead. Angel was bright eyed, her mouth a little open, her nipples hard points beneath her top. Both puppies were staring: Bitch in sympathy and understanding, Fifi's expression working between regret and relief.

At last Kay shook herself and started to rise, no longer Patch. I helped her up and led her indoors, knowing she'd want to wash, and to have some time to get her head around what she'd done. It had been so sudden, maybe half-an-hour from her transformation to a puppy-girl until she'd been brought to orgasm with a bellyful of supermarket own-brand dog food. At first she was looking at the ground, and as we came into the kitchen she managed a wry grin, and spoke as we mounted the stairs.

'I am a dirty bitch, aren't I?'

'The best.'

It was the answer she wanted, and it wasn't just empty reassurance. We'd come a long way since she'd accepted her first gentle punishments and learnt to come over her own submission, but I knew she'd always felt a little unsure of herself, especially with Sophie, who simply revelled in being a slut. Perhaps that was why she'd eaten the dog food, or at least partly so.

'Now you,' she said as we reached the landing.

For a moment I thought she meant she wanted me to do what she'd just done, and my heart jumped because I knew I could not possibly refuse. Only when she stuck her tongue out and wiggled it did I realise she just wanted to lick me. Her face was a mess where she'd licked the bowl, so I led her into the loo, pushing my jeans and knickers to my ankles before taking my seat, my thighs wide to her face as she got to her knees.

She went forwards, her face pressed to my fanny and she was licking me, my reward for letting her utterly degrade herself: ecstasy. I let my eyes focus on her, watching her pretty face, framed in golden-brown hair, her little tits quivering in their rubber casing to the rhythm of her licking. Her eyes were closed, her arms around me, holding me to her face, her bottom well stuck out so that I could admire the full swell of her rubber-clad cheeks with the gentle valley between and the black puppy-dog tail wagging gently to her motion.

It was one of the things she loved the best: kneeling to lick my fanny, providing me the pleasure of her tongue and of her body, at my feet. She was always good, and all the better for a spanking or a dose of my hairbrush: more thorough, more conscientious. Only now her bottom was fresh, but her mouth wasn't, anything but. Her mouth was still full of the taste of dog food, dog food I'd made her eat, down on her knees with her face in a plastic bowl, gobbling down cheap nasty dog food for my amusement and arousal, so our friends could watch her do it, watch her eat and watch her swallow, watch her play at puppy-girls to the point of utter, filthy degradation . . .

My orgasm was so long and so hard I had to bite my lip to stop myself from screaming so loudly it would have alerted the Biltons even if they weren't in, even if they were in the next county. Kay just kept on licking, her face buried between my thighs, holding me as I bucked and shook in her arms, telling her I loved her and calling her a dirty bitch over and over, until at last the sensation broke and I settled back, limp and happy, against the cistern.

* * *

We'd barely begun the day and both Kay and I had come, and over a really strong piece of humiliation. By the time we'd showered and changed and come back out on to the lawn the others had been through two more rounds of catch training, only with spankings for the losers instead of a bowl of dog food, and had also been making Bitch and Fifi fight over the rubber ball. Patty and Angel were laughing so hard they could barely stand, with their arms around each other's shoulders as the two puppy-girls rolled and wriggled on the lawn, snapping at each other and at the ball.

It was the same for the rest of the morning, alternating between serious attempts at puppy-girl training for the show and just mucking about. Kay had changed, but was soon back as Patch, as frolicsome as the others. We tried to make them do jumps, which was a disaster but extremely funny, and practised having Bitch covered, with Fifi as a stand-in for Rubba Dobie. It looked both bizarre and obscene, and if we might not necessarily win, at least nobody could say we hadn't given the opposition a good run for their money.

When Bitch and Fifi needed to pee they simply squatted down over a flower bed, letting it all come out without the least trace of self-consciousness or shame. It seemed a good thing to include in our routine, so long as the judges seemed right, and when Patty suggested it to Bitch the response was a happy barking.

By the time we went indoors it was nearly one in the afternoon. We were all hungry, especially the puppies, all three of them whining and begging with their paws as we sat down around the kitchen table. Patty cooked up some pasta shapes and tomato sauce, which we made the puppies eat from bowls on the floor, leaving them with their faces smeared red, or in Bitch's case her muzzle smeared red. They were badly in need of a clean up, so we took them outside again, to hose them down, and left them there, all three soaking wet.

Leaving the puppies to play, we put the final touches to our programme over a bottle of cold wine. Sakura seemed the real threat, and in direct competition with Patty and Bitch, so we determined to try to bribe Morris to let them go on first, then try to outdo whatever they came up with. At the minimum, Patty would put Bitch through a more elaborate version of the routine she'd used before: a display of obedience, catching doggie treats in her mouth and the bowl of dog food. Bitch could pee too, if it seemed the right thing to do. We could also have her covered by Rubba Dobie, with Patty actually guiding the big rubber cock up Bitch's fanny for the sake of effect. Lastly there was the option of having Sophie dragged out of the crowd and mounted, and me decided that if we did it, she should pretend to fight until the cock was actually inside her body.

Before the fucking, Angel would put Rubba Dobie through his normal routine, only this time when he humped her leg it would leave cream dripping down her boot and he would get a proper whipping for his disgusting behaviour. It was good, no question, both elaborate and extremely dirty, while Rubba Dobie's dog suit was better than anything we'd seen on the net or elsewhere, and Bitch's not so very far behind.

We went back outside, where the puppies were still messing about, with Bitch and Fifi head to tail, snuffling at each other and trying to lick. Patty brought out a new bottle and our glasses, and we curled up on the lawn to watch, and drink. It was going to get rude, with all three of them close together, nuzzling and licking, faces to bums and fannies, tongues to eager little holes. It didn't surprise me at all when Angel unfastened her trousers and pushed them down, as I wanted to masturbate myself, but she had other ideas.

'Would you do me, one of you?' she asked casually, spreading her lean brown thighs to show off the shaved lips of her fanny between. 'Amber, I think. Nothing against you, Patty, but she owes me.'

Patty mumbled something conciliatory, but I couldn't find an answer at all, taken completely aback by the suddenness of her demand that I lick her fanny.

'Come on, girl, get licking,' she demanded, pointing to her open sex. 'I like it on my lips first, and kisses, your tongue up my hole too.'

I nodded weakly, wondering if I should refuse, or at least ask to go head to tail, but feeling a bitch for my own response. After what I'd done to her, it was little enough to ask. I shrugged and scrambled around, on to all fours. She gave a pleased purr and moved around a little, putting her back to an apple tree so that she could watch the puppy-girls at play while I licked her. Her thighs were wide open, with not just her fanny on show, but the dark crease of her bottom, and a hint of her anal star. I crawled in between her thighs, catching her scent – perfume and her own natural musk – before going down, to kiss the soft bulge of shaved brown flesh above her fanny.

As I began to attend to her sex I was telling myself it was perfectly reasonable for her to want me to lick her, but it was impossible not to feel I'd been put down, at least a little, especially with Patty watching and in front of the girls. All I could see was Angel's bare brown skin, the folds of her sex and the low bulge of her belly, but I could hear the giggles and gasps from behind me. Angel was watching them at first, my job simply to make her come, but then her hand had closed gently in my hair, pushing me lower to make me tongue her hole.

'Put your tongue well in,' she told me, 'then you can clean my arsehole.'

A shiver ran right through me at her words, but my tongue was already probing her fanny, my face pushed hard to her wet flesh as I tried to get as deep in as I could, as instructed. She wanted her bottom hole licked, cleaned she'd said, and I could no longer pretend. My acceptance wasn't enough. She wanted my submission.

I hesitated, feeling put out because I'd been enjoying being in charge, but I had done it to her, and not just made her lick my bottom, but spanked her, stuck vegetables up her, peed over her bottom and in her mouth . . .

She gave a long sigh as my tongue found her bumhole. Her fingers were locked in my hair, but she hadn't made me. I'd done it because it was only fair, maybe . . . because she wanted me to, maybe . . . because it was nice, maybe . . . but whatever the reason, my tongue was on her bottom hole, lapping at the little bumps and crevices of flesh, and burrowing into the tiny crevice.

I could taste her in my mouth, and my resentment was fading quickly to pleasure. My guilt at what I'd done to her and at her being only nineteen was fading too. She'd wanted her fanny licked and I'd done it. She'd wanted her bumhole licked and I'd done it, using my tongue where she used loo paper, deep in, wriggling up the little hole and wanting to just push my jeans and knickers down and rub myself to heaven . . .

'I think I'm probably clean now, Amber, make me come,' she ordered, and pulled my head up by the hair, right on to her clitty.

Her thighs tightened around my head, the grip in my hair grew stronger, and I was being smothered in wet, musky girlflesh, my own senses reeling to her scent and the taste in my mouth. The girls were still playing, and I knew she'd be watching them, enjoying the view as I gave her tongue service. She began to moan and I licked harder, full on her clitty, rubbing my tongue against the tiny bump until my jaw ached and I could barely breathe. I was rewarded in moments, her thighs contracting around my head, her bottom cheeks squeezing tight, and she was there, coming in my face as I licked urgently at her sex, in complete submission to her will.

170

I came up the moment she let go of my hair. My face was sticky and wet, but her arms were open, welcoming me for a long hug and an open-mouthed kiss, sharing the taste of her fanny and bumhole. Patty was watching, bright-eyed and urgent, her hands on the button of her jeans, but hesitant. I went straight to her, eager to taste her too, opened her jeans and pulled them down as she lifted her bum, knickers and all.

The puppy-girls were still playing, in a tangle of limbs on the lawn, Bitch mounted up on Fifi, head to tail. They were licking each other, with Patch's face pressed firmly in-between Bitch's bottom cheeks, tongue to bumhole, just as mine had been. Patty rolled her legs up, holding herself behind the knees to let me get at her fanny and still watch. I went down, to kiss the tight knot of her bottom hole and draw a pleased sigh from her before my face went to her sex.

She was gasping and moaning immediately. I slid two fingers in up her hole and began to tickle her bumhole with a third, licking all the while. From the corner of my eye I could see the puppy-girls, intent on each other, all three licking urgently, while Patch was rubbing her fanny through her rubber pants. Bitch began to twitch and shiver in orgasm, and rub her bottom in the others' faces. She'd come off Fifi's fanny, but only for a moment, burying her face again while she was still in orgasm.

I felt Patty's muscles start to tighten and knew she was near orgasm. She'd snatched up her top and her hands were on her breasts, kneading them through her bra, then bare as she tugged them free. I licked harder, finger-fucking her as her moans rose to cries of ecstasy, and she was there, and Angel's hands were on my jeans.

As I licked at Patty's fanny I was being stripped, my jeans were pulled down, all the way to my ankles, and then my knickers. My top was hauled high, my bra too, and my boobs were bare, with Angel sucking hard at

171

one nipple. Even as Patty was coming down I heard another cry of ecstasy, from the three on the lawn. I spread my thighs, inviting a lick from any one of them, and, to my delight, Patty climbed on, still trembling from her orgasm as she went down on me.

I closed my eyes, letting it all come together in my head: puppy-girls and spanking girls, being licked and licking, Kay's tongue on my clitty, and Patty's, my own tongue up Angel's bottom. Already I could feel my orgasm coming and, as a soft, wet mouth closed on my other nipple, I was arching my back and my thighs were tightening around Patty's head. I felt a leg brush my hair, and the coarse texture of Fifi's fur as Sophie mounted my face, her bottom spread, her bumhole to my nose, her fanny to my mouth, and I was licking.

Patty stopped, briefly, leaving me right on the edge, but only for an instant and her tongue was on my clitty once more, licking urgently even as Kay's face pressed in, lower, her tongue wriggling in to lick my bottom. Somebody's fingers slid in up my fanny, and I was there, coming under a tangle of giggling, laughing girls, being licked and sucked, my mind a welter of rude images, and all of them female.

My orgasm left me weak and shaking, spreadeagled half-naked on the lawn as they climbed slowly off me. All six of us had come and, while Kay was still toying lazily with her fanny through the rubber puppy pants as she rolled over on to her back, the rest of us had had our fill, at least for the moment. Angel didn't even bother to dress, but peeled off her clothes to go nude, lying back on the warm grass with her arms limp at her sides and her eyes closed. Patty went in to get some juice and I rolled on to my side, still bare from my chest to my ankles and vaguely thinking I ought to go in and shower.

In the end I did, along with Sophie, who'd had enough of being a poodle because the carpet material was beginning to irritate her skin. Gemma had taken off her spaniel outfit too, but stayed nude on the lawn, using the hose to wash herself down, and Kay and Angel too. Sophie and I could see them from the window, and we came down in the nude, knowing full well we'd get squirted whether we were dressed or not. Patty was in the kitchen, giggling and mischievous as she whispered in my ear that she wanted me to give her a special treat later, but she wouldn't say what.

I got the hose right in my face the instant I stepped from the kitchen door, from Gemma. I didn't know if she was angling for a spanking or not, but she was going to get one and, as she dropped the hose and ran, I gave chase, with her squealing and laughing as she tried to dodge, only for Angel to stretch out one lazy arm and trip her up.

I got straight on top of her and dealt with her then and there, spanking her little pink bottom until her cheeks were rosy and she'd begun to howl and babble apologies. She was pouting beautifully as she stood up to rub at her sore bottom, and went straight to Patty, only to get upended and spanked a second time, with such a glorious look of consternation on her pretty face that I was unable to stand properly for laughing. My sides were hurting, and I had to close my eyes to stop it, opening them only when the sounds of Patty's palm on Gemma's bum cheeks and the others' laughter stopped abruptly. I looked up.

Jean de Vrain was standing in the kitchen doorway with a face like thunder.

Patty froze, one foot up on a garden chair, Gemma upside down over her knee, hand still lifted to lay in the next spank. Jean crooked a finger and went back indoors. Patty helped Gemma up, gave us a single glance compounded of appeal and fear, then followed her grandmother. My hands had gone to my boobs and fanny, covering myself by instinct, no longer nude and playful, but naked and embarrassed.

For a moment we stood looking at each other, four naked girls and one in a rubber dog costume, all looking as embarrassed as we felt. Suddenly I needed my clothes very badly indeed, and started for the house. The others followed. As I made for the stairs I could hear voices from the front room: Jean's raised in anger, Patty replying, contrite but also sulky.

'Why must you do these things? I specifically told you not to play outdoors because we're overlooked, and —'

'But we didn't go where the Biltons could see, Granny. We were really careful.'

'I told you not to play outdoors. The Biltons —'

'They're not even there,' Patty wailed. 'I checked.'

I paused, wanting to help, because there was real fear and consternation in Patty's voice, and it was as much my fault as hers. The conversation stopped and I hesitated, shuffling from foot to foot, not at all sure what to do as the others hurried past me, up the stairs, except Kay, who came up beside me, biting her lip. Jean spoke again, and it was an order.

'Come here, Patricia.'

'Granny, no,' Patty answered, and there was real panic in her voice.

It was obvious what was going to happen. She was going to be spanked, spanked as a genuine punishment. I had to try to help her.

There were various coats hanging up in the hall, and I took one, a blue duffle coat. I pulled it quickly on, to find the hem barely covered my bottom, and one sleeve was inside out, getting me in a tangle. It was still better than being stark naked, and there was no time to change, with Patty babbling out apologies and pleading not to be punished but getting nowhere.

'. . . no, Granny, it's not fair, not in front of my friends. Do it later if you really must, but —'

'Come along, Patricia. Best get it over with and perhaps they won't see.'

'They'll hear. Granny, please, they don't even know I get spanked, not by you. It's a game to them, just play –'

'Patricia.'

Jean's voice was patient and firm and brooked no refusal. Patty's answer was a sob of misery and consternation, just as my sleeve finally gave way. The duffle coat would barely close over my boobs, and I had to hold it, making me acutely conscious of how silly I looked as I stepped into the front room, Kay following faithfully behind.

Jean was seated on the same two-seater sofa I'd occupied the night before, bolt upright, her legs extended to make a lap. Patty stood in front of her, pink with shame and still arguing, but obviously just about to get down across her grandmother's lap. Jean looked up and Patty turned around, closing her eyes in embarrassment as she realised I must have heard. Jean obviously expected me to speak, but it was a moment before I could find anything to say. I couldn't just demand she stop, I had no right to, not if Patty accepted it, but it really wasn't fair to do it with us in the house.

'I . . . I'm not sure this is very fair, Jean,' I finally managed. 'Not that I'm trying to interfere with your personal choices, or –'

'Precisely,' she interrupted me, her voice cold and definite, 'you should not interfere. This is between Patricia and myself. Please leave the room.'

'Yes, but . . . I mean, no . . . I mean, it wasn't even Patty's fault. I went out first. I put the hosepipe out.'

'Are you saying you are the one who should be punished?'

'No! I'm saying nobody should be punished, not . . . not like that! It's –'

'It's not right? Is that what you were going to say?' she asked. 'You yourself advocate corporal punishment.'

'Yes, but with consent.'

175

Her eyebrows lifted a trifle, and her reply was addressed to Patty.

'Patricia, do you consent to my right to punish you?'

'Yes, Granny,' Patty answered, a whisper full of shame and very real contrition. 'Please just leave it, Amber, you're only making it worse.'

'Maybe do it later then?' I tried. 'When we've gone.'

'I think not,' Jean answered. 'Now please leave us. Undo your trouser button, please, Patricia.'

I held my ground, trying to tell myself that it was grossly unfair for Patty to be spanked, but with both reason and instinct against me. The only even remotely sensible argument was that I should take her place, or really, be spanked as well, but that was not something I was going to admit to in a hurry. Patty had undone her trousers and was about to go over her grandmother's knee, waiting only for Kay and me to leave. The choice was between that and admitting I needed spanking myself, but I just couldn't . . .

As I stepped back to leave a voice spoke from behind me, Sophie.

'You're right, Mrs de Vrain. We were wrong to go outside when we might have been seen, especially with your court case coming up. Only it's not right to spank Patty because we were all equally at fault. If you're to spank Patty, you should spank me too.'

I looked at her in horror. She didn't think she ought to be spanked at all, she just wanted to be spanked. I could see it in her face – a mock contrition very, very different from Patty's real emotion. She'd even put a skirt on to make absolutely sure her bottom could be bared easily.

'Sophie, this isn't the time –' I began, only to be cut off.

'Thank you, Sophie,' Jean said quietly. 'You are a very sensible and honest young woman, something all too rare in this day and age. However, the responsibility lies squarely with Patricia. So if –'

She stopped and drew a sigh. Gemma had come in, now in jeans and a skinny top. Angel was standing at the door, also dressed and looking hesitant. Sophie spoke again.

'I am at least as responsible for what happened as Patty, Mrs de Vrain. What you're doing is unjust.'

It was a blatant lie, and I opened my mouth to say so, then shut it, because if anybody was responsible other than Patty, it was me.

'I appreciate what you are saying,' Jean answered, now somewhat impatient, 'but this is my house and Patricia is my granddaughter, so if you wouldn't mind –'

'Please!' Patty broke in suddenly. 'I can't bear it, I –'

'I'll take your place,' Sophie said quickly. 'I should, shouldn't I? Patty told me not to go outside, Mrs de Vrain, but I wouldn't take any notice. It's not fair to punish her and not me, and you said justice was important.'

She was lying through her teeth, just to get her bottom spanked as a real punishment. I could have done it to her myself, I was so cross with her, but if she wanted it in Patty's place . . .

Patty didn't want it, for all her acceptance. She was already close to tears, and shaking. Jean looked up at her.

'Well, Patricia?'

For an instant, Patty's face was working with emotion, and I could just imagine her raging guilt with the prospect of escape open in front of her if only she lied. Finally, she nodded. Jean heaved a heavy sigh and spoke again.

'Very well, Sophie, if I have your permission, and on the strict understanding that you accept punishment from me?'

Sophie nodded, and how Jean managed to miss the sudden expression of ecstasy that passed across her face I couldn't imagine. Perhaps she didn't miss it at all.

'And the rest of you?' she asked. 'Do you have Sophie's honesty? Gemma?'

Gemma made a face, but she didn't answer. Kay glanced at me, her eyes full of guilt, but she said nothing. I felt the same, wanting to own up, knowing I should, but quite unable to submit myself to the indignity of a punishment spanking across Jean de Vrain's lap. With Sophie there, never mind the others, it would be round all my friends within days, and would eventually get to people like Mr Protheroe. I could already see his red sweaty face as he tried to make me go over the story. I held my tongue, but I was promising myself that once I got Sophie alone she was really going to suffer. When it was obvious none of us was going to answer, Jean spoke again.

'Very well. I shall spank Patricia, also Sophie. The rest of you may watch, and I hope you feel ashamed of yourselves. Come across my knee, Patricia.'

'In front of them?' Patty wailed.

'In front of them,' Jean echoed. 'I think it only suitable.'

Nobody answered and, for a moment, the silence was broken only by a single miserable sob from Patty as she laid herself down across her grandmother's lap with her hips lifted so that her jeans could be pulled down. Jean made short work of it, hauling on the waistband to peel them down, and the seat of Patty's knickers was showing – pink ones with a slight frill. Gemma spoke, her voice so quiet it was barely audible.

'I . . . I should be punished too, Mrs de Vrain.'

Jean's response was a nod of acceptance, and she began to spank, applying firm, hard swats to the chubbiest part of her granddaughter's bottom, thorough and matter-of-fact, her expression showing only determination to see a job done properly. I watched, boiling with emotion, pity and chagrin, but mostly guilt and a horrible sick feeling for my own cowardice as Patty's ritual continued, her bottom warmed just enough to get what was happening to her right into her head before her grandmother's hands went to the waistband of her knickers.

'Not bare, please, Granny,' Patty said softly, pleading.

Jean didn't even bother to answer, pushing the little pink knickers down, only for Patty to suddenly snatch them back, gripping them determinedly, although the top half of her bottom crease was already showing.

'No, please, not bare, Granny, not bare!' she wailed.

Still Jean didn't answer, her face set in very real anger as she tugged hard at her granddaughter's knickers, hauling one side right down, to bare a single cheek and most of Patty's crease. Patty began to kick and struggle, in real panic, saying no over and over again.

'You know your pants are coming down, young lady, now let go!' Jean hissed.

I couldn't see the fuss, when we'd seen everything, but it mattered to Patty because she began to cry, little choking sobs with her face buried in her free hand, still clinging hard on to her knickers with the other, although they were already so far down her fanny showed from the back as she began to buck and squirm. Jean gave a click of her tongue, perhaps expressing irritation that Patty was taking it so badly, perhaps trying to hide sympathy, then I realised.

Patty's cheeks had come far enough open to show her anus, neat and pink and perfectly clean, but with a piece of string hanging from the hole, a piece of string that ended in a small black plastic ring. She had anal beads in, the special treat she'd asked for from me: probably having them pulled out as she came, perhaps after a good spanking. As Jean took hold of the ring I realised that was more or less what Patty was going to get, only in very, very different circumstances.

'Patricia, really,' Jean sighed, and pulled.

The string began to emerge, a good six inches before Patty's anus started to pout and a bead appeared, a round black bulge in the open pink ring. I could feel for her, with a vengeance, imagining myself held over my own grandmother's knee as she slowly extracted a string of pleasure beads from up my bottom. It didn't bear thinking about, and Patty was sobbing bitterly as the beads were pulled slowly free of her anus, emerging one by one as her little wet ring spread and closed. As each one popped free she gave a little gasp, until the final one was out and her bumhole was left wet and sticky. Jean held up the string of beads, inspecting them with a look of disgust mixed with patience on her face. They were quite dirty.

'Gemma, if you would,' she stated.

Gemma took the beads and ran from the room. Patty had let go of her knickers when the string in her bumhole was discovered, and they were quickly taken down, all the way to her knees, where her jeans were already tangled. Utterly defeated and crying bitterly, she lay limp across her grandmother's lap, until the spanking began again and she'd begun to kick and jerk to the slaps.

I was staring at Patty's bottom, watching her cheeks bounce and ripple as she was spanked, with her skin going slowly red and every slap adding a fresh sob to her crying. She kicked a lot, for a girl getting spanked by hand, with her knees together and her lower legs pumping or kicking out at right angles to each other. Her fanny and bumhole showed, despite her best efforts to keep her legs together, because she was just too slim, a thoroughly rude display, and it was impossible not to think of myself in the same awful position. She was wet too, her fanny juicy and open, her bumhole moist in the middle where the beads had been pulled out, which made it so much worse because it was her own grandmother spanking her.

The spanking wasn't that hard and it wasn't long, maybe a hundred firm, purposeful smacks, meant to hurt and to teach her a lesson, not to turn her on. It worked because when she finally got up she was streaming tears and went straight to the corner, to stand with her face to the wall and her hands on her head, red bum showing, the same humiliating finish to the ritual of spanking punishment as outlined again and again in *Slap Happy*.

Patty was still sobbing, her head hung low, and she didn't even turn around as Sophie stepped forwards to take her turn. Kay moved close to me, holding my arm as Sophie laid herself submissively across Jean's lap and lifted her bottom to have her skirt pulled up. She was shaking with excitement, and I found myself wanting to teach her a lesson more than ever. I could see her face, her eyes closed in utter bliss as her tarty red mini was turned up to show off her knickers, but Jean couldn't.

I was furious with her, but it was false, a deflection of my anger and guilt, because I knew that if anyone should be spanked at all, other than Patty, it should be me. Refusing was going to make me feel awful. So was accepting, but maybe not as much, and there was an awful inevitability about the ritual as it began, with Jean applying a dozen spanks to the seat of Sophie's little white knickers. Gemma came next, and then who? Kay? Angel even? Me?

Sophie behaved like the slut she is, lifting her bottom to have her knickers pulled down more easily and moving forwards to keep it up and make sure her fat little cheeks were wide enough apart to show off her bumhole and the rear pouch of her very wet fanny, absolutely revelling in her own shame and exposure. She barely squeaked as she was punished, just making little mewing noises in her throat as each smack fell, and even staying in place when she was done, hoping for more.

Jean must have realised Sophie was enjoying it, but she was standing no nonsense. Sophie was sent to stand next to Patty, nose to the wall and her hands on her head, her chubby peach flushed pink and squeezing a little in her excitement. Jean took no notice, but patted her lap for Gemma, who'd come back. She went over, but with none of Sophie's enthusiasm. The ritual began: jeans taken well down, a few firm smacks to the seat of a pair of diminutive blue knickers, knickers down with the jeans, bum up high enough to make sure every last scrap of her modesty had been taken away, the spanking, a hundred or so hard swats that had Gemma kicking and mewling with her little shaved fanny and tiny bumhole on plain view, against the wall to show her red bum and think on her punishment.

It was done: three girls lined up against the wall with their smacked bottoms on show, three girls standing fidgeting and biting their lips, knowing they deserved the same, knowing they'd lose something of their friends' respect and their own if they didn't take what was coming to them. I knew what I should do, but there's a stubborn streak in me. There was in Angel too, because I knew she wouldn't give in, not after the state she'd got in over her wrestling punishment, not the girl who was worshipped as a goddess by just about every submissive man in London and the home counties, not . . .

. . . the girl who stepped past me and laid herself passively across Jean de Vrain's lap with her bottom lifted to allow her trousers to be taken down. I could only gape, feeling betrayed and amazed. Even Jean looked a little surprised because she'd seen Angel at the puppy show and knew what she was like, or rather, what she was like in a club. Not that it stopped her – one hand was immediately pushed in under Angel's waist to get at her jeans – but she did at least ask.

'I do not wish you to feel obliged to accept this, Angel, but if you are certain?'

Angel nodded her head, no more. I felt my breath

come out in a little gasp and she turned, looking right at me, her expression completely serious.

'It is right, Amber. If Patty was wrong so were we.'

I didn't answer, I couldn't, but stood watching, dumb with shock, as the ritual began again. Down came Angel's jeans, exposing her little brown bottom with her cheeks already bare because all she had on was a tiny green thong that covered next to nothing. She got spanked with it up anyway, the same dozen or so firm, even swats. The thong came down, all the way to her knees, and she was showing behind, her bumhole still wet with my spit. She was spanked, methodically, without emotion, at least on Jean's part, Angel trying to hold herself, but producing a series of little yelps and squirming her bottom as if she had an itchy fanny. As soon as it was over she went to stand in line by the wall, jeans and knickers now around her ankles, her dark bottom flushed purple. Kay and I stood alone.

'Amber, I think –,' Kay began.

'Just do it.' I sighed.

She went and I was alone. Jean gave a knowing nod as Kay got down across her knee, rubber-clad bottom stuck well up, ready for spanking, her little tail poised over it. Finally, the ritual was broken, which gave me a quite pointless but satisfying sense of rebellion. *Slap Happy* said nothing about the punishment of puppy-girls.

Not that it seemed to faze Jean de Vrain for more than an instant. She simply applied her first few swats to the straining rubber seat of Kay's puppy pants and then rolled them down, exposing the sweaty, talc-smeared skin beneath. Kay's rear end was in a fine state, her skin wet, her tiny brown anus slippery, her fanny swollen and caked with juice from her orgasms. It made no difference. She was spanked exactly as the others had been, only with more of a fuss, kicking and squealing, with her fists thumping the sofa and her legs flying wide to show off the full spread of her sex. Then it was into the corner to join the line-up and I was standing in front of Jean, who was looking up at me, questioning.

'And Miss Oakley? I suppose you are too ... too dominant to accept what your friends have taken?'

I was stammering out my reply immediately, struggling to find reasons I knew did not exist.

'No, it's not that, not at all, it's ... it's just that I don't think it's appropriate –'

'Not appropriate? Yet it is appropriate for your friends?'

'No! I mean, yes ... they make their own choices, but ... but –'

'Whatever is the matter? One would think you'd never been spanked before.'

'Of course I've been spanked, you saw –'

'You've never been spanked by another woman?'

'Yes. Many times, but –'

'Then why so much fuss?'

'I ... I ...'

'Amber,' she said, 'I have been spanking women since long before you were born, and I assure you that you are no different from any other, only perhaps rather more stubborn than most. You have nothing I've not seen before, and considering your behaviour on the lawn I hardly think you need give yourself airs. Nevertheless, if you do not feel you should be spanked, I –'

'OK, do it,' I snapped. 'Just do it.'

'Are you sure?'

'Yes.'

'Quite sure?'

'Yes, Jean, quite sure. You can spank me.'

'Very well, but that's Mrs de Vrain to you, I think, as I'll shortly be taking your pants down.'

'I don't have any on,' I replied, my voice every bit as sulky as Patty's had been before.

'Nor you do,' she answered.

184

I looked down, realising that the sides of my duffle coat were a little open, showing my bare fanny beneath. My face was already screwed up in humiliation, and I felt it get worse at the thought that if she made me take my coat off I'd be the only one in the nude. Sure enough.

'I think you had better take Patricia's coat off, don't you?' Jean suggested.

'Yes, Je ... Mrs de Vrain.' I sighed, and shrugged it free from my shoulders to let it fall to the ground.

She coughed. I bent to pick up the coat and laid it carefully across the back of a chair. She patted her lap and suddenly the lump in my throat was so large I couldn't swallow and couldn't speak. I came to her, burning with humiliation for what was coming to me, for the fact that I was stark naked, for the fuss I'd made when all the others had at least shown some grace, but above for all for the fact that I was going to be spanked and that there was nothing special whatsoever about it. I was just the latest in a long, long line of women put through the same shameful ritual, the only difference was that I didn't have any knickers to pull down.

I could feel my tears welling up in my eyes as I laid myself down across her lap and lifted my bottom into what I knew was the required spanking position, raised enough to let me show behind and ensure that there was no modesty left to me whatsoever. I felt the cool air on my fanny and I knew she could see – the rich gold puff of my pubic hair, my plump, pouty lips and the knots of flesh between, my wet hole ready for use because I'd become excited. My cheeks came apart, slightly sticky, and my bumhole was showing too, pink in a dark ring which I always feel makes me look as if I'm dirty.

My bottom felt huge – and let's face it, fat – a great wobbling split sphere of girlflesh so much bigger than anyone else's in the room, let alone the woman who was about to punish me. My boobs felt agonisingly prominent too: fat and heavy and pendulous beneath my chest; embarrassingly, shamefully large, and bare. My belly even felt big, and I know it's not, but it still felt that way, one more terrible detail to my exposure.

Jean's hand settled on my bottom, just gently, somehow kindly, and I just burst into tears, absolutely howling as my spanking began, a pathetic, miserable blubbering as my big fat bottom began to bounce to the slaps and my boobs began to swing and slap together. I couldn't control myself, I didn't even try, my legs kicking wide and my fists pounding the sofa and the floor, my head shaking to scatter hot tears on to my arms and over the carpet.

It hurt so much, even though I'd had harder many a time before. Every slap stung like fire, until my whole bottom was aglow and I was gasping and begging her to stop, to slow down, anything to relieve the agony of my shame and the furious heat of my rear end, and all the while blubbering incontinently, showing less dignity even than Patty, and in front of all of them, even my own girlfriend.

The state I was in didn't matter, not that I was crying, not that I was in the nude, not who was watching, nothing. I was spanked, just like the others, no less hard, no harder, no less long, no longer, and when it was over I was let up and sent to stand against the wall, just like the others. My hands went to my bottom, clutching my hot cheeks, and I was feeling desperately sorry for myself as I walk across to join the end of the line of spanked girls.

We were left there for ten minutes by the clock on the mantelpiece, feeling utterly ashamed of ourselves. At least I was, for the awful fuss I'd made, both about being spanked at all and for the way I'd behaved during my spanking. It was worse for me though. At least they had some clothes on, I was naked, not just bare behind, but nude, red bottomed and in the nude, still snivelling as I listened to the gentle ticking of the clock and wished I could cover myself or at the very least take my hands off my head and soothe my poor, spanked cheeks.

I'd never known ten minutes to pass so slowly, but finally Jean spoke and I realised the time was up.

'I think a little quiet time would do us all good, don't you? Up to your bedrooms, all of you, until teatime.'

We went without a murmur of protest, six bare-bottomed girls trooping up the stairs in a line. I knew from her magazine that she'd once accepted girls who wanted to be spanked, for whatever reason, and wondered how many punished women had climbed the same stairs. Plenty, I was sure, some full of relief or feelings of absolution, some angry, some in tears, some aroused, most with their heads spinning with a combination of contradictory emotions, just as mine was. I knew what I was going to do though because for all the chagrin the knowledge brought me I couldn't help it: I was going to masturbate.

I took Kay's hand as we reached the landing. We went into the bedroom together, to lie down on the double bed, side by side. She'd left her puppy pants rolled down anyway, but quickly pushed them right off. Her top went the same way and we were both nude. Our thighs came open, our hands slid down across each other's bellies, our fingers burrowed into the wet grooves below. She began to rub in my crease and I in hers, with never a word spoken. My eyes closed and I took one breast in hand, feeling how big I was, how heavy, caressing my hard nipple as Kay briefly slid a finger in up my fanny to pull out some more juice.

My guilt and ill feeling were gone. I'd been wrong, completely wrong, to resist, even for a moment. I should have been the first to volunteer, accepting my responsibility, and if Patty had to be spanked, then so did I. Not that it mattered because I'd got what I deserved in the end, what I needed, and it felt so good.

I'd had my bottom spanked and been sent to bed. My bottom was hot and my girlfriend's fingers were working me towards orgasm, as mine were her. I was in the nude, and I'd been in the nude while I was spanked, stripped and punished ... stripped and punished over Jean's lap ... over Mrs de Vrain's lap ... stripped and punished over Mrs de Vrain's lap with my fat, wobbling bottom stuck up in the air, my fanny on show, my bumhole winking in my pain, in floods of tears, blubbering pathetically over a strong woman's lap as my bottom was spanked ... spanked ... spanked ...

As I came, I cried out, calling Kay's name as at the last instant my mind turned to the fact that she'd got it too, the same bittersweet ritual applied to her own sweet little bottom, she and I spanked together by a woman strong enough to deal with us both and four more besides. We'd been spanked together and now we were masturbating together, our minds full of the pain and the shame we'd been through, so awful, and so wonderful.

My fingers were still hard at work on Kay's fanny as I came slowly down from my orgasm, but her muscles were already tightening and, in another moment, she came too, calling out my name as it hit her, just as I had hers. For a long moment her whole body was rigid, before she sank down on to the bed with a contented sigh and at last rolled over to cuddle up to my chest.

Five

Our weekend at Jean de Vrain's had been a success by any standards. We had the whole routine for the international puppy show worked out in detail, we had great fun together, I'd made friends with Angel properly and I'd been given one of the most emotionally intense spankings of my life. Unlike Mr Protheroe, I didn't regret it at all, and the fuss I'd made beforehand just seemed silly, even if I knew that given the circumstances I was quite capable of making just as big a fuss again.

We'd even worked out how to take our revenge on Morris and Melody for the betting scam. Morris was not stupid, and he would know perfectly well we'd want to get back at him for what he'd done. It would amuse him, and yet that wouldn't stop him doing his best to outwit us because that would amuse him even more.

There was going to be a rematch at the club night in Belfast, both to open the evening with a bang and to decide on a winner for the annual competition, which he was determined not to abandon. That meant me wrestling either Vicky or Mel. Vicky would be favourite, Mel a close second and me well behind, but not as far as I'd have been before my fight against Angel by a long way. After London, Morris would be playing it a little carefully, but there would still be betting. There always was.

We had several options. Vicky could be persuaded to lose against me, or against Mel. Possibly Mel could even be bribed, but it was the hard option and one that would inevitably involve my submission to her, and probably Kay's as well. We could arrange any number of double and triple bluffs, with rumours circulating about all sorts of things. All of them were possible, and all of them were completely useless because anything we could think of, Morris would have thought of already. He would just turn the tables on us. He ran the book too, which gave him a major advantage.

We had a much better solution. After the wrestling and the puppy show, when all the money was in and the doors closed, the club would be at its peak, but with a another two hours before it closed. The night's takings would be in a strongbox in whatever Morris was using as an office, guarded by two of his regular bouncers. Sophie knew them both, very well, and was often sent in to give them a treat. She'd ask to be taken at each end and they were sure to comply. They also knew me, and it would be the work of moments to borrow the strongbox.

Morris would go berserk when he found out the money was missing, and we'd leave him to tear his hair out for a few minutes before telling him we had it and demanding Melody's surrender for its return. He'd be genuinely angry, but Mel would take it the way it was intended, hopefully. In any event, Angel was keen on the idea, and it was her revenge more than mine.

The three weeks passed quickly, with nothing out of the ordinary going on and everything ready to go. Morris had provided every detail we could possibly have needed to get to Belfast and the venue where the puppy show was to be held. He'd even covered the cost of our flights and rooms, in a hotel near the university. The actual club was to be held in an old theatre, and when I saw it I had to admit it was perfect. We'd flown from Stanstead, which is very easy for me, and had come over early to have a look around and to do what we could to secure an advantage. Morris, Melody, Harmony, Hudson Staebler and the lawyer, Mr Montague, were drinking in the hotel bar when we arrived, and they took us straight over to the theatre.

It was great, all fading gold paint and red plush, providing a wonderfully baroque feel, perhaps most suitable for wild orgies with debauched men and fleshy young women, but with far more style than the warehouses and old factories Morris generally used. There were three tiers of boxes, a great sweep of stalls, and the gods above, which he'd closed off with crimson drapes to provide a play area well stocked with bondage equipment. The stage was already set up, with the wrestling ring in place, while the backstage area was perfect for storing all the props. There were even proper changing rooms, into one of which Kay and I dumped our stuff, locking it and pocketing the key.

The Japanese man and Sakura were apparently already there, having come over several days before. Morris seemed impressed, praising her beauty and also her manners, which knowing him meant she'd offered to suck his cock without having to be asked more than once. Mistress Leash was also rumoured to be in Belfast, but nobody had seen her, only the apparently limitless supply of men she had at her beck and call. There were several other competitors from abroad too, most of whom had used the event as an excuse for a longer trip. Morris had a programme printed out, which showed Sakura being exhibited third and Bitch seventh, positions that had cost Sophie a long, slow buggering the week before.

We managed to find where Morris' office was before leaving the theatre, a room in behind the booking office, which was ideal for our purposes. The two bouncers were there, along with the security guard for the theatre, a heavyset man called MacCruiskeen. All three tried to flirt with us, and I couldn't imagine any of them being a problem for Sophie. MacCruiskeen also had a Rottweiler, but it was old, also smelly, and which didn't even pause in licking its balls when we came in. The theatre was also full of all sorts of odd little nooks and crannies, ideal for our wicked scheme. Best of all was the props room, entirely full of ropes, furniture, scenes, old costumes and general junk, the ideal place to take Mel for her punishment.

I was feeling deliciously naughty as we walked back to the hotel, brimful of anticipation, and apprehension too. If everything went to plan it would be a truly glorious night, and I was even resigned to being thoroughly humiliated in the wrestling ring. After all, if it was by Vicky I could take it out on her anytime I liked, with the full cooperation of her husband Anderson, and if it was by Mel it would make our final revenge all the sweeter.

It was mid-afternoon and the hotel bar was relatively empty, with one group and a few serious solitary drinkers, all apparently locals. Kay and I joined the others at a table and accepted drinks, all seven of us discussing the coming evening. Morris' programme showed twelve competitors for the puppy show, among whom I was familiar with only four, but as we'd suspected, Mistress Leash and Sakura were the serious competition. There was also the matter of who would be making the decisions.

'Who did you choose for judges in the end?' I asked Morris.

'Ourselves,' he answered, gesturing to Hudson, 'and Miss Barbara, who's from Dublin.'

'We couldn't agree,' Hudson explained, 'but it works OK this way.'

I nodded, thinking. Miss Barbara was a reasonable choice, not an expert perhaps, but getting there. She was genuine anyway, and game, having gone in for the wrestling and helped at the auction. Morris at least I knew, and if he regarded bribery and corruption as all part of the game, then at least we were on a level playing field. There was only one problem.

As we'd already agreed in the car on the way back down from Lincoln, the judges were to be offered oral sex as a bribe, especially if our competitors seemed to be up to the same tricks. It seemed that they were, probably – Sakura at least – but Kay and I were the only people there, which left the question of which was worse, giving my girlfriend to Morris Rathwell to suck his penis or doing it myself, unless I waited. I decided to wait.

Hudson Staebler was something of an unknown quantity. I was sure his bluff, honest Uncle Sam act was superficial at best, because after all he spent his time amusing himself by putting girls on dog leads, but that didn't mean he'd take kindly to an open offer of bribery. Possibly he'd be better approached diplomatically, with an offer to suck his cock but no explanation as to why. That way he could politely decline if he wanted to, and no harm done. The offer would also look better coming from Sophie, Kay or myself, as we were known to be supporters of Patty and Angel, Rubba Dobie and Bitch, but weren't actually competitors. Again it seemed best to wait for Sophie.

Miss Barbara I could take care of myself, although, again, I had no idea if she was corruptible. As with Hudson, it was probably best to make the offer and then play it by ear, while choosing her to service gave me an excellent excuse to avoid sucking cock, something I try not to do if I can possibly help it.

I found myself sitting next to Mr Montague, making me wonder how Jean de Vrain's court case was going. She was a mad old cow, but I was fond of her in a way, and she had given me one of the most intense spankings of my life, while the decision was evidently important for everyone into kinky sex, or plain old-fashioned spanking for that matter. After all, if the trial went badly the wrong way she might even end up in prison.

'You're handling the *Slap Happy* case, aren't you?' I asked as he began on his second bottle of stout.

'I was, yes,' he answered.

'But not any more?'

'Oh, no. Didn't Morris tell you? The Director of Public Prosecutions wouldn't take it up.'

'But I thought charges had already been brought?'

'It doesn't work that way.'

'No?'

'It's a quirk of the system,' he explained. 'There has to be an arresting officer, who therefore takes on a number of responsibilities as regards the case. Once an arrest has been made there is considerable pressure to bring charges, but that doesn't necessarily mean the DPP will support those charges, far from it.'

'Oh.'

'This.'

'This is a typical case. Take an over-zealous rural constable, perhaps with a bee in his bonnet about sexual offences and certainly no understanding of the ethics of sadomasochism, and he's likely to wade in with all guns blazing, metaphorically speaking, of course.'

I took a healthy swallow of my own drink. The implications were more than a little humiliating. Had I realised that the whole thing was likely to have been dropped, the auction to support Jean's fighting fund would have seemed a good deal less important. I could even have avoided my ignominious public spanking from the appalling Mr Protheroe. The memory made my stomach tighten and my fanny twitch, bringing back the feelings of submission my punishment had inspired.

An hour later and there was still no sign of the others, while the alcohol, thoughts of what I'd been put through by Protheroe and what I was likely to be put through by Vicky or Mel had begun to dwell on my mind. Just hours to go, two cocks to suck and a fanny to lick. I knew I should do it, or at least one, if only to get myself in the right headspace for the wrestling, but couldn't bring myself to make the first move. It wasn't necessary. When I went to the bar to get a fresh round of drinks, Morris followed me.

'Let me help you with those,' he offered, coming up beside me as the barman began to put the glasses and bottles out on the counter.

'Thank you,' I replied, a little surprised at the offer.

'Puppy show's looking good,' he remarked. 'I hear you went up to help Patty Whitworth give Bitch her final training?'

'Yes,' I admitted, blushing at the memory of my spanking and hoping it hadn't filtered back.

'You on the team then?'

'I suppose so . . . yes.'

'Cute girl, Gemma, flaky, but cute. Maybe not quite as cute as Sakura.'

'We have a good routine.'

'So do they, believe me, very good. You've got some stiff competition there, Amber, very stiff.'

I sighed. He might have been more obvious, but only by getting his cock out at the bar.

'That's Gemma's job, really,' I told him, 'or Patty's.'

'A bird in the hand is worth two in the bush, Amber, or right now, a bird in Unrshaw's Hotel is worth two at Birmingham International. Room twelve, first floor. See you in ten minutes.'

I nodded, still hesitant, but telling myself I could hardly expect Patty or Gemma to do it if I wasn't willing myself, and he had asked. Still my stomach tightened at the prospect of taking his cock in my mouth. There was no point even in hiding what was happening, except possibly from Hudson Stabler. Morris would certainly tell Mel, and if she beat me in the wrestling she might make my punishment that much worse, but no more. I put the drinks I'd carried over down on the table and swallowed my shot of Irish whiskey in one.

'I'm going up to take a bath,' I told them. 'See you in a minute, Kay.'

She nodded, her eyes briefly questioning. I made for the door, my stomach tying itself in knots at the prospect of what I was about to do. Rationally, I knew I was being silly, but rationality has nothing to do with it. I was going to have to suck cock, and not just any cock, but Morris Rathwell's. A little voice at the back of my head was telling me I was a slut, and only looking for an excuse, but it wasn't true, not really.

We were on the third floor, which gave me no justification whatsoever for hanging around on the first-floor landing. A man passed on his way up, and gave me a glanced compounded of lust and contempt. I was blushing immediately, realising he must have mistaken me for a call girl, and would have said something, only it wasn't really that far from the truth. I was waiting for a man, for sex, and if I was paying a bribe rather than doing it for the money, it was a small enough difference.

By the time Morris appeared I was fidgeting badly and about ready to give up. He grinned as he opened the door and patted my bottom to steer me inside. His room was a lot bigger than mine: a suite, with the bathroom and bedroom opening off to one side. Assuming he'd want me on the bed, I started across the room, only for him to flop out his cock and balls and sit down in an armchair, his legs well spread.

'Down you go, love,' he stated. 'Been a while since you had a dose of the happy stick, isn't it?'

I nodded, looking at the skinny little cock in his lap, already stirring, but I could see I was going to have to suck him erect, on my knees too, kneeling for him. Down I went, on to the soft carpet, still with the image of myself as a call girl in my head, sucking cock for any man willing to pay my price. He was smiling as I shuffled close, more amused than excited. I pulled my top up and quickly took off my bra, leaving my boobs bare and heavy on my chest. He gave an appreciative chuckle as I took them in my hands, showing him what I'd got. He smiled, then spoke.

'Why do girls always get their tits out when they suck cock?'

Fresh embarrassment welled up in me, but I said nothing. My breasts felt very big, and very sensitive, also vulnerable, and my nipples had come erect. Morris licked his lips and slid a little further forwards in his chair, his cock and balls right in front of me, ready for my mouth.

'Open wide,' he said, 'and in goes the lollipop.'

My mouth came open, and I'd done it – taken his penis between my lips, then right in. He sighed in pleasure and my mouth filled with the taste of cock as I began to suck, mouthing on him and pushing my tongue on to his shaft until he'd begun to swell. His hand came down, curling around his balls as he started to stroke himself, and, with his cock fully hard, to masturbate into my mouth. He was quite small and thin, what he called the ideal cock for girls' bumholes, something he put to the test whenever he could. Eager to bring him off quickly, I made a slide of my lips, taking him as deep as I could, with the rounded bulb of his cock head pushing into my throat.

'Nice,' he said and sighed. 'You want me to fuck your head, yeah?'

He'd already taken hold of me, by my ears, and he began to pull my head up and down on his erection, fucking in my mouth. Every push was jamming his cock head into my throat, and I was struggling not to gag, but let him do it, willing to take my mouthful but hoping I wouldn't choke on his spunk, or worse, be sick down my tits. It would make him laugh.

I really thought he was going to come when he stopped, suddenly, still holding me by the ears, with his cock well in.

'How about a good buggering?'

I shook my head on his cock.

'Come on, love, it won't take a minute, and you're going in the bath anyway.'

Again I shook my head, my bumhole twitching and my cheeks tightening in my knickers. He began to fuck my head once more, with slow, deep strokes.

'Oh, well, your lose as well as mine. I buggered Sakura last night, with her bloke watching. Dirty bastards, the Japs; very considerate though. Gave her an enema, he did, before he let me up her arse. Let me watch it come out, too, in the bath. What a laugh.'

I closed my eyes, thinking of the poor Japanese girl, kneeling in the bath tub with her bottom hole spurting filthy water as her master and Morris looked on. Morris would have laughed, I knew, and I could almost feel the well-lubricated hose sliding in up my own bum. His fucking grew suddenly urgent, his grip tightened on my ears and, as he spoke again, I knew he was going to come.

'She's great ... arse like a peach ... tiny, but so round and juicy ... tight too –'

He came, full down my throat, his cock rammed into my windpipe, his mind not even set on me, but on Sakura's bottom. Shame and resentment bubbled up in my head as I struggled to swallow his spunk, only for everything to be pushed aside as some went down the wrong hole and I went into violent spasms as I jerked back, coughing up spunk and mucus and spit all over my top and tits as Morris calmly finished himself off in my face.

I was dripping spunk. Some had gone in my eye and bits were hanging from my nose, while my top was foul and my tits badly soiled. Morris just chuckled as he took a handful of my top to wipe his cock clean. I let him, as I needed to change anyway, biting down my resentment in the knowledge of a job well done. As I ran for the bathroom his voice followed me.

'That was great, thanks, not that you need have bothered. Sophie had already seen to it.'

I couldn't answer because I was still coughing up spunk. He'd tricked me, but as I thought of the revenge we'd planned and the state he would get in, my reaction was one of grim satisfaction. I took my top off, and my bra, both of which were soiled, and spent a moment washing down my breasts. Morris could see me, and watched with interest, enjoying the simple fact that I was topless despite having just come. As soon as I'd washed my mouth out I put a question to distract him.

'How are the odds for the wrestling tonight?'

'No betting tonight, not a proper book anyway,' he answered. 'Too many stroppy types after last time, and half of them are over here. That guy Protheroe lost really badly, and he won't leave it ... That's a thought – you wouldn't spend the night with him, would you?'

'No!'

'Didn't think so. No harm in asking. He knows he won't get his money back, so he's angling for some action instead. I'll have to send Sophie round.'

'Do you have to prostitute every woman you know?'

'No, but it's a laugh. For the wrestling, we're going to do tag teams.'

'Tag teams?'

'Yeah, you know, two in each team, and you've got to touch hands to bring your partner back into the ring.'

'Yes, but why? Shouldn't it be Vicky and Mel, then me against the winner?'

'Yeah, but the thing is, it's not fair if Mel and Vicky have just been in the ring and you're fresh. So what I reckon is this: you go in all together, as tag teams, you and Vicky against Mel and Angel. If Mel and Angel win, then Mel goes in the final against you, if you and Vicky win, then Vicky. Fair?'

'Fair enough, I suppose. Is, um ... is Hudson Staebler ... is he –'

'Corruptible? Not really, no. I'll send him up and you can suck him off, if you fancy him? Might do you some good.'

I hesitated just too long before refusing. Morris had put his cock away and was making for the door.

'Hang on,' I called out. 'You don't . . . I mean, could you ask Kay to bring me a clean top and bra? I mean, later, that is –'

'Sure,' he answered, and shut the door.

I went to sit on the bed, wondering exactly what I was doing, sitting in a Belfast hotel room waiting for men to visit me so that I could suck their cocks. It was a horribly sleazy thing to do, but I couldn't deny that it was turning me on. Hudson Staebler had a nice cock too: big and smooth and pale. I thought of masturbating, just a quick rub before he came up, because if I did it while I was down on him he was sure to want to fuck me. Maybe I'd let him . . .

The door went, suggesting that Morris had more or less swapped places with Hudson. Everyone would know what was going on, and I was blushing pink before I could tell myself they'd have guessed anyway. I lay back, wanting to look a little more relaxed and seductive, just in time, as the door opened. He walked in, big and cool and easy in his white suit. I didn't know what to say, so rolled on to my back, taking my boobs in my hands.

'Morris said you might appreciate a visit, and it looks like he was right,' he said, his voice full of satisfaction. 'I feel privileged, seeing as how I'd heard you only liked girls.'

I shrugged, then spoke as he began to undo his belt.

'Just your cock, please, Hudson.'

'Fine.'

He pulled it out, fat and white and heavy in his hand. I scrambled over, to sit on the edge of the bed and take him in my hand, then my mouth, sucking eagerly. He began top swell, his thick foreskin rolling back against my tongue and the head within slowly emerging. I was playing with my boobs as I sucked, and wondering why I was feeling so dirty. Erect, he was every bit as fine as I remembered, thick and smooth and pale, very suckable. I wanted more too, a good fucking while I had the chance, or a man at each end, mouth and fanny as I brought myself to ecstasy under my fingers ...

I would have masturbated, but before I could get over the last of my reserve he'd come, full in my mouth. He was holding my head, and all I could do was swallow, struggling a bit in his grip, but at least half willing. It left me feeling a little sick and a little dizzy, but eager for more, and I knew there'd be no real trouble in coping with whatever Vicky or Mel had in store for me.

We chatted for a while before Kay brought my top and bra up. She gave me a studied look: a little disapproval, a little gratitude. The first was because I'd been with a man, and been pretty submissive at that. The second was because if it hadn't been me, then it should have been her.

Decent again, and feeling pleasantly aroused and in just the right frame of mind for the night ahead, I went back down, with Kay and Hudson. The bar was considerably more crowded, with several people there I recognised, including Patty, but she was on her own and did not look at all happy. Kay and I went straight over, to ask the question that had immediately come up in my mind.

'Where's Gemma?'

'She's not here.'

'Not here?'

'Not here. She threw a paddy. It was at the airport too, and we missed our plane arguing about it. I had to pay extra for the later flight and everything ... Shit! What am I supposed to do?'

'Don't get in a state, Patty. Sophie will do it, she'd love to, and she knows the routine.'

'Well ... yes, I suppose so,' Patty said and sighed. 'Where is she?'

'She's not here yet,' I answered, 'but she will be. I spoke to her last night. Do you want a drink?'

'Yes, badly. Shit!'

I went to fetch her a drink, leaving Kay to try to calm her nerves. My mouth was still full of that salty, slimy sensation, despite a thorough rinse, and I bought myself another double Irish whiskey to get rid of it.

Back at the table, Kay was explaining to Patty what had been going on.

'... couldn't agree, so they're doing it themselves, with Miss Barbara.'

'Could be worse,' Patty answered. 'I suppose we'd better do our best to bribe them.'

'I've done Morris, and Hudson,' I said, sighing. 'I haven't seen Miss Barbara.'

Patty looked at me in surprise.

'You've done Morris and Hudson? Blow jobs?'

I made a face. Kay reached out to stroke my hair.

'She's been an angel.'

'Speaking of Angels?'

'She decided to come over on the ferry, and she's not here yet.'

Even as I spoke the bar doors swung open and Angel stepped in, immediately followed by Miss Barbara. Both had their bags with them, and they shared a brief but quite intense kiss before Angel started towards us. I gave her a questioning look.

'We met up on the ferry,' she explained, 'and shared a cab. I licked her out in the back, and, girl, you should have seen that driver's face! I thought he was going to crash.'

'Lucky he didn't,' Patty answered her. 'That's our bribery and corruption done for the evening then. Is Greg here?'

'Yeah, somewhere about, he called me.'

'Then we just need Sophie,' I put in. 'Gemma isn't here.'

Angel had been casting puzzled glances between us, and once more I had to explain that I'd already sucked both Morris and Hudson, and Patty that Gemma wouldn't be there. I also told her she'd be wrestling, which came as a surprise, and that we'd be on opposite teams. Immediately, she was rubbing her hands in glee, delighted by a further chance to revenge herself on me. Morris was coming towards us, grinning happily, and he spoke as he arrived.

'No draw this time. It's school uniform, in pink blancmange, nice touch, huh?'

Morris' idea of school uniform would have had any real schoolgirl sent home on the spot. My pleated, red-tartan miniskirt didn't even cover my bottom, leaving my big white school knickers showing front and back, with plenty of flesh spilling out because he'd deliberately chosen ones several sizes too small. I had no bra, thanks to a piece of logic Denis Humber would have been proud of – just as adult baby-girls didn't need to wear tops because they had nothing to hide, adult schoolgirls didn't need to wear bras because, supposedly, we had nothing to put in them. Mel and I certainly did, with our blouses stretched taut across our bare chests and our nipples showing through the thin cotton, and all four of us looked thoroughly indecent. The long white socks and shiny black shoes were at least straightforward, but only because Morris hadn't been able to think of a way to make them any ruder.

Standing to one side of the stage listening to the thump of the music and ebb and swell of the crowd noise, I felt rude, and naughty, as if one of the Jean de Vrains of this world was going to catch us and spank all four of us at any moment. That was probably just as well, with four men working to fill the wrestling ring with pink blancmange, an enormous quantity of it, in which I was very likely to end up, nude. If I was on the losing team, that would just be the start of it, and with the final still to come.

Morris appeared behind us, his hands closing on his wife's bottom and mine.

'All set girls?'

'What are the rules?' Vicky asked.

'Standard tag,' he answered. 'One in the ring at a time, and a touch to let your partner change places. You stay in until both girls in one team are nude. Teams are Vicky and –'

'Oh no you don't,' Vicky cut in. 'We'll toss for it, winner gets to choose her partner.'

She'd taken a ten-penny piece from the breast pocket of her school blouse. Morris shrugged.

'Your call, Mel,' Vicky offered.

'Heads,' Mel answered and Vicky flipped the coin high, catching it neatly on the back of her hand.

'Heads it is,' Vicky announced as we craned close.

'I'll take Amber,' Mel said immediately.

Vicky made a face and we drew apart, into our two teams. We seemed pretty well evenly matched to me and, in school uniform, with ties, skirts, blouses, knickers, shoes and socks, it would be the best team who won. Already Morris was walking up to the microphone and, as the music died, he began his announcement. I leant in close to Mel.

'How about tactics?'

'OK. First off, don't worry about Angel unless she's going to get you. Concentrate on Vicky, and get rude with her. Try to get her panties off first, and spank her, maybe try and sit on her face –'

'But –'

'She's a sub at heart, right? Turn her on and we've won. Piss her off and she'll slaughter us.'

I nodded, because I could see the same tactics working on me and Vicky is mainly submissive, which

I'm not. Mel went on, quickly, as Morris was about to announce us.

'Once Vicky's stripped, we can take Angel in our own time.'

I nodded, and took her hand as Morris called out our names. The crowd raised a loud and dirty cheer as we stepped onto the stage, clapping and wolf-whistling and calling out obscene suggestions as always. I could barely see beyond the edge of the stage for the powerful spots bearing down on us, most of which were directed onto the wide, quivering lake of pink blancmange in the ring. Mel climbed up into our corner and I followed. My throat was dry and my skin had already begun to prickle with sweat from the heat, so I gratefully accepted water from Annabelle as she held up the tray chained to her wrists.

Opposite us, Vicky and Angel had climbed in, and I found my apprehension rising. Next to Vicky, and out of her heels, Angel looked slim, a waif, and yet she'd given me a run for my money before. Meanwhile, Vicky looked tougher and fitter than ever.

'Remember, go for her arse,' Mel advised as Vicky began to climb the ropes. 'Go on, you first.'

I hesitated, thinking to argue, but Mel was supposed to be the team captain. Climbing into the ring, I stepped gingerly forwards, the blancmange squashing out around my shoes and quickly slopping back, to soak into my socks. Vicky made a face, glancing down, before her eyes met mine and we began to circle. I really did not want to end up in the blancmange, but I had little choice. She came at me suddenly, gripping me hard around the waist and hurling me to the side. I just managed to twist, so that I ended up on top, and we hit the blancmange with a splash that drew cries of surprise and disgust from around the ring.

Not that I heard because I'd just had my blouse ripped wide and my boobs were out. Vicky's next motion had my blouse down my back, trapping my arms, even as the blancmange closed over her face. I hurled myself away and she came up, spluttering pink muck and completely blinded. My hands were up under her skirt in an instant, clutching for her knickers, catching the waistband and hauling with all my strength. Off they came, leaving the dark bush of her fanny on show to the entire crowd for just an instant before the blancmange oozed in to cover her modesty and soil her flesh.

She was trying to get to the ropes, slipping in the blancmange, and, as she turned, her bottom lifted, her skirt up, her slimy cheeks on full show. I caught her a cracker, splattering myself with blancmange, and another, spanking her furiously as she slithered in the mess, to the delighted laughter of the crowd and Mel's yells of encouragement. Angel reached out, touched fingers with Vicky and began to scramble quickly in. I gave back, eager for a rest, and waded quickly to my corner, to slap hands with Mel.

Just seconds in the ring and I had blancmange all over me, plastered up to my knees and spattered elsewhere: in my face and in my hair, all over my uniform and all over my chest. As always I had to leave my boobs showing, and for all that I could barely see them I could feel the gaze of the crowd on my heaving chest and my stiff nipples. It was worse just standing there than fighting, but Mel was doing well, and didn't look in need of my help.

She'd got Angel in an arm lock, face down in the blancmange, with one knee planted firmly in her back. All Angel could do was squirm in the mess as she was casually, methodically stripped. Her shoes and socks were pulled off, her skirt removed, her knickers pulled down and off. Each time she tried to resist Mel would simply dip her face in the blancmange for a while until she stopped struggling.

I thought Angel would end up nude, but Mel was enjoying herself too much, and paused to spank the wriggling black bottom beneath her. Angel gave a single, frantic lurch and Mel lost her balance, sprawling in the blancmange. Both came up fast, but neither one fast enough to gain an advantage, and Angel darted for the ropes, where Vicky was ready, her face wiped clean.

Mel could have run to me, but she stayed put. They came together, both struggling for a grip, Vicky to get Mel down, Mel to get Vicky in spanking position. Neither succeeded, unable to break each other's strength, and they were still locked together when the bell went to signal the end of the round. Mel came back to me and we shared a slippery hug before taking stock. My blouse was open, but we'd lost no clothes. Vicky was knickerless and Angel bare from the waist down, a good start by any standards. Vicky's bottom was also pink with more than just blancmange.

The moment the bell went again I came out, eager to get to grips as Angel was my opponent. She was wary, and tried to feint me off balance, but I caught her wrist and tugged hard, sending her sprawling face first in the blancmange, to the delight of the crowd. I was on her back in a moment, tugging at her tie, which she caught, leaving us in a slippery tug of war neither one of us could possibly win. She was half up, fighting to rise with me her back, and when I let go, suddenly, she went down hard, even as I wrenched the sides of her blouse open and jerked it down.

Her collar was out of her tie, her arms trapped. I had her, twisting the remains of her blouse to calm her struggles and pulling her tie back around her neck so that I could work on it with my teeth. She fought like anything, kicking and trying to bite, but the tie was soon off. Her blouse followed, wrenched off her arms, and she was stark naked, her slender body slippery with blancmange, her hair utterly soiled, naked, but not out, and even as her blouse came away she was snatching out for Vicky's hand. I beat a hasty retreat, slapping hands

207

with Mel an instant before Vicky's fingers closed on my ankle.

They were already facing up to each other as I scrambled out, and went down in the blancmange almost immediately. For all Mel's tactics, Vicky was fighting furiously. In a moment, Mel's skirt was off, then her knickers, simply torn loose, but Vicky's blouse was open too, as they went down, sideways, their bodies barely distinguishable in the pink mess as they tore at each other's clothes. Mel swore as her blouse was ripped wide, her heavy brown breasts bounding free, but she had Vicky's tie, jerking the knot free and slipping back, to sit down in the blancmange with a meaty splat. I reached out, but she was too far away, and Vicky was on her in an instant, mounting up, and they were fighting for Mel's tie as the second bell went.

Mel and Vicky separated reluctantly, and once again we took stock. Angel was nude, Vicky in shoes and socks, skirt and open blouse. Mel was about even with Vicky, in shoes and socks, bare bottom, but still with her tie as well as her ruined blouse. I'd done best, my blouse open but otherwise untouched. If we just concentrated on Vicky we had every chance of winning.

Inevitably, Angel came out first, and I went to meet her. She had nothing to lose, already naked and covered from head to toe in blancmange. I let her grapple me, holding her arms to stop her getting at my clothes before going down on my knees so I wouldn't fall over and taking her down with me. It was still a struggle, slipping in the blancmange and fighting to keep her claws off my skin. I never even realised we were up against the ropes until my skirt was suddenly hauled high, by Vicky.

Even as I twisted around to protest my knickers had been pulled out behind. Angel changed her grip and I was stuck, unable to let go without losing my blouse and maybe more. As my skirt was tucked up behind, Mel was screaming out for a foul, but Morris was in fits of laughter and took no notice. I tried to push Angel back but she clung on, and Vicky had scooped up a big handful of blancmange and dropped it down my knickers. I felt the cold, slippery muck down in the crease of my bum, and more, a second handful to join the first.

I could let them soil me or get stripped in double quick time, and I hung on, trying to break free as Vicky loaded blancmange down my knickers, handful after soggy, cold handful, until my pouch had began to bulge and sag, with the slippery mess squeezing up around my pussy and between my bum cheeks. Kicking just made it worse, and I had to take it, until at last they were satisfied and Vicky let go.

My waistband closed with a snap and the whole revolting mess was hanging heavy in my knickers and I sprawled forwards, on top of Angel. For one instant, my overloaded knickers, bulging with blancmange held well in by the tight leg holes, before Vicky landed a cracking spank full across my bottom. Blancmange exploded from the hems of my knickers, in every direction. Some went up my fanny too, cold and slimy, and, as I screamed out in shock and disgust, I let go of Angel. Instantly, my blouse was down my back, trapping my arms.

I hurled myself sideways, only to lose my blouse and sit down hard. There was a thick squelch as my bum hit the mat, and my mouth came wide as yet more blancmange was forced up my open fanny hole. Angel had my legs, grappling a shoe, and it was off before I could get control of myself. I pushed her off, slipping in the mess as I tried to get to Mel. She was quicker, tagging Vicky, who vaulted over the ropes and caught me by one ankle with my fingers an inch from Mel's.

My second shoe came off even as I was hauled back, both my socks, and I had twisted around, to catch

Vicky's blouse and jerk it up, covering her head. She fought back, but I wasn't letting go, and clung on one handed as I tore at her skirt, wrenching it down around her hips. She clung on furiously, a grip I couldn't break, and we were still struggling as the third bell went.

I was a state, nude but for my knickers, which were squelching with blancmange, and my tie. Mel hadn't even been in the ring, and it was very definitely her turn. She agreed, only for Morris to declare a free-for-all. In we went, Mel against Vicky, Angel against me, coming together quickly to go down in a welter of blancmange and soggy clothing. For a moment, my face was under the blancmange, but I'd got Angel around the waist and clung on hard, using my weight to keep her down and mount her.

Half blinded, I could see Vicky and Mel, grappling each other. Vicky's back was to me and, in an instant, I jerked her blouse down. Mel grabbed her, tugging at her clothes. Shoes came, and socks, before Angel unseated me, but I still had Vicky's blouse, Mel her skirt and, as we hurled ourselves apart, we simply peeled her from both ends. Angel had pulled my knickers down at the last moment, but it no longer mattered. They were both stark naked and we were victorious.

I stood, unsteady, to hold Vicky's blouse aloft in triumph, even as Mel straddled her and, an instant later, released the full contents of her bladder. Vicky just opened her mouth, letting it fill until the piddle had begun to bubble out at the sides, more than happy to be peed over now that she'd lost. Before Mel's stream had finished, Vicky was masturbating, rubbing herself in shameless ecstasy as the crowd hooted and cheered and the hot pee ran down over her filthy body. The moment Mel was done I took over, straddling Vicky's body and waiting until she had begun to gasp and shiver before giving her everything I could over her tits and in her mouth.

She came while I was still doing it, but I didn't stop or move aside, finishing off over her belly before dropping a neat curtsey in her face to let her kiss my bottom. Her lips met my anus to the wild cheering of the crowd, and it was done, or at least, I had helped earn Mel the right to meet me in the final.

Mel and I left the ring with our arms around each other's waists, much to the delight of the crowd, and I let my mouth open briefly under hers as we kissed in the showers at the back. I knew she might be playing mind games though, and when her hands moved to my bottom I took them gently away. She grinned as she went back to rinsing bits of blancmange out of her hair.

'I'll have you yet, Amber,' she said.

'Very likely,' I admitted.

She just chuckled, and no more was said as we finished washing. Kay had come in and, as I towelled myself down, she told me that Sophie's plane had been delayed but she was now in the air. It was cutting it fine for the puppy show, but I had the wrestling to think of first, and put it aside. Morris appeared just as I was putting my robe on, grinning and rubbing his hands.

'Great fight, girls, great fight. I knew you'd do it, love.'

'I didn't,' Mel admitted, 'and I'm not sure I wouldn't rather have lost.'

'Lost? Why?' I queried.

'Don't you know what we're wrestling in?' she asked, in genuine surprise.

'No,' I admitted. 'I'd assumed we'd be drawing for it, but –'

'Too much trouble getting all the gear over,' Morris explained.

'So we're in nappies,' Mel said and sighed. 'Nappies and plastic pants, and little frilly pinafore dresses, and booties.'

'Nappies?' I echoed, horrified.

211

'Yeah, it was that git Humber's idea,' Mel told me, shaking her head.

'Neat, eh?' Morris said happily. 'The crowd'll love it.'

'And what will be in the ring?' I asked weakly. 'Not baby food, Morris, please.'

'Nah, Humber managed to get a few commercial volume tubs of some cream you use for nappy rash. It's good stuff, great for opening up bumholes.'

Mel made a sour face and Morris winked at me as he turned away. I shook my head, wondering exactly what I'd let myself in for.

'The gear's in my room,' Mel said with a sigh.

I followed her to the changing room she'd chosen, just two down from mine. There was a huge bag, and she began to pull out our outfits: puffy pink disposable pull-ups with yellow teddy bears just like the ones Sophie had bought, knitted booties – one pair pink, one pair yellow – and the pinafore dresses, which were utterly babyish and perhaps the most humiliating garments I had ever seen. For one thing they were transparent, so everything would show right from the start. The top was pleated at both neck and waistline, leaving the material bulging over our bare breasts. Below the waistline, which came only just below our boobs, they flared wide, with the hem held out by layer upon layer of nylon frills, and so short that our nappies would show front and back. The plastic pants were no consolation at all, also frilly around the leg holes, and in the same colours, baby pink and primrose.

We exchanged a look.

'Pink or yellow?' Mel asked despondently.

The yellow seemed marginally less humiliating, until I realised that the colour had probably been chosen to make it less obvious if I wet myself.

'Pink,' I sighed.

We began to dress, Mel complaining as she squeezed her bum into the tight pull-ups, and looking at herself in the mirror with an expression of utter horror when she'd finished. I'd have laughed if I hadn't looked equally single, while my tawny curls just made it worse. My boobs looked every bit as prominent and every bit as ridiculous as I'd imagined, while from behind the bulging seat of the plastic pants made my bum look enormously fat, if not quite as big as Mel's.

With a final despairing glance we took each other's hands and made for the backstage, to find Morris already at the microphone and a man with a large spoon scooping out a gigantic pot of nappy cream and flicking it down on the canvas. I could smell it, reminding me of playing in Loughborough, wetting my nappy and watching Sophie wet hers, Humber fucking her with her terry and plastic pants pulled down at the back, changing her . . .

I wondered if Mel knew that the pull-ups were designed to tear open at the sides to make them easy to remove when they were wet or dirty. It seemed unlikely, as I was pretty much certain Humber hadn't had her in them before. Just possibly I had an advantage.

We stepped out as Morris announced us, to a roar of encouragement that changed instantly to laughter as they saw what we were wearing. I felt the blood rush to my face, and I was cursing Humber bitterly as I climbed into my corner. Even Kay was struggling not to snigger as she passed me up a water bottle, and I wagged a rebuking finger at her. She just stuck her tongue out.

The ring was covered in heavy blobs of nappy cream, but that was not all. There were toys: little rubber balls, miniature skittles, various objects with suspiciously rounded handles, what was presumably supposed to be a rocket but looked more like a hastily painted dildo – all things selected for their ease of insertion into well-lubricated fannies and bumholes. There were also several baby bottles, on a scale more suited to an infant hippo than a human, and all full.

213

Across from me, Mel was waiting and, for all her absurd costume, she looked strong and confident. As the bell went I was thinking of what she might do to me when I'd lost: pee on me at the very least, spank me, lube up my bottom hole and feed some of the rubber balls into my rectum, ask for new nappies and change me . . .

At the very least I had to fight, and my only chance was to go in fast and furious, and to hell with giving the crowd a good long fight. I screamed as I came out of my corner, hurling myself at Mel, only to tread on a blob of nappy cream and go headlong. I caught the astonished look in her eyes even as I grabbed at her pinafore dress, not to strip her, but for support. It came anyway, ripped clean off her body even as I went face down at her feet.

Before I could recover myself she'd caught my dress, by the back, hauling in the hope it would rip away as hers had. Half of it did and, as I rolled clear and quickly bounced to my feet, she was left with the lower part in her hands. I was left in just the top, a ring of transparent pink material girdling my chest and bulging out over my boobs. I'd lost a bootie too, and she was coming at me, crouched low, bare and black and powerful, for all the absurd puff of pink nappy around her hips.

I gave back, just a little, before rushing in again, grappling with her. Our arms locked, struggling to throw each other, but neither strong enough to gain an advantage. She kicked out, trying to trip me. I jumped, pulled, landed in some nappy cream and we went down together, rolling on the slippery mat, clutching at each other's nappies. She had me, trying to pull my nappy down, at both sides, a mistake. I grabbed one side of hers and tore the tab wide.

She gave a yelp of surprise and rolled away to protect herself, leaving me with the back of my nappy halfway down over my bum but otherwise as before. Both her

214

booties had come off, and I kicked my other one free as they were just making it harder to stand up. We faced off, Mel now cautious and with her thighs close together to stop her torn nappy from falling down, circling, each waiting her moment . . .

. . . and diving forwards at the same instant, shoulder to shoulder, struggling to push each other back and grappling for a hold. She disengaged, suddenly, gripping what was left of my pinafore dress at the last moment, ripping it free and sending me sprawling in the cream, topless. I rolled, too late, and she was on me, my arms trapped, her nappy-clad bum right over my face, then in it. She was laughing wildly as she sat down, the soft nappy seat squashing in my face. I was kicking madly, struggling to break her grip as she started to pull my nappy down my thighs . . .

. . . and I had a mouthful of her nappy, ripping at it with my teeth. The filling erupted in my face and mouth, even as my nappy was hauled high, up my thighs, to my knees, and I was fighting to keep them together in a last desperate effort to stop myself being stripped nude, my teeth snapping at her nappy, wrenching, my mouth full of absorbent granules, and pulling the whole thing away, to sink my teeth into the firm black flesh of Melody's bottom.

She jerked up, just one of my arms came free and I tore her remaining tab wide. Her nappy came away, leaving her bottom bare in my face an instant before my own was wrenched up off my ankles. We were both nude, but I'd won, stripping her just a fraction of a second before being stripped myself. I was also underneath her, with her broad black bottom in my face, her cheeks spread wide and my nose well in up her sweaty, slippery bottom hole.

I heard her triumphant yell and realised she was holding my nappy high to show it off to the crowd. As she made herself more comfortable, wiggling her bottom down into my face, I was struggling to protest. Her fanny was pressed right to my mouth, and I could barely breathe, let alone speak. She lifted her plump, shaved sex right over my mouth and, as I began to point out that I'd won, she just let go, right in my mouth, a great gush of piddle, most of which exploded straight back out of my nose as I began to choke. All I could see was her bum, her tight black anus pouting a little and, for one truly awful moment, I thought she was going to do to me what Angel had threatened and load my mouth, before I caught Hudson Staebler's rich American accent from somewhere above.

'Say, Melody, I think you'll find you lost there.'

'I did not!' she answered, and this time her own sister answered her.

'You did, Mel, by about half a second. I've got it on film.'

My mind filled with gratitude for Harmony, but Mel didn't get off me, or even try to stop her flow, still arguing and barely seeming aware that she was still pissing in my face and over my chest. Only when Morris joined in did she finally give way, by which time she'd finished anyway and I was lying in a wide pool of her piss, my hair sodden, my mouth full of it and bubbles of yellowish mucus frothing from my nose. She shrugged as she stood up.

'Sorry, Amber, I really thought.'

'Just get down here, Melody. You've had it.'

She gave another shrug, apparently indifferent, and got down.

'On all fours, bum to the audience,' I ordered.

She gave me a wry look, accepting her fate with just a touch of warning, but she turned around, lifting her full, meaty bottom to the audience. I left her for a moment to accept a bottle of water from Kay, most of which I poured over my head, and a towel. Only after taking a few deep breaths did I turn my attention to Mel, first to make a quick inspection of her rear view, to be sure her fanny showed, which it did, and that her cheeks were open enough, which they weren't.

'Dip your back, Melody,' I instructed her, 'let the boys see what they've paid for.'

She gave a little sigh, but pulled her back in, to make her magnificent bottom open, showing her anus, if not in the full, rude detail I would have liked. It would do, at least for her spanking, which was how I intended to start off her humiliation. Shuffling close, I took her around the waist and began to stroke her bottom. I could smell her even through the nappy cream: cocoa butter and girl sweat and fanny – an intoxicating mixture, arousing too.

I began to spank, enjoying her bottom as much as punishing her, but still doing it hard, to make her big cheeks wobble prettily. She took it in silence, at first, until I curved my arm down under her tummy, slid a finger in among the wet, mushy folds of her sex and began to masturbate her. Soon she was gasping, as her control began to slip, and squeaking to every spank, no more reserved than any other girl with a smacked bottom. I began to do it harder, rubbing on her clitty, and to spank lower, on the chubby swell of her bottom, right over her fanny.

She was going to come, at any moment, just as I stopped, to haul her cheeks apart and show off her wet, open fanny and the tight brown knot of her anus, both twitching in the onset of orgasm. A low moan escaped her as she realised she wasn't to be allowed to come at all, but that I was merely adding to her suffering by showing how excited she was. I was going to make her come, of course, but not until she'd been fucked, and more.

The toy skittles were ideal for my purposes: the smooth, bulbous ends just about small enough to be accommodated in a girl's bumhole, but big enough to be worth pushing up a fanny. I took a blue one and

217

pushed it in up Mel, her own natural lubricant providing an easy passage. She grunted as her fanny filled, and again as I began to fuck her, pushing the skittle deep to make her hole stretch wide, easing it out to leave her gaping, so wide I could see the little pink mouth of her cervix, and again, before I left it in and scooped up some nappy cream on one finger.

'Now for your bumhole, Miss Melody,' I told her, and once again hauled her cheeks wide apart.

Her anus was winking, with the shame of her exposure and in fear for what I might do. As I touched her ring she tightened it, but I merely rubbed the cream on to her anal star and into the little hole and she soon went loose again. Up I went, my finger sliding up into the hot tube of her rectum, probing a little to get her good and open. Despite herself she was sighing as she was buggered and, after a while, I pulled my finger out and stuck one of the miniature skittles up instead. It went, just, as I watched her ring spread to what must have been capacity around the rounded yellow plastic, with a thin line of white nappy cream between straining bumhole and skittle. She took it gasping and shaking, making little whimpering noises in her throat as I began to bugger her, and finally speaking, in a broken, urgent whisper.

'Make me come, Amber, like this, just like this –'

'Uh, uh,' I told her, 'I'm not finished with you yet, Melody Rathwell.'

As I spoke I eased the skittle free, to leave her well-buggered rectum a gaping pink tube into her bottom for a moment, before her anus closed with a soft, wet fart. Briefly, I rubbed her fanny, until she was breathing in little ragged gasps, close to orgasm. When I stopped, she let out a little sigh of disappointment, and turned her head to look as I reached out for one of the over-sized baby bottles. Her eyes came wide.

'Not an enema, Amber, please!'

'Sorry, Mel, but this one's for Angel.'

'Amber, no . . . please, no . . . please –'

Her final plea broke to a sob as I eased the teat of the bottle in up her well-lubricated anus. The scale on the side of the bottle told me it held two litres, and it was nearly full, plenty for a girl's enema. With the teat wedged well in up her bum and Mel gasping and wiggling her toes in an agony of reaction and embarrassment, I squeezed the bottle, hard.

Mel gasped as her rectum began to fill with warm milk. I squeezed harder, forcing more of the milk up her, and more. With maybe a litre up her, her muscles begun to contract, squeezing the skittle out of her fanny, which stayed wide. She had begun to wriggle her toes too, and squirm her bottom on the intruding teat, in helpless reaction to the growing pressure in her rectum. Still I squeezed, filling her until milk had begun to ooze from her buggered ring and she was gasping and clutching at the mat, her feet kicking in pain as much mental as physical. At last it was too much, and she began to babble.

'No, Amber, please . . . stop . . . that's all I can take –'

'Nonsense,' I answered soothingly, 'a big girl like you should be able to take two litres easily.'

'No, really, I can't . . . I can't hold it anyway . . . I –'

'You're not supposed to hold it, silly! You're supposed to expel it, for the audience. Now stick that lovely bum up and let's get a nice high squirt, because I'm nearly done.'

She responded with a broken sob, but her bum came up, lifted high as I squeezed the last of the milk in up her rectum. I held the teat in her for a moment, just watching her ring squeeze on it, before pulling it free, slowly, so that she'd have time to clench and prolong her agony. Dropping the bottle, I wrapped an arm around her body, holding her, to comfort her as she expelled, and to be ready to frig her off. She was babbling incoherently, and her bumhole was already dribbling milk, a thing white trickle running down to either side of her fanny and into the open hole. As her anus begun to pout her words grew clear.

'I ... I can't hold on ... I can't ... I can't, Amber ... it's coming ... hold me!'

I was already masturbating her. Her voice broke off in a last cry of helpless despair and her bumhole simply exploded, spraying milk out in a high arch clean across the ring and over the ropes, to patter down on the bare boards of the stage a good three yards behind her. I held on, rubbing hard on her clitty and keeping her bum cheeks good and wide so that everyone could see the milk squirting from her open hole. She was gasping and whimpering as it came, her cheeks and fanny in spasm, her anus too, so that her spray broke to a series of spurts. Her bumhole was sucking in and out as she struggled vainly to hold herself, only to explode once more in a fresh squirt of milk and solid too as her orgasm hit her.

She screamed the house down, her whole body in violent contractions, milk and her own mess squirting from her bumhole, and from her fanny where it had trickled in. I held on tight, rubbing her and spanking her too, and laughing, with pure sadistic joy for what I'd done to her and for her utter inability to control her own ecstasy. Even when she'd finished coming her bumhole was still oozing, and the mess behind her was appalling. I didn't care. I wanted people to see what she'd done while she licked me out.

I went to her head, pulling her up by her hair and spreading my thighs in her face. She began to lick immediately, tonguing my clitty, the mess still bubbling from her bottom hole, the crowd in uproar. I'd done it, beaten her. However absurd I'd felt in my nappy and pinafore dress, I had won, and even if I was naked and sodden with her piddle, at least I hadn't been given a public enema and made to come with dirty milk bubbling out of my well-buggered anus . . .

The crowd roared as one as I came, my teeth locked tight in ecstasy, my fingers clawed into Mel's hair, her tongue working urgently on my clitty. The moment it was over I stood, unsteadily, to raise my hands in triumph, ducked down to pull Mel's discarded nappy on over her head, and walked from the ring to thunderous applause. Kay hugged me as soon as I was down, then Angel, and the three of us walked from the stage, deliberately swaying our hips in unison. Patty was waiting for us in the wings.

'Sophie's still not here.'

'She's supposed to be in the air,' Kay said.

'Well, that's no fucking good, is it, not unless she's got a parachute. Sorry, Kay –'

'She might still make it,' Angel suggested.

'In half an hour? It takes that long to drive in from the airport.'

'Maybe by the time you're due to go on stage,' I tried. 'You are seventh.'

'Maybe . . . just –'

'Or we can find somebody else,' Angel suggested. 'Maybe you, Kay?'

Kay immediately began to stammer.

'I . . . I . . . I can't . . . I would . . . you know I would, but –'

'She couldn't cope,' I said, 'not in front of a big audience.'

Patty drew a heavy sigh.

'I would,' Angel offered, 'for you, but I've got to lead Greg out. Amber?'

'Me?' I managed.

'Why not?'

'Well –'

'Amber, please,' Patty begged, and her eyes were beginning to fill with tears.

'We need you, Amber,' Angel urged.

I glanced at Kay, but I knew I couldn't ask her.

'I did help you with my corset, in the wrestling,' Patty urged, 'and I came and got you in Loughborough.'

I nodded, completely unable to refuse, despite my head being full of images of Gemma and Kay with their faces down in bowls of dog food. Yet they'd done it, and I'd enjoyed making Kay do it, and Patty was right, I owed her a lot. Only a complete and utter bitch would have refused, and not the doggy kind. Yet I could hardly bear the thought. Fortunately, there were still problems.

'I would,' I answered her. 'I will, if you really want, but how? I can't fit into Gemma's spaniel costume.'

'We ... we can make you into a poodle,' Patty answered, 'a white one. All we need is some glue and lots of cotton wool. There must be a chemist's somewhere, a newsagent's even.'

I hesitated, but really I had no choice, whatever my feelings.

'Oh God,' I said and sighed. 'All right, get the stuff, and if Sophie doesn't turn up on time I'll do it – except for Rubba Dobie, I really don't think I could bear to be fucked by Rubba Dobie.'

'Thank you,' Patty breathed, 'thank you so much. You won't regret this, Amber.'

'I won't?'

'I'll help you with the gear,' Angel put in. 'Let's go.'

I'd thought I looked ridiculous in the adult baby-girl costume. I hadn't even understood the meaning of the word. As a French poodle, I looked truly ridiculous, absurd, a ludicrous, obscene parody of woman and dog, at once comic and erotic, extraordinarily farcical and extraordinarily lewd.

Inevitably, Sophie hadn't made it, and I'd no choice but to agree to be Bitch for the show; Bitch because that was the name on the competition sheet and it was too late to change. I also had to go through with the awful, humiliating routine, as far as it took, and I was painfully aware that I myself had suggested several of the most agonising details.

I'd had to strip stark naked and go down on all fours. They'd drawn marks on my body where the cotton wool was supposed to go: around my elbows and wrists, my ankles and knees, my neck and my hips, my chest. Angel had painted me with glue as Patty stuck on the cotton wool, first to make rings of fluffy white fur around my limbs and neck, then on the main areas. For my chest there was a broad band across my back, but underneath they had circled my breasts, to leave them dangling, pink and fat beneath me, like two great udders. For my hips they had covered the lower part of my back and belly, my pubic mound, most of my bottom cheeks and a little of my inner thighs, in a shape like a pair of big knickers, only split at the rear to show off the crease of my bottom, my anus, and my fanny – no, let's face it, my cunt.

More cotton wool had gone on top of my head, a huge puff that covered my hair, and a last ball on a piece of rolled white leather to make a tail with a pompom bobbing jauntily above my unspeakably lewd rear view. It was done in my changing room, and just being with the girls had me in an agony of embarrassment, which grew abruptly worse after Patty had put me on her collar and lead and led me out to the wings.

The other competitors were already there, and turned to look, setting my face hot with blushes. Most I didn't know at all, but we had at least identified our real competition. Sakura was obvious, a tiny, exquisitely pretty Japanese woman, and ever so cute in her little doggy suit with the little round bum and budding breasts on show. Her master was a lot older than her, very poised and correct in a dove-grey business suit, as if he was merely walking his dog before going to work.

Angel had just taken hold of Rubba Dobie, who looked as grotesque as ever, and obscene, with his huge rubber cock hanging from his belly along with the swollen rubber scrotum behind. Nobody else's dog suit came close, and I knew that for skill alone, they were the best.

Mistress Leash was also unmistakable: a slim woman, immaculately dressed, in all body leather and satin, in unrelieved black, save for the brilliant red of her lipstick. Her perfectly made-up face looked out with utter disdain from behind a black gauze veil. Her heels had to be six inches high, and yet she only just topped Angel. Around her were no less than sixteen men, all stark naked but for their absurd cartoon masks, collars and leads, and sat back on their haunches so that their cocks and balls hung out between their open thighs. She gave me a single glance, amused, contemptuous and above all superior. I thought how easily I'd have defeated her in the wrestling ring, and how satisfying it would have been to force her painted lips apart and piss right in her mouth.

Morris had already called out the first pair: two gay men who focused on obedience rather than look. A man with two naked girls with puppy ears and tails replaced them, and I settled down to wait, thinking bad thoughts about Gemma and Sophie, and even Kay, but unable to escape the irony of the position I'd got myself into.

One puppy followed the next. The theatre rang with cheers for Sakura even as she came out, and I watched with a sinking feeling as she performed, a routine both delightful and rude. She fetched and begged, rolled over to have her tummy tickled, rubbed herself on her master's leg, and, as a finale, squatted down with her open bottom to the audience and let them watch her pee, bitch fashion, to leave a broad yellow puddle on the stage as she walked off.

The crowd were in raptures, and I knew Patty was going to have to put me through the whole routine for us to stand a chance. Really, she should let Rubba Dobie fuck me, but I couldn't bring myself to ask for it. Just the sight of his huge, pink cock swinging beneath him set me sick to the stomach, and yet it was impossible not to imagine it inside me, pushed in right up to the fat rubber knot, with the cream from the bloated scrotum pumping up my fanny with every shove . . .

I only realised we were on when Patty's lead pulled against my neck. It was more than I could bear even to look up, but I trotted out at her side, with a huge lump in my throat and my stomach churning. A wild cheer went up at the sight of me, and not a few gasps of astonishment. I heard my name called, and the run of a whisper, that the all-girl wrestling champion was now a puppy-girl on her mistress' lead.

Every detail of the routine was fixed into my head, and I forced myself to follow it, and to show willing, every bit the eager, obedient little bitch I was supposed to be. I rolled and begged, flaunting my spread fanny to the audience, came to Patty's heel at her call and sat still on my haunches with my tongue lolling out of my mouth as she patted my head and told me I was a good girl.

By the time I was ready to pee my head was swimming with humiliation so strong I was choking back my tears. I played up though, letting Patty take me to Sakura's puddle and sniffing at it before going down in a bitch squat above it and squeezing out my own, with my funny white bottom spread wide to the audience, my pouted anus and dribbling cunt bare for all to see.

It left me weak with reaction, but my ordeal wasn't over, not be a long way. I'd done the easy bit, utterly humiliating but not actually unpleasant. Next came the feeding. Patty had a large bag of doggie treats: big, bone-shaped ones meant for large dogs. I'd suggested them myself, so that the audience could see what Bitch was being fed. Now I was Bitch, and I was wishing I'd suggested something smaller.

She ordered me to stay and walked back across the stage. She held up the bag of doggie treats for everyone to see. She tore the top open and dipped her hand in, to pull out a big brown biscuit. I caught the doggy smell and my stomach tightened even as she gave the command.

'Here, girl ... good girl, Bitch ... Bitch catch ... Bitch catch in mouth.'

Too late I remembered what a useless throw she was. She'd tossed the biscuit up far too high, and well to my left. I jumped up, but missed by a mile, landed badly and ended up sprawled on my back with my cunt spread as the audience went into hysterics. As I righted myself, I gave Patty a filthy look, to which she responded by stepping forwards, taking me firmly by the collar and applying a dozen hard swats to my bottom as she told me off.

'Bad Bitch! Bad! Smacked bottie for Bitch! Now sit!'

I sat, absolutely burning with humiliation, as Patty once more stood back to extract a second dog biscuit. Determined not to spend the next few minutes alternately missing the biscuits and having my bottom smacked while the audience laughed at me, I watched carefully to see where the biscuit would go, and leapt in good time, rising to catch it neatly in my mouth.

A fraction of a second later, I was regretting my decision. The biscuit tasted utterly foul, the way Mac-Cruiskeen's Rottweiler smelt, and it was gritty and dry too. Nobody had thought I might need water, and I was forced to chew it up and swallow down the foul pulp, all the while pretending I was hugely enjoying the treat my loving mistress had provided. When I did finish, it was to find Patty holding the next one ready.

'Good girl, Bitch, nice doggie treat! Good girl ... catch ... catch it, Bitch!'

226

I missed, deliberately, and got my bottom smacked again, this time after having my back turned to the audience so that they could appreciate the obscene rear view of my fanny and bumhole among the thick white poodle fur. She did it in my crease, and it stung, but left me fighting the sense of arousal that was flaring in my head. As she stood back, she pointed at the two biscuits lying on the stage, one right in the middle of Sakura's and my pee puddle.

'Eat up! Good girl, Bitch! Yummy treats for Bitch!'

She was pointing to the dog biscuit in the pee. I looked up, pleading with my eyes as I wondered how I could ever have mistaken her grandmother for a mad cow when she was quite obviously the real thing. In response to my plea, she put her hands on her hips and shook her head.

'Bad Bitch! Very bad! Eat up, now!'

Her hand came up, lifted to smack me, and I backed quickly away, to nuzzle up the clean dog biscuit. My mouth was already dry, and the horrible dog taste filled my senses as I struggled to make saliva. Patty had come to stand over me, and watched as I chewed and swallowed, chewed and swallowed. I was praying she'd let me off, but the moment I'd finished she pointed to the second biscuit.

'Go on, Bitch! Eat it! Good girl, Bitch!'

I went, and the crowd were hooting with laughter as I nuzzled up the dog biscuit. It was soggy with pee, and I couldn't help but screw up my face as I munched on it, the rich, hormonal flavour of our urine mixing with the taste of dog. Patty stayed above me, watching and, the moment I swallowed, she was pointing at the pee puddle once more.

'Drink! Drink, Bitch! Lap it up!'

My mouth came open in horror, and again I tried to plead with my eyes, but she merely wagged her finger in my face. Down I went, out came my tongue and I lapped up Sakura's and my piddle and swallowed as best I could. I could really taste us, her and my sex as well as piddle, and I couldn't stop it getting to me, or what Patty was putting me through. She made me clean it all up too, waiting until there was no more than a sticky stain on the smooth surface of the stage before taking me by the collar and pulling me up.

I felt sick, but my head was swimming with arousal, submissive arousal, as Patty marched me a little to the side. She had the dog bowl, a red plastic one with 'Bitch' on one side, and the food, the same cheap, economy-sized tin of supermarket own brand as I'd made Kay eat. I could only watch in horrified fascination as she scooped it out: a thick, greyish-brown paste with that same horrible doggy smell. I remembered how I'd enjoyed having Kay eat it, how I'd delighted in the fact that once she swallowed it down there was no going back. She'd eaten dog food, and it became part of her. Now it was my turn.

Patty stood back, to ruffle my poodle fur.

'There we are, girl. Come on, good girl, Bitch, eat up!'

My eyes fixed on the pile of dog food, and I knew I couldn't do it. I glanced at Patty, but her expression was set and firm. When she spoke again there was a stern edge to her voice.

'Eat up, Bitch! Nice dog food ... nice ... there's a good girl.'

I went onto all fours, moving my head a little closer, telling myself that if I could make Kay do it I could do it myself ... I must do it. The smell caught me and I backed, only to have Patty's hand catch firmly in my collar, and before I could react my face had been pushed into the dog food.

'Eat it, Bitch! Bad Bitch!' she snapped, and I was doing it, my mouth open, a piece of dog food inside, and closed.

'Good girl,' Patty said, now stroking my head as I

began to gobble up the smelly, meaty paste, filling my mouth . . .

. . . and swallowing, to fill my stomach, and just like Kay, and like Gemma, I was truly a bitch puppy, part of me forever dog food, something I could never, ever lose. I felt my tears break free, but I wanted to come, to come with my face well down in the bowl and my stomach bulging with cheap dog food. Patty was still stroking me, trying to soothe me as I blubbered out my emotions, but what I wanted was for her to rub my cunt, to bring me to ecstasy in my utter disgrace, with the whole crowd watching as I did it. After I'd swallowed a second mouthful, I managed to speak from the side of my mouth, a covert whisper.

'Do me, Patty, now. My fanny, as I eat.'

She nodded and to my surprise stood away. I went on eating, fighting down the last of my resentment as I prepared to be brought off in my disgrace. Patty whistled, I heard the thump of rubber doggy paws, and too late I realised what was happening, that she'd misunderstood, even as his weight settled onto my back: Rubba Dobie, mounting me, his suit slick against my sweaty skin, his monstrous rubber dog cock pushing at my cunt hole, and up, deep in me . . .

I cried out as my cunt filled with the thick rubber penis, a moment before I lost my balance and my face went into the bowl of dog food with a thick squelch. For a moment, I was trying to fight, but my fanny was full of cock and he was humping me at a furious pace, too good to stop, and I just broke. My mouth closed in the dog food and I was eating it again, now eager to fill my belly as I was fucked. I was going to come too, whether I liked it or not, because the fat rubber plug of his knot was stretching my hole wide, sending jolts of pure ecstasy to my clitty.

He was growling as he fucked me, and the powerful pumping motion was rubbing my face in the dog bowl even as I struggled to eat up the filthy contents. It was all coming together in my head: the utter, delicious degradation of being made into Patty's poodle, Bitch; of being made to snuffle up doggie treats from a pool of pee; of being fed dog food from a bowl marked with my name; of being mounted and fucked by a man in a grotesque dog costume . . .

It stopped, leaving me gasping, bits of dog food falling from my open mouth, and dizzy with need. Out came the cock, drawn slowly from my body, and I found myself babbling, all my pride and all my modesty completely gone as I began to beg for my fucking, no longer even caring that I was supposed to be a dog as long as I got Rubba Dobie's cock back where it belonged.

'Don't stop . . . please . . . fuck me . . . just fuck me . . .'

He gave a low growl, something cold and slippery was pushed in between my bumcheeks and up my hole, nappy cream, and I realised I was to be buggered even as Patty skipped back, laughing happily to see my face as I turned it to her, and the audience. I could see, just about, row upon row of staring faces, full of lust and glee and shock and disgust as the wrinkly tip of Rubba Dobie's cock began to push in at my bumhole.

'Oh God, no,' I gasped as my anus began to spread, wanting it to stop, and at the same time wanting it to happen more than anything else in the whole world.

My ring was too slippery to stop him anyway, and up he went, deep into my rectum, eased in inch by painful inch as I gasped and shook to my buggery. Only when the knot met my gaping anus did he stop, unable to get it in. Not that it mattered, with my rectum already bloated out with a foot of heavy rubber dog cock, and as he began to move in my gut, the scrotum started to swing and to slap on my empty cunt. My face went back

230

in the dog bowl and I was eating again, my orgasm rising once more as the pace of my buggery picked up.

As my tits began to swing my nipples were rubbing on the floor, in the mess of dog food that had spilt from my mouth. My stomach was full of it, my face and hair caked with it, and still I ate, eager to feel my belly swollen with what would become part of me. Every push as he rammed the huge rubber cock home stretched the mouth of my poor aching bumhole wider on the massive dog knot, until at last it began to squeeze in, even as I reached orgasm.

The pain hit me first and I screamed, but he never even stopped, jamming himself into me, right in, bloating my rectum, with the fat scrotum smacking on my cunt lips, faster and faster. Then the knot was up me, and I felt my bumhole close behind it and the scrotum was pulled tight to my cunt. I was wriggling on it immediately, squirming my buggered bottom on the huge load inside me, screaming my head off and beating my fists on the floor, tossing my hair and rubbing my face in the dog food as I came, with the cream pumping in up my bottom as the scrotum squashed to my empty, dripping cunt.

As I jerked and shook in ecstasy I was thinking of how well and truly used I'd been: made into a dog, a French poodle, called Bitch and made to beg and roll and flaunt the most intimate parts of my body; fed dog biscuits and made to eat them soaked in piddle; fed dog food and made to swallow so that my degradation would for ever be a part of me; mounted and fucked from the rear, doggy style, covered, a bitch in heat fucked by the top dog; and, finally, buggered and my rectum pumped full of warm, sticky cream . . .

It took ten minutes, about a pint of nappy cream and the assistance of two nurses from the audience to extract Rubba Dobie's dog knot from my rectum, an experience almost as humiliating as my buggering. Once it was out my bumhole wouldn't close properly, dribbling cream down my thighs as I stood to make an embarrassed thank you to the nurses.

To make matters worse, the first person I saw after crawling off stage with Rubba Dobie still on my back and the rubber cock wedged up my bum was Sophie Cherwell. She had arrived as I was being fed the doggie treats, and had seen everything. Or rather, she'd arrived backstage while I was being fed the doggie treats, because she'd spent twenty minutes chatting up the bouncers and MacCruiskeen in the office, when she could have been getting into Gemma's costume.

We had at least won. Even Sakura's master came over to congratulate Patty while Rubba Dobie's cock was being extricated from my bottom, and stated firmly that he considered it an honour to give way to us, and would do so even if they were voted first. As it was he came in third, behind Angel and Rubba Dobie in second, and Patty and me in a triumphant first. Triumphant at least for her because while the awards were being given I had a large Irish nurse up to her elbow in my rectum, checking to make sure I hadn't been hurt. Mistress Leash had placed fourth, and stormed from the building in a temper, leaving her sixteen dogs behind.

Kay brought me the news, runnning back and forth between the stage and the impromptu medical room where I was being examined – or possibly fisted, because she was certainly taking her time about it, or maybe both. I was still dribbling a mixture of nappy cream and UHT, which was what Rubba Dobie had had in his scrotum, and was about to make for the shower when Sophie came running in, babbling.

'Amber, we have to get to the office, now.'

'Sophie,' I protested, 'I can hardly walk.'

'Yes, but –'

'I've just been buggered, Sophie, I –'

'Never mind that. Now the prize money's been given out, Morris is about to have the takings sent down to go into the nightsafe at the hotel. There's a security van coming, Harmony just rang to confirm.'

'Oh, shit. Look, Sophie –'

'Amber, come on. It won't take a moment.'

'Oh, God, OK, but if anyone ever needed her bottom whipped, Sophie Cherwell, it's you.'

'I know. Now come on.'

I grabbed the robe they'd put out for me and went, waddling badly, with a horrible slippery sensation between my bum cheeks where the assorted creams were still oozing out of my bumhole. Sophie at least knew where she was going, via dimly lit passages and oddly shaped halls, quickly arriving at the office. I hung back as she reached the door, and ducked down into the cashier's booth, listening. Sophie spoke first.

'Hi, boys, how's it going?'

One bouncer merely grunted, the other answered.

'Boring, in here. I hear that posh bird, Amber Oakley, just got one up the dirt box from some guy in a dog outfit. What a laugh, eh?'

'You missed something there,' Sophie agreed, laughing. 'Anyway, Morris was worried you boys weren't having much fun, so he sent me out.'

'What for?' a thickly accented voice answered, MacCruiskeen.

'Sex, silly,' she answered.

'Blow jobs all round, yeah?' one of the bouncers chuckled.

'Blow jobs it is,' Sophie confirmed. 'Come out front, and I'll take you in the booth, or you can watch if you like?'

Realising I'd chosen the wrong hiding place, I moved quickly back into the corridor and hid.

'Watch?' MacCruiskeen queried. 'Watch some other bloke getting a blow job?'

'Why not?' Sophie responded. 'Like in a porno. You watch pornos, don't you? Come on, I want you to watch.'

'I don't know –'

'Watch, or no blow job. Come on, wouldn't you like to see me with a great big cock in my mouth?'

'Yeah, mine, but –'

'OK, you can spit-roast me, how's that? Like footballers do.'

'In front of each other?' one of the bouncers said, doubtfully. 'Sounds a bit gay to me.'

'Nah, not if footballers do it,' the other answered him.

I shook my head, wishing they'd hurry up. My bottom was dribbling badly and my poodle suit was starting to itch, while the van was likely to turn up at any moment. Sophie spoke again.

'Look, either you come in the booth and you get to fuck me, or you stay here and you get nothing, OK?'

There was a pause, one grunt of acquiescence, a second, and then MacCruiskeen spoke.

'What about the cash?'

'Don't be stupid, you great Paddy,' one of the bouncers answered. 'If we're in the booth, nobody can get in, can they?'

For one awful moment, I thought they'd start arguing, but Sophie must have done something rude because MacCruiskeen swore softly and then the three of them were trooping out and across to the booth. The door closed and I nipped quickly forwards, to find myself in the office, and face to face with MacCruiskeen's Rottweiler . . .

. . . who was asleep. My heart was hammering as I crossed quickly to where a big, red cash box had been pushed in on the bottom level of an ornate table. Flinching at the stink of dog, I got down, crawling in under the table to lift the box. I heard the click, and felt the cold iron of the latticework closed around my waist, the shock of realisation hitting me too late, far too late.

I was trapped, in some diabolical device of Morris', my waist clamped and my bottom stuck out towards a door through which two bouncers and an Irish security guard would be walking in ...

I heard the click of the latch, and a voice – Morris.

'Hello, Amber. We thought we might find you here.'

I turned my head, looking sheepishly around to find him in the doorway, his expression thoroughly smug. Mel was behind him, Harmony and others back in the corridor.

'Oh, shit. Morris, look –'

He raised a finger. I shut up. He spoke.

'You're a very naughty girl, Amber. Play is play, but money is money. You should know that. Now, what do you think we should do with you?'

'Let me go?'

'Hardly. Mel has the little matter of a public enema to discuss with you for one thing, and I'm not too impressed myself. At the very least I shall expect to give you a good buggering.'

'Morris, please, no! You saw what happened to me in the puppy show –'

'Yes, I did. I imagine it's left you nice and slippery.'

'Yes, but –'

'Then stop whining. I'll give you two choices. One – you take me up your bum and Mel gets her own back. Two – you take Sophie's place servicing the bouncers and the security men. There are eight of them in all.'

'How about just letting me go?'

'Would you, if you'd caught Mel about to play a vindictive trick on you?'

I shook my head. Morris nodded. There was genuine anger in his voice, and I felt my guilt rise in response.

'You always were an honest girl at heart, Amber. Oh, and there is one other small matter ... well, not small exactly –'

Mr Protheroe's big, sweaty moon face appeared, leering in over Harmony's shoulder.

'Oh, God, no, please –'

'Don't worry, he just wants to watch, and perhaps a blow job afterwards.'

I shook my head, but it was a weak gesture. Morris came up behind me, my robe was thrown up and my bum was bare once more, or rather, the seat of my poodle costume. With the gown up I could barely see, only clutch onto what I now realised was a modern bondage table, specifically designed to trap a girl around the waist so that she could give oral sex to anyone sitting at it, while her bottom was left vulnerable behind.

All I could was hang my head, defeated, knowing I really deserved what I was going to get. There was nothing I could do anyway, slumped down, waiting, and listening to the gasps and grunts from the cashier's booth as the bouncers and security men used Sophie. I could hear the wet, smacking noises too, as Mel or Harmony sucked Morris erect. Cream was still oozing from my bumhole, on blatant view to all of them, including Protheroe. Maybe he was being sucked hard too, cock readied for my body ...

I gasped as I felt strong male hands take me firmly by the hips: Morris, his grip very different from Protheroe's clammy embrace. The rounded head of his cock touched my bumhole and he slid up, easily, sighing with pleasure as he drove the full length of his erection in up my rectum. I was panting immediately as he began to bugger me, unable to stop myself enjoying the sensation of taking a man's cock up my bottom for all my shame. My eyes were closed, but they came open again at the scrape of a chair, and I looked up to see Mr Protheroe pulling his gross body in under the table, seated, his fat thighs spread wide, right in front of my face.

Morris increased his pace up my bum as Protheroe's hands appeared, fiddling with his fly to flop out his big ugly cock for my mouth, adding a strong man scent to the stench of MacCruiskeen's Rottweiler. I knew full well that if I didn't suck him off he was likely to put it up my bum, whatever they'd said, and the feel of Morris' erection working in my bumhole was just too much. My mouth came open, I took him in and I was sucking Mr Protheroe's cock, to the tune of the twins' laughter and the squelching noises from my buggered bottom hole.

Soon Protheroe was erect, his cock thick and stiff in my mouth, and I was struggling with my feelings, half hoping he'd bugger me when Morris was done, half dreading it and cursing myself for my weakness. By the time Morris gave a final grunt and spunked up in my rectum, I was mouthing eagerly on Protheroe and taking my time. He'd pulled his balls out, and I began to suck on them in between sessions with his cock. Morris pulled out, leaving my bumhole pulsing and dribbling spunk as well as cream.

He was replaced immediately: a long, fat cock driven in up my cunt for a fast, hard fucking, before one of the girls took him in hand, giggling crazily as she guided his erection to my bumhole. Up it went, deep in, and I was being humped, fast and furious, my whole body shaking to his demented thrusts, my tits swinging and slapping together and, as I felt my bumhole forced suddenly wide and his dangling ball sack began to slap on my empty cunt, I knew what they'd done to me.

When Mr Protheroe took my head and began to fuck in my mouth I just took it, lost in my buggering and already rising to a helpless orgasm. My bumhole was straining again, and then I had taken everything and his big balls were right on my cunt, rubbing the slippery groove of my lips, right on my clitty. I started to come, the twins' demonic laughter ringing in my ears as my body went into powerful contractions, my empty fanny blowing air, my anus squeezing on the big cock inside me, sucking spunk deep in up my rectum . . .

Mr Protheroe erupted in my mouth at exactly the right moment, catching me just as my orgasm broke. I tried to swallow, but couldn't, and the whole lot exploded from my nose an instant after it had been ejaculated down my throat. It didn't stop me coming, my body jerking in the iron lattice that held me trapped, my fat boobs bouncing crazily under my chest, my buggered anus on fire and so open, the spunk and cream had begun to squelch in my hole once more despite my filling.

I just rode it, snatching and slapping at my dangling boobs, sucking up spunk and mucus from Mr Protheroe's cock and balls, delighting in every slap of the great leathery scrotum on my fanny, in every hard thrust up my bloated, cock-filled rectum, in the slippery, sticky mess running down over my cunt lips and into my hole, in the knowledge that my belly was still bloated out with dog food, in Melody and Harmony's demented laughter, in being put in nappies and in school uniform and done up as a French poodle, in being named Bitch and made a bitch, in being trapped and buggered and forced to suck cock, but, most of all, in my final, perfect initiation as a puppy-girl.